# WOAD

## JAMES ISAAC

MONTAG

First Montag Press E-Book and Paperback Original Edition November 2022

Montag Press ISBN: 978-1-957010-20-5
Design © 2022 Amit Dey

Montag Press Team:

Editor : John Rak
Cover Ilustration : Zlivkun
Managing Director : Charlie Franco

A Montag Press Book
www.montagpress.com
Montag Press
777 Morton Street, Unit B
San Francisco CA 94129 USA

Montag Press, the burning book with the hatchet cover, the skewed word mark and the portrayal of the long-suffering fireman mascot are trademarks of Montag Press.

Printed & Digitally Originated in the United States of America
10 9 8 7 6 5 4 3 2 1

# DEDICATION

For those who want to go on an adventure with me.

# CONTENTS

# ACKNOWLEDGMENTS

I want to thank:

*Mo*ntag Press, for helping me to stitch these words together. John Rak, for giving it all a thorough going over and casting a bit of sorcery over the pages. Charlie Franco, for his nth level grammar mastery.

My Mum and Dad. Mum, you always supported me, especially when things went wrong no matter how often that may be. Love you. Dad, you always loved history and passed that love of it on to me, which has helped me write this book and see the wonder in the world. Love you.

My brother, Douglas, for funny jokes and being a best friend.

My brother, Robert, for always being someone to look up to.

Family. All of you, because family is the soul for better or worse.

Recent and passed friends, who, at times, filled and fill my world with life.

Our cats, because animals are better than people.

The students and kids I taught. Those thirsty learners, who are still infectiously amazed by the world around us.

My island home, a true place of myth and magic, despite what many people say in this day and age. You merely have to open your eyes and see...

*Cheers!*

# WATCHING THE WEAVE

Under her sack-cloth cloak and hood, Cerridwen the Crone mumbled curses. Something wasn't right. Although the nearby warriors laughed and yelled with their usual blood-filled glee, their notes rung with something...*discordant.* But nothing appeared untoward.

Still, the warriors raged while the wounded held in their guts, rolling on the greenest of grasses with the greatest of smiles. Still, severed limbs reknit, mortal wounds folded until healed and the should-be-dead got up to fight again. And still, pale, wispy elves, with their delicate features and elegant long limbs, fawned upon these warring men. They laid out a most succulent banquet of meat and fruit on straw blankets for when the warriors tired, needing to feast before re-joining the fray. Everything *looked* fine. Yet, Cerridwen knew that sight was the least reliable of all the mortal senses. She pulled in a breath, letting the air wash through her, and a rotten, bitter-sweet something tainted Avalon's natural honeyed fragrance.

Bent-backed, the Crone hobbled to one of the many apple trees just outside her modest shack. Musty decay followed behind the teeth-clenching grate of ancient bones. Spitting on the trunk, she hissed up at the branches, "Children of Fate, birth into the world from the seeds of fortune and hope. Let me assess the health of the future."

Apples trembled all along the branches. The skins started to ripple, then bubble, before swelling like boils. Stick-like arms tore their way from the insides, growing as they pulled out from the ether and into existence. Finally, dropping from branches and screeching, a dozen of the creatures known as boggarts (among other things) landed cat-like, on all fours. Immediately, the green, pointy-faced creatures sniffed the air. Grabbing each other's crotches, they quickly descended into a mad rutting spree, eager to procreate in the more *mundane* way. Momentarily ignoring the off-putting display, the Crone mulled over the current problem.

"The land is thriving, but..." The words caught in Cerridwen's throat. Up, in the tree, an apple remained. "Curses, curses!" The Crone squinted to get a better look. *Why had it not answered her call?* The dangling apple appeared fully ripe. Could it be a boggart caught between emotion and magic? A misspoken and miscast spell?

"Get that apple," she hissed to the nearest boggart. "Bring it to me."

"Curses, curses!" The boggart giggled and flexed its claws before bounding gleefully up the tree.

In the Crone's shack, made from a great fist of knotted and still growing branches, Cerridwen examined the unfinished tapestries which adorned her walls. At present, all were embroidered with a forest scene of dancing nymphs and great, ancient trees. Loose threads were slowing, knitting each image into completion. With a bony, crooked finger, the Crone traced one of the weaves until she groomed a loose end. She started to wind it around her finger. Suddenly, her breath rattled, her body jerked, and she clenched her eyes shut. Perhaps it was fate, magic, or the gods, but whatever caused it was familiar to Cerridwen. Entwined between worlds, Avalon and Albion, on the precipice of possibilities, the Crone sought to empty her mind.

Old bones cracked in defiance as tapestry threads lengthened and laced around her, but she refused to be distracted. She whispered the sound of the wind as it rushed through leaves. Magic took an even greater hold as Cerridwen scried the fate of the mortal world. Her consciousness pulsed unseen across faerie roads, the leylines of Albion, in the waking world. Great Albion, the last land of Faerie, positively rumbled with tension. It *sweated* with unnatural humidity. The land was anxious, shuddering as it awoke from a nightmare. Now Cerridwen probed further. Visions of a giant, double-headed eagle filled her mind. The creature sated itself on forests and hills before squawking shrilly and taking to the air, leaving behind a barren waste.

An even shriller squawking shattered her concentration. It was like lightning had forked into the depths of her ears! "Curses, curses!" It was a damn, mocking boggart, a pock-marked thing, particularly ugly—the one she had sent to get the apple.

Pleased with itself, the boggart held the apple aloft. A large bite had been taken out of it, exposing rancid, brown flesh. Immediately, though, the boggart's attention shifted to the loose threads hanging from the tapestries. It chattered its teeth in contemplation.

With her free hand, the Crone took the apple and drew a sharp breath. Couched inside the boggart's bite was a maggot squirming through the pulp. *An apple of Avalon, rotten to its core...?* Again, Cerridwen was shaken from her concentration by a boggart-yap.

"Curses, curses," the boggart tugged at the loose threads, spinning in mad glee as a tapestry unravelled.

"Shoo, blighted runt," snapped the Crone, while the thing ran playfully around her feet. Clenching the gummy remains of her teeth together, Cerridwen focused her energies. She would summon magic enough to obliterate this annoying pest across Time and Space. Pure power tingled her vocal cords and wetted the very tip of her tongue. However, something bade her to bite against uttering the syllables of destruction.

A loose thread recoiled from the boggart's grasp, leaving the creature stunned, and began to reknit the tapestry. A stain of red, a bloody background against which stood a golden image, wove together stitch after stitch, without a guiding hand. Bright and bold, a double-headed eagle emblazoned the tapestry.

"Bah," spat the Crone, pushing her spirit into the ether, using her magic to rip the tapestry off the walls, to scrunch it up. Fresh branches sprouted from the walls of her shack. Never had a tree moved so quickly! Like a hand swatting a fly, the bark fingers pinned the petulant boggart to the floor.

"Curses, curses." The green, scrawny thing's voice was a pitiful whine.

The screwed-up tapestry ball spun towards the creature, pushing into its mouth, choking it, spilling down its throat and into its stomach, and making a fine pot belly. "See if this keeps your gob shut." But a twinkle of intelligence in the boggart's eyes caused the Crone to, for a second time, spare the creature. *Lucky pest...* "I wonder, can you make yourself useful?"

Trapped under the sturdy branch hand, the boggart spat and gagged as it fished at a thread in its throat. It began reeling the tapestry out of its insides. However, the thread snagged. The boggart's yellow eyes watered and blinked. It gargled a plea for mercy.

"Go to Albion, then. Find me a way to stop this eagle. Go. We will let fate decide the rest."

# CHAPTER ONE

# A KNOT IN FATE'S THREAD

*Britannia, 61 A.D.*

Abandoned. Broken. Defeated. An absence of feeling at first, building to a timid growl, then to a ravenous beast's roar devouring all other feelings. Except one. *Rage.* Artos tried to fuel himself with that rage, just enough to carry him through the swamp and to keep up with the creature bounding ahead; a scrawny, but pot-bellied, boggart. Known for the size of its mouth, big even for its kind, the tribesmen had taken to calling it 'Gobba.'

A dented legionary helm clattering from side-to-side on its small head, a belt of string and thimbles clinking around its waist, Gobba's large yellow eyes glowed like a beacon. Stopping for a moment, it looked back and spoke with a rasp and a cackle. "Hurry, quick. She is calling us to safety. Quick!" Then Gobba skipped onward without the slightest tremor of fatigue.

1

Mere man could not keep pace; Artos' chest screamed for breath. *Conquered...*

Just months before, a renewed Albion had triumphed over Rome. Artos' tribe had joined the great host of warriors spilling into the Southeast. They joined Boudicca and the Iceni, in retribution against Roman impositions, torture, and rape.

On a moonless night, surely gifted by Cerridwen, the Crone of Fate, ancient Fey marched with rebellious tribes. Along the banks of the Marsh River, those with druid-blessed eyes followed the blazing faerie light of the leylines.

The vengeful army stopped only once, spending a night in chalky fields thick with the yellow flowers of the woad plant. There, they prepared the blue dye that cured their wounds, stained their skin, and stoked their ire. Men and women became Woad Warriors.

Deep into Roman Britannia they went, scouring freedom into grass and mud with every footstep. On every bend of the river Marsh, at every guard post, Woad Warriors materialized from the blackness to slit legionary throats. Stout and bearded dwarves, those fabled 'Knockers' of the mineshafts, burst from tunnels, craftily undermining any fortified point, with picks ready to bury any who swore allegiance to the Eagle. Even forest creatures taunted, distracted, bit and tore at those who threatened the land.

Finally, where the Marsh River fed into the river Tamesas, on the approach to the new Roman town of Londinium, the great host halted and gathered. Artos hid among tribesman in the surrounding forest, all in the guise of night-demons with faces and bodies darkened by the thickest, bluest woad and hair spiked white with lime. The air thrummed with excitement.

Not so for the night-watch, Artos recalled the legionnaires clinging to their torches as they patrolled the riverbank. Twitchy from the inauspicious omens cast by the absent moon, a slow breeze carried their nervous whispers: *'Brittunculi,'* a term of abuse, a Latin nonsense. Artos had smirked at their discomfort, but it was anger that curled his lips into a smile of vicious knowing. Below the legionnaires, the night-blackened river bubbled and burped as half-submerged boggart-folk slipped free their short blades.

Just at that moment, the breeze had ceased as if the whole British Isles held its fogged breath. The Roman patrol huddled together, their torches aloft as they squinted into the darkness. Silence gave way to a rustle in the surrounding forests: the bark of dogs, the lowing of cows, and the roar of larger things. At the edges of the torchlight, shadows winked in and out of sight. A lone shooting star arced across the sky.

The forest boomed with the magic chants of faerie. Fire spells whipped flames into the sky. Black earth frothed like the sea as dwarves sprang from their positions. Elves rushed from the trees, leading a stampede of black cattle. Bears and wolves lurched from every direction.

Fire glinted against the smooth, green bodies of the boggarts as they emerged from the riverbank. Flashes of knife and light coloured the night. A lone legionary horn sounded before cutting out, a desperate whimper to stir the barracks and call reinforcements. Bleary-eyed men ran from their bunks to grab any available arms. Yet the hurry and the chaos left them without enough time to don armour and present an effective fighting formation.

From the very darkness itself sprang forth yet more boggarts. Muses of hospitality and hearth when bade to steer the path of helpfulness, or spiteful goads of misfortune- never would the wise ignore such creatures. The boggarts had truly unleashed their spite. Dashing like bees from a disturbed hive, trailing their curses, they whispered the enemy positions on the wind, screeching distractions just long enough for tribesmen's spears to stab true.

Artos remembered the flickering heat on his face, the glowing embers, and the black ashes floating against a backdrop of yellow flame. He remembered the thunderous bellows which announced the arrival of ogres, hill-sized loners from the far western mountains, which all but assured the route of Rome's forces. He would never forget that day, the day Londinium burned.

Victory had swollen on a chorus of song, a battle chant deep and proud enough to make the land rumble. The song charged the air and watered the land, sprouting glittering faerie grass from the scorched earth in but an instant. A great, new beginning had pulled together the threads of fate and knotted Time and Magic into one. None could doubt that, forever after, this would anchor the leylines and resonate as a beacon of power. It would be a shrine for druids, Fey, and all those who followed the spirits of Albion.

*Victory...*

*Fleeting victory.*

Human and faerie had fought as one and smeared Roman civilization across the south-east like the entrails of a wolf's kill. *Glorious days!* The great goddess of victory, Andraste, had swaddled her warriors with blessings and carried fearless hearts and deadly spear-points deep into enemy lines.

*But only when the enemy was outnumbered and unsuspecting.*

It had taken only a few short months to blunt the euphoria, with rumours of an ocean full of wooden ships drawing up to the white cliffs of the coast. Under the banner of the eagle, metal-armoured men spilled over the beaches in numbers enough to replace every grain of sand. That was when the fight turned hard. That was when the old gods proved lacking.

◇※≪≡══════════≡≫※◇

That was why Artos fled into the western marshes, with the warriors and priestesses of decimated tribes, praying that the young boggart they followed knew enough of Albion to get them *properly* lost so they could find one of the sacred groves. "This way. I hear the whispers of fate, I do," it rasped, moving with sure purpose and flipping upwards into the branches of a gnarled oak. Nearby, apple trees marked the edge of the marsh and the onset of firmer ground.

Bulrushes pricked the stagnant bogs. Occasionally a frog burped. A chill vapour hung just above the surface and swallowed the shadows of other survivors; warriors collapsed on blood slicks with nothing left but their prayers for revenge or mercy. Artos would not fall, though. With scolding thoughts of defeat, he punished his body as he punished his soul, and this ignited the rage in his core to fuel every screaming muscle.

Each splitting and fraying fibre ignited new agonies, yet still he ran. Away from the memories of splintered wooden shields, of unbreakable legionary formations, of wild woad warriors chipping away at the metal edges of Rome, only to die from a gleaming gladius or pugio between the ribs. Not even the rolling death-thunder of Iceni chariots, rattling from the fog like monsters, dented the enemy lines. The cries of galloping horses soon accompanied those of cut-down men. *We have been conquered.*

"Conquered," Artos hissed, just to feel the word prickle in his mouth. It left his spit cloying and bitter.

Running on through the sucking marsh, spear held tight as if it was his only purchase on a cliff edge, he damned those who had fled before that last battle, cowards who sensed the fear of their gods in the wind. Doubt and paranoia had faded the up-rush of sudden victory. But not for Artos. On the day of battle, he had not been found wanting.

Fighting like a mad dog, he took down legionary after legionary even though the air grated against his skin as if it was exhaled by a foreign god who meant only to salt his wounds. But, as the centurions had bellowed, 'Nothing stops the march of Rome.'

At least Artos survived. He was sure of that. This stagnant bog, writhing with the drones of thousands of flies, could not be the Afterlife. Avalon existed without pain, a place to rest after death before re-joining the fray. Pain was a thing of the living and Artos would not stop living until he reached the lost places, the ancient forests where faerie would knit him together again. He didn't want to die, to only come back many years from now to face a new enemy. What mattered was Rome, to fight against Rome. Until the world ended, if need be.

As sludge dried into earth, the limping rhythm of his feet carried him onward, a dull repetitive thudding in time to the land's heartbeat. Everything blurred into one great stretch of mud and an ever-darkening shade of green...

A filigree of white pierced that dark green. Blinking to make sense of it all, Artos found himself lying on a bed of twig and leaf mush. It took him a while to realise the light was that of the sun, oozing through a forest canopy. Somehow, running after that boggart, he had made it into the oaken heart of Albion. Or died. *Maybe they are one and the same.*

Breath hushed around his ear, "They marched through my forest, severing us from the leylines as they went. It itches like an infection. Artos, comfort me."

The words pushed into his mind, scintillated his nerves, and immediately inflamed his desires. *Surely magic of some sort.* A body pressed warmth against him. A veil of black hair swept over his face and the scent of woman surrounded him. Within his stomach, chest, and loins, Artos felt lust coil and tighten. Birds twittered; childish giggles echoed from all around. Many pairs of yellow eyes watched him intently.

Pale and wonderful, suddenly the woman was on top of Artos, a raven-haired beauty amidst a dozen points of light like daytime stars. But not stars, sprites, tiny girl-things with wings buzzing and soothing. Then more lights, all around, from the circular engravings covering the trees, the faerie eyes blinking open to sate curiosity. In the bushes, nymphs looked on, naked and taut, charming senses and minds with tra-la-la melodies.

Pain exploded into wet ecstasy, an ongoing rush that defied anything Artos had ever felt. The world became skin and pink, tongues and sweat, before that dark-greenness took him away again.

---

A raven's harsh caw woke him. A lady stood over him, as pale as the moon, and smiled. Artos knew her from the stories of druids and war maidens, from the totems engraved on his spear shaft; she was Andraste, the Goddess of Victory. Artos sat up and rested on an elbow, unsure if he could even trust his mind to balance him.

"We soothed each while they murdered the land. You can stay here, warrior, to guard me and remain safe in the magical forest." Her voiced cooed enchantment, but the peacefulness of this glade snagged against a barb of bitterness in Artos' core. *Safe?*

"I saw your ravens through the fog of battle, looking down with their beady eyes. Looking as we died. Just looking, nothing more."

The lady only smiled as she leaned in close. Her eyes swelled and rippled like slow-green water, leading him into that infinite dark point at the centre... *Trickery!*

"You did not join us!" Artos shouted, to affirm possession of his words and thoughts. "Together we could have struck a great blow and reclaimed our lands."

With her fingertips, Andraste traced Artos' cheek and soothed her way to his mouth, gently massaging his lower lip. "Hush now, warrior. We cannot risk ourselves in doomed battles. You must understand, we and the Fey are the souls of Albion. Hunted from the great land-sea to the East, we have engrained every mote of these islands with our essence. If we are wiped away these isles lose everything."

The forest haze sharpened in Artos' eyes. *Their islands?* "You manipulate blood feuds for your own amusement, but when war arrives you hide. Omens for petty squabbles, is that all you are good for?"

"Victory takes time, and we must build up our strength. But we are weakened on soil claimed by Rome. It breaks the cycle of power. Do you understand?"

But Artos could only clench his jaw and attempt to douse his temper. *He* was not claimed. No Roman claimed the rebellious earth which clung to his body. More so, atop the forest mulch of leaves and twigs rested his spear. The point and upper shaft, flaked with dried blood, were proof that he remained free.

Grabbing it, shifting it in the dirt so he could push himself to his feet, he found his body healed from wounds and pain. A curious strength broke from his core, entwining with agitation as if he faced the calm before a storm of battle. The forest clarified into pinpoint focus. Earwigs scurried around tree trunks, leaves trembled from the leaps and feints of red squirrels. Gleaming strands of spider silk knitted between branches and the dilated eyes of nymphs, elves, and other things stared from overgrown foliage.

Artos gripped his spear tightly until the bones in his hand hurt. He spat at the ground.

"You are 'Victory.' You were supposed to be there, to punish the Roman rape. But you did nothing."

"You do not understand." But now Andraste's eyes flared with fright, her glowing paleness dimming. She looked smaller. Artos raised his spear and sensed a pull toward action.

"For generations, this spear has been a living judgement in personal combats and battle, ingrained with the sweat of family, the blood of foes, the water and dirt of these lands. This spear has tasted victory for a hundred years. It is more Albion than you. I am more Albion than you!" The goddess lunged forward and tried to throw her arms around the warrior to calm him, but Artos side-stepped and watched her fumble pathetically.

"I sacrifice you, Goddess of Victory, to any other god or goddess who will give me what I want, be they on this isle or the next."

With a snap of his arm, Artos' jabbed his spear point through Andraste's breast. Half expecting the fates to turn against him, for the goddess's ravens to gouge and peck him into a pulp, instead there was...nothing. Only weakness.

Opening her mouth just as lenses of water burst from her eyes and trailed down her cheeks, Andraste let out a final sob. Her green eyes held Artos' own for a moment, before rolling back. Lips twitching with a silent lament, Andraste slid from the spear shaft into a heap on the forest floor. In seconds, she disintegrated into sods of rich black earth.

Great cracking noises echoed from beyond the forest like the far-off mountains had been struck with a giant pickaxe. Suddenly, trees surged contrary to the breeze, their branches reaching for Artos. Something malignant cast its gaze on his back, he could feel his skin crawl. The warrior swung around; spear poised to stab at whatever preyed upon him.

Instead, he gasped at what he saw, a cloaked figure winking into existence from a cone of swirling leaves. Despite a hood concealing her upper face, Artos recognised her gaping, toothless maw and crooked frame: the Crone, Hag of Fates. Sweet rot clutched at his senses; images of maggots flickered in his mind. Insides churning, he heaved but swallowed back the bile.

"Unless first victory is absolute, are not victory and revenge two faces of the same?" Croaking with every word, the old thing's after-breath was like a sucking wound.

"Cerridwen, Crone, I have no wish to hurt you, passive witch of prophecy as you are." Artos' voice shook.

Out of her voluminous sleeves creaked a grey hand. It clutched, like a claw, around a translucent green stone, which had a peculiar, neat hole in the middle from which string could be laced. She offered it to Artos. "See what fate you have woven, God of Victory. See your last moments."

Hesitating, daring not to touch such a tainted Fey-thing, Artos nonetheless stared at it. The tiny hole in the middle of the stone swelled in his mind's eye. Crystallising, it formed an image that scared and confused, a nonsense picture of a town that had never been, lifelike but thoroughly alien. Huge pillars stood over houses, which squashed and leaned like drunks in mid-tumble, and billowed fire. A filthy place teeming with running children and faerie. But what caught his eye was a spire above a well, a bizarre circle of gold stuck to that spire. Around the circle someone had affixed symbols, Roman-looking sigils which Artos had observed on military eagles and banners.

"A man cannot be at war with all things at once," said the Crone. "Maybe it is better to grow patient, young warrior, just like Andraste told you. See how the children of humans and faeries play together? Is that not worth fighting for? Have faith, and maybe your crime can be reversed." Snatching the stone away with surprising alacrity, Cerridwen tucked it beneath her hood where it clacked against what must have been dozens of the things

With awkward movements, the hunched crone turned her back to Artos and hobbled away. Almost hearing the scrape of bone against bone, Artos winched. Only when Cerridwen disappeared into the shadows of the deeper forest did Artos regain his composure, his spear almost humming in his grip to reaffirm his warrior's pride. Silence returned.

Suddenly, as if they had been waiting to make sure the Crone had gone, a dozen or so little green boggarts, pinched-nosed, and long-eared, sprang from burrows in earth and hollows in tree trunks. Their bulbous, yellow eyes focused on Artos, while they huddled around one of their number, Gobba the big-mouthed boggart with the Roman helmet. This particular boggart proved braver than the rest, approaching Artos with tentative curiosity. "You stink of resentful dead things. Powerful, like a god. We think you are entertaining."

More slowly, lithe elves appeared from behind trees, their eyes glassy. They looked at Artos, a few slowly nodding as if to ask for his permission. Artos returned the nod and watched as the Fey joined hands and encircled him. Hesitantly, they walked around Artos, walk turning to skip, unsure faces creasing into smiles.

Artos matched them, raised his arms to the heavens, and spun around. Faster and faster, laughing now, a mad guffaw to the gods. A whirl of energy and celebration overtook that forest grove, the Fey tumbling in a jolly Fey dance.

*My first followers?* Artos remembered Cerridwen's words. *Is it true, am I now the God of Victory?*

Of Andraste, only heaps of black mud remained. As the wind kicked up to join the celebrations, the mud spiralled into the air, sparkling with the brightest green Artos had ever seen.

# CHAPTER TWO

# OMENS

*London, 1861 A.D.*

A knife-edged wind blew through the docks. However, hardy breeds of sailors wouldn't be sent scampering indoors by the threat of prolonged winter. Sol watched them from the rooftop of a warehouse, straining to ignore the distraction of the clippers and steamships bobbing on the Thames, with their forests of smoke, masts, and ropes. From those ships, the produce of the world would be unloaded into the insatiable bowels of London.

Sol often passed away the hours staring at the mishmash of dockside humanity, dark men and women, tanned and blond-haired men and women, men and women in dirty rags or theatrically bright cloths. The stink of damp and salt mingled with the thrust of spices and the choke of rubber. It always sent Sol away to a land of dreams and adventure. But his purpose here was not to dream, his purpose was to trick and con. Below him, on the board walks where a crowd of fresh-off-the-boat men huddled, a girl called Shammy played a theatre of deceit; she was the hook and the reel.

With her almond-shaped eyes and skin of either summertime golden tan or wintertime snow-white, Shammy always attracted the stares and comments of Londoners when in other boroughs of the city. Among the far-flung human bric-a-brac of the docks, however, exoticism was not, in itself, a cause for resentment or malice.

Dressed in an old but slightly too-large, once red but long since faded pink, silk dress, Shammy knelt upright on a cushion. In front of her rested a wooden crate, covered in red cloth, on which she laid her hands, palms upward and splayed open. Both Sol and Shammy understood the art of the 'mislead,' how the sight of a young eastern girl conjured up mystery and superstition. How even men of learning, who thrilled to declare 'charlatan' at every opportunity, held back their words when presented with a mystic from the oldest of nations, a Han in touch with ancient truths and able to see through the veneer of European logic and science.

The sing-song syllables she plucked, like random strings on the voice instrument in her mind, fooled the audience into believing they listened to the authentic speech of Mandarins and Celestials. Grubby dock workers and prim-and-puffed gents all returned the gesture when Shammy bowed as if she was a dockside princess and they her motley court. At present, she had pierced the attentions of a dandy-dressed sailor with rings in his ears. The sailor tossed a coin Shammy's way, flipped it high into the air so it spun and glinted from flashes of a cold sun; today's con, the simplest game of 'heads or tails.'

Sol felt the pull of fate as soon as the coin left the sailor's palm. He watched it spin, shimmer, and then blur around the edges, all signs which he regarded as a physical manifestation of his 'good luck.'

With bravado and a drunken slur, the sailor called 'Heads.'

Sol whispered, 'Tails,' and imagined the word fluttering into the ether, into the invisible ear canal of some deity of fortune. And, for the thirty-first time that day, the coin spun back to earth and landed neatly on the red cloth in front of Shammy. She would smile sweetly and let the coin, clearly showing 'tails,' speak for itself. Audience mutterings, mixed with a few claps, accompanied her pocketing of the coin. She bowed her head, respectfully. It worked the same with cups and balls, or cards, or any petty game of chance. Apart from the odd deliberate loss to cool mobs or up the ante, the 'mark' never won the toss.

This was Sol's gift, to own an instant, to think of an outcome and manoeuvre time and space as if luck obeyed him when he needed it. It always came with a shimmer of air, the smell of grasses, a flash of green, and a lost moment like a blink of sleep. But Sol couldn't be the frontman to his and Shammy's con-game. Gaunt with narrow eyes, a dirty street urchin, the crowd would call him a cheat and thief if he personally dared to trick their coins away. They would call the Peelers, and the dockside constables were far quicker than Rozzer Jim back in Sol's borough, the Marsh Worm Mile. Or they would noose him or beat him until he couldn't walk. He had seen that done to others. No, Shammy was Sol's partner in crime, his accomplice ever since Artos had found them both as babes, like a hundred others, by the old well. That was a place where Ladies and dollymops dumped unwanted reminders of sailors' visits before the seafarers disappeared into the vast ocean blue.

Sometimes the con did go wrong. Sometimes one of the marks *would* call Shammy a cheat, usually a drunk who thought the girl too helpless to defend herself. As it so happened, the big sailor with the rings in his ears was not only one of those drunks but a petty conman who hated the tables being turned.

"Little street rat, that was me double-headed coin! Weren't no 'tails' on there to begin with." With a jarring rush of motion, he stomped through Shammy's makeshift table, the wooden box splintering, the red cloth bunching up under his boot. Sol heard the man shout a colourful variety of curses. The crowd joined in, anticipating a fresh round of 'street entertainment.' A few, though, backed away, shiftily surveying the scene, perhaps, to see if a Peeler lurked nearby.

Shammy flinched; head jerked back as her charade melted into harsh reality. A second later, after she turned and caught sight of Sol skipping over a slate roof just next to a warehouse, she smiled a challenge to the sailor.

With heart-pounding, Sol jumped down onto a window ledge and kicked off onto a drainpipe. *Must be quick.* Scanning for escape routes while he shimmied down to the boardwalk, as soon as he hit the ground he yelled, "Oi, Trouble! I've got us our way out."

Struggling to stand, Shammy's tied-back dress bunched around her knees and caused her legs to zigzag in a series of awkward angles, like a trapped stick insect in a heavy breeze. The angry sailor leaned in, imposing his size against her petite frame. But Shammy found her balance and stared straight up into his face. She lifted an arm into the air, held it above her head, and pinched at the wind. The crowd suddenly quietened.

Fingers twisting invisible nothings, Shammy closed her eyes and started to shriek harsh-edged syllables of sing-song nonsense. The sailor stepped back, eyes darting to the remains of the crowd, afraid that he might be the target of some sort of spell.

A burly dockworker on the edge of the crowd barked a quick laugh. "Go on, get her, quick. Before she gives you the evil eye and curses you down to the Dark Alley."

The crowd watched Shammy's fingers weave their mystical secrets, while her other hand slipped unseen behind her back. She loosened the clasp holding the silk dress with a flick, allowing the material to flow airily around her legs, giving her room to move. Her careful movements at once exploded into a full-blown sprint. She headed toward Sol, who calmly waited at the entrance of an alley. Grabbing Sol's hand as she rushed by, Shammy yelped with excitement as they passed into the alley, really a street made narrow from towers of splintered warehouse crates.

Lost in the thrill of the chase, they barely noticed the frost on the wind until it whipped in streams through the air. It slowed them down, their shoes-slaps echoing dully on the boardwalk. Sol looked at Shammy and pushed a finger to her lips. "Hush." Then, just as the angry sailor appeared, cursing and spitting, with a couple of rough-faced mates behind him, Sol pointed to one of the stacks of warehouse crates.

"What's wrong, don't you like me?" His voice was a sea-shanty accent from a thousand ports. For a stolen moment, time seemed to blink. The edge of one of the crates shimmered and blurred against the clarity of the brickwork behind it.

With a whoosh of her silk, a turn of her lips, and an impudent smile, Shammy stepped towards the men and said, in hard-edge Bow Bell cockney "How can I help you, gents?" All at once, the crates came crashing down, blocking the way and pinning the sailor underneath.

Hand-in-hand, Shammy, and Sol strolled from the alley, back home to Chavver Street, giggling even as the wind stung them with its chill.

## Marsh Worm Bridge, London 1861 A.D.

Although Victor's rough-hewn, inside-out robes warded against evil, they did little to fend off the unseasonal chill. His breath clouds cursed the cold and his metal pike shaft ached in his hands. It hadn't seemed like glove weather earlier, when midday chatter rang with the happy notes of springtime. Markets waxed street-slang majestic about sun rays and sweet pollen, how it made their produce juicier than before, how it blessed their potions with potency. But, to Victor, the sunlight had seemed too delicate, as if it might shatter somehow.

Nonetheless, the faint whiff of grasses converging on London and the Marsh Worm Mile had hinted at a languid Spring stretching awake from hibernation. Then, as suddenly as the morning thaw, a host of patchy muscular clouds and the vicious winds of renewed winter rushed in.

Censers swung from clasps nailed into the wooden frame of Victor's guard house. The rolling veil of blessed smoke had long since evaporated; the dull orange embers inside the censers turned the air bitter instead of flavouring it with the usual sweetness. The little silver bells on Victor's leather belt tinkled in the wind.

The large man stared across the echoing stones of Marsh Worm Bridge. Something about the way the wind moaned and whistled around the iron guardrail made him uneasy. Even just a few years back, the Faerie mobs would have swarmed the bridge by now; refugees on the cusp of spring fleeing the grunts of industrial machines which fed on their ancient habitats. Whole squads of Hymn Whisperers used to stand guard to ensure no evil magic slipped through into London. Maybe the Forest Fey had learnt that passage was not worth the price, to give up old-world life for gainful employment under suspicious human eyes. Maybe, as rumours had it, the Fey had finally become extinct beyond the borders of the city.

Victor would happily let any Fey in though, even the magic ones, if they could show how their gifts could be used for practical purposes. Like brewing good gin or making bread plumper and more delicious. *Ward off the curses and welcome the blessings...* After all, London was the world in a city, but the borough of Marsh Worm Mile had the dubious distinction of being the final destination on the last leyline of old vanished Britannia. Marsh Worm Mile, the only place in the whole United Kingdom, if not the world, where men and Fey lived, worked, and prayed to, or in the very least *observed,* the ' one' Christian God together.

Victor shivered. The forest on the far side of the bridge thrashed wildly, trees whipping like the arms of a maddened crowd. A fell feeling worried at his nerves. Due to his size and temper, everyone thought him to be fearless. Really though, Victor knew how to hold fear inside. If his fear ever did so happen to break to the surface, well, then he knew magic *must* be responsible. The bad sort, curses and the like

As he wept from the frost stinging his eyes, Victor's emotions twisted and grew heavy in the cold. He tried to warm his soul with thoughts of the upcoming Sea Nymph Carnival, but his mind kept wandering to colder things...Like loneliness, an almost despairing pine for anyone to say anything to, but everyone had cleared off not long ago and Victor only guarded against portents and signs. The few knocker merchants allowed at the Marsh Worm Gate had packed up shop when the weather took a turn for the worse.

Gritting his teeth, the large man began to hum one of the Holy Cathedral dirges. It steeled him, inspired him to do his duty, and to push back the tide of parasitic evils which flaked from every pore of the unwary Faerie folk who still worshipped the old gods; the omnipresent rust waiting to stain a soul.

*What was that?* He blinked at something other than frost.

Crumples of brown leaf circled and zipped. Tiny twig-breakings putter-pattered irregularly against the guard house. Across the river, the trees lashed ever more wildly as if calling for someone to free them from the ground. Leaves surged from between their trunks until a rolling wave of dried brown gusted from the forest, spilling onto the bridge.

"Holy things protect me," whispered Victor. He took a hand from his pike to fiddle with the nozzle of the hose tucked into his belt. It linked to a tank on his back, full of well-water blessed by a Christian priest and cursed with forgetfulness by an elf-witch.

*Dead autumn leaves and a winter wind during the first week of spring?* This confusion of seasons was surely an evil omen. The smell of vegetable rot trailed into Victor's nostrils, ash smeared his palate and he coughed to spit it out.

The tide of leaves blustered along the bridge and broke around Victor, lashing against the walls and collecting in niches. Deciding on the pike over the hose, Victor swung ineffectively at imagined creatures bearing ill-omens, swatting what he could, blinking against the black bits barraging his eyelashes. The leaves swirled and twisted into faces with mocking open mouths. He smashed through them with unsatisfying ease.

Like a caught breath, the wind suddenly stopped. The brown rush fell into motionless heaps. The overcast sky split, breached by a dozen rays of slow-warming sun.

*What boggart curse is this? Those pests were, of all the Fey, the most prone to mischief.* What evils could have been on that wind to make him so fearful? Squeezing his steamship broad shoulders into the narrow guard house, Victor placed his pike in an iron rack. Loosening the hose, the cylindrical iron tank on his back rung as it knocked against the door frame. When he re-emerged onto the bridge he aimed the hose, the nozzle made from silver and engraved with crosses and fishes and cows and waves. He aimed it at a heap of leaves. Out sprayed a fine mist of forgetfulness, freeing the leaves of whatever evil contaminated them, burning away any bad-luck boggarts and old-god curses hiding underneath.

Beaten by the spray, the leaves collapsed into tighter heaps, crumpling into remnants. Victor held his breath at the sight of boggart scrawl under where the leaves had collected; graffiti-faerie-eyes, evil eyelets for malevolence to thread through into the city. Just one of a myriad of petty nastiness. The scribble hissed away as the pavement forgot the taint. All the while Victor remained vigilant over his thoughts in case something wished to manipulate or possess him. The internal battle to control his anxiety was almost too much. Spiked evil pricked at the edges of his holy humanity. Guilt pulled at his conviction as if he'd just done something very, very wrong.

Just as his tank and hose spluttered on empty, and to Victor's eternal relief, the new Hymn Whisperer shift arrived; another brother-in-arms, though a right rotten one at that. A lad as big as Victor called Shiv, who ran with the Marsh Mob Boys and not Victor's favoured Guinea Dreadfuls. Dressed in his own inside-out brown cloak and clinking with silver charms, Shiv inanely babbled about the weather and failed to notice the concern on Victor's face. Victor barely understood a word Shiv had said anyway, his mind so dizzied, but he caught a single phrase, 'Winter's last gasp.'

Shiv continued to talk while checking his equipment and refilling the censers. Victor grunted: a low rolling growl loaded with danger. Only then did Shiv stop talking, squinting at the large man with uncertainty.

Victor's eyes narrowed; his unease bubbled on the rim of anger. Forcing himself to recoil from the snap of violence, he tightened his jaw. "Beware your mind. Evil lurks on the wind."

Shiv frowned and shrugged his shoulders. "Ain't nothing. Just that you Dreadfuls scared of the cold."

Victor grunted again. With tunnel vision, he pushed past Shiv into the empty streets, to the sound of little bells.

*What had happened to cause that ill wind?* Victor should have refilled his tank and blasted the whole bridge clean. Instead, he quickened his pace, walk breaking into a jog through the thread-alleys of the redbrick, earthen and wooden maze of Marsh Worm Mile. He thought only of oblivion and escape, of answers at the bottom of a bottle of gin. One night of broken temperance wouldn't hurt, the boggarts couldn't possess him that easily. Tomorrow he would be 'Hymn Whisperer Incarnate' again, an impassable guard at the gates of Humanity's soul. Tomorrow he would do that. Tonight, though, he would forget it all, and dream of the excitement of a good ruck at the Sea Nymph Carnival.

<hr />

Back at the guard post the following afternoon, Victor was a closed fist of apprehension. The water in the tank on his back sloshed while he fidgeted. The stark white light of the afternoon sliced sharply into hangover-eyes. Every creeping noise, scrape of debris against the ground, or scurry of rats in a corner made him jump. Hell, he'd even prefer to venture into the Dark Alley than stand there on guard that afternoon.

*I bet I've only gone and been bloody cursed by those evil eyes.* Another worry to add to the list; how best to 'cure' himself? Victor hated the needle pricking mischief of those pesky, flapping sprites, or all the knot-tying and tarot card trickery of witches. Sad to say though, that always seemed to be more effective at removing curses than a blessing and splash of holy water.

Where a Hymn Whisperer should find cast-iron resolve, Victor found only a withered, soft thing. *Do your job and wait for the time to pass. Afterwards, I can drink again...* Everything was so... *unholy.* The knocker market, behind the gate to Marsh Worm Mile, still echoed with emptiness. *Suspicious that.* Those Fey-folk had surely heard warnings whispered on the bitter winds of the past few days.

*Come on, puff out my chest, get on with it.*

Passing the time as best as he could, Victor hummed church songs and sprayed walls free of graffiti evil eyes. The holy dirge reverberated in his chest, rubbing out the black blot of gin on his soul and reconfirming his purity of purpose. But all went to waste when a whistle broke the therapeutic hiss of his tank and hose. A figure emerged from the forest on the far side of Marsh Worm Bridge, a stooped outline of a man-thing, with large sacks of something or other, slung over his shoulders.

*What is this now?* Victor squinted against the light and noticed a white shock of spiked hair on a naked torso, a scrawny man of tight wired muscle walking barefoot. Levelling his iron pike and gritting his teeth, the fire of potential conflict instantly burnt away Victor's earlier tension. He grunted loud enough to jolt nearby cats from hiding places, the threat in his voice carrying a dozen questions across the Marsh Worm Bridge.

The approaching man looked up, his face hollow-cheeked and dirty, with wild grey eyes and moss of red stubble. "I can see by your aura that the drink has weakened your resolve. What if I'm some foul ancient thing, forced from my home by hungry factories, and bent on revenge against human filth?" the man shouted, voice scratched and thin. "What if I refuse to turn back?"

"Then you take the test and I run you through." Yes, the words felt good. A return to manliness against the malicious whispers of the wind.

"And would you enjoy it?" The white-haired man, closer now, beamed a smile and winked.

Victor's heart ran faster, he let his pike point fall a few inches. *No, it couldn't be?*

"Answer me, lad, would you like it? To run through an elf about to give you the Evil Eye? Would you claim Marsh Worm Mile for your own kind?" The white-haired man's face held youth behind the blue stain of woad, his white hair just a lime-styled façade. Walk turning into a jog, the man abandoned his sacks and opened his arms wide, exposing a network of tortures and scars over his body.

Then Victor roared, "Artos!"

Leaping the last several feet, Artos flung his arms around Victor's broad shoulders, flooding the large young man with clean scents of sap and forest. Rot followed, crawling deeper into Victor's mind, becoming that ash that had made him cough a few days ago.

Smothering Victor's fire of violence into cowed confusion, Artos pulled away but still held the Hymn Whisperer by the shoulders. "Boy, Victor, you've put on weight. A big strong lad you are. I knew you were Hymn Whisperer material, steel gauntlet over a woollen mitten if I'm right, lad? Not a trouble-maker but a trouble-ender. Soft touch and a hard man. A perfect companion to build a new future free from faerie lies."

The words pricked Victor's conscience. This didn't ring true. Holy Humanity and Good Faerie, not boggarts and curse wielders, were one and the same in the Marsh Worm, at least that was what he had been taught – what Artos himself had taught them all. Fey were not the enemy, only evil magic, and evil magic was as bad as human hatred.

"You doubt me, lad? I found out the Fey are cuckoos in the nest, all of them – every last one."

Victor searched his mind for memories of Artos, of the man who left the Marsh Worm Mile five years ago with a whole company of followers, and recalled how those grey eyes could cast away all fears, how they brought hope to every orphan of Chavver Street. Now they seemed made of stone as if nothing in the world could surprise them. "Where is everyone else, Artos?"

Leaning in so his lips almost touched Victor's ear, Artos whispered like a man fermenting revolution. "My bear, my murderous bear, I can see your past lives. An axe swinger on northern shores, a warrior not a general. You are not to ask questions; those things are not your worry. Just know my path is to make us all gods of the Mile."

"I don't understand. I thought you went to trade with the lost faerie and bring us together…" Before Victor could finish, Artos let go of his shoulders, turned his back, and walked to his discarded sacks.

"Things change, my friend. You are my man now, too good even for the Hymn Whisperers. I will make a new brotherhood of you all, to help cure this city of new *and old-world* corruption. Pray remind me, lad, who are the orphans you run with, your gang? You don't run with a faerie mob, do you? I remember a celestial girl, what's her name?"

"Shammy." Curiosity getting the better of him, Victor found himself following Artos, although he didn't relax his grip on the pike.

"Could be. And another lad. Some soft little prick, not a warrior like you."

"Sol, he is my friend." Victor couldn't help the half-smile crawling up one cheek. Nobody ever said anything bad about Sol. Somehow it lifted his spirits, eased his suspicion. "Artos, there's been foul things on the wind."

"Yes, the purge before wholesomeness. We must cure the evil within. That is deadlier than the evil without. My lad, my boy, my bear, you will learn to be a warrior of woad, a warrior of Welsh bogs and Chalk Cliffs. And I bring gifts for you to share, to make you feel good, and to weed out corruption. Pass it around to all your friends and come running back to me if any hidden faerie mischief turns up."

Artos delved into a sack where green shone through brown stitching, disturbing the contents and creating a haze of pollen and dust. Pulling out a fist-sized bundle of cloth, he tossed it to Victor. The Hymn Whisperer's pike rang against the stone bridge when he dropped it to make the catch.

"Those without the sand to fight write their own deaths. This will help me see what you see. Run along now, lad. Enjoy yourself, spread the word that the Lord of Marsh Worm is back," said Artos.

Victor was intrigued by the little cloth pouch in his hand. Green dust puffed out of the cloth bundle. A second later, Victor felt a tingling behind his eyes, a pleasant fizzing that massaged his mind. He smiled and nodded before taking a big sniff. He felt good... *like a... God or something.*

# CHAPTER THREE

# PEERING THROUGH THE ETHER

*London, 1861 A.D.*

Shammy and Sol laughed and gasped for air, nestled within the soft afternoon shadows cast by the tall, broad wooden warehouses. Their breath clouds merged with the yellow tinge of city smog. Between them, they caressed a roast potato, the snatch-and-run prize from a street vendor, and relished the faint warmth in their palms. As always, they had escaped with ease, Sol leading Shammy to safety as if he followed a good-luck thread through any nook, fence, or coincidence. Never had irate traders cornered them, never had the Peelers snagged them by collar or cuff despite several close shaves.

Always the fortunate ones, he and Shammy avoided the worst depravities of the street, coddled by Sol's blind luck and the lingering remnants of absent Artos' fearsome reputation. Living lives of playful mischief and plentiful stealing not once had they ever had to resort to selling their innocence to drunks or gentlemen of unsavoury tastes. Even now, both having recently turned their eighteenth years, they played like children.

Shammy's brown eyes flashed with mischief and excitement; her cheeks rosy from the run. During times like this, and increasingly of late, Sol felt as if he might blow or slip away if it wasn't for the great anchor of raw feeling in his chest. Collecting cuts and bruises the way a good thief collected purses and watches, Shammy was always a tomboy. But though her tomboy attitude remained, her puppy fat had smoothed into something... *else*, her sparkle and smile often inspired Sol's thoughts to dwell on other possibilities. *Romance* ...? Inexplicable feelings he pushed away. For all this coming of age though, Shammy seemed as happy as ever to continue making street-urchin mischief.

The potato crunched crisply, and steam rose in lacy white tendrils when Shammy squeezed it. "Mine, that is." Her eyes narrowed and her top lip curled.

"You better watch yourself. You don't know who you're messing with," Sol shot back. But when Shammy pressed into him, twisting her body, entangling their arms, and pulling them both down, Sol let himself fall. The day's copious wages jingled in Sol's pockets and they laughed and strained to hold the potato at arm's length so as not to let it touch the dirty boardwalk.

In truth, Sol could easily wrestle or chance the potato from Shammy's grip. If a larger lad had tried to take the potato, Sol would've sent a minor mishap his assailant's way: a stubbed toe on a rusty nail or a momentarily blinding pigeon shit, anything to cause his foe's grip to loosen and allow Sol to claim the potato in victory. But when Shammy gripped Sol's wrist and yanked, he gave in. "Ow," he yelled, the now battered potato leaking fluffy whiteness like ripped feather pillows and dropping into Shammy's hand.

At once, she sprang up and teased with the potato. Sol knew the drill, something built upon layers of memory from when Shammy would play rough, bite and scratch like a wild cat. Shammy didn't bite and scratch Sol any more. These days, Sol was faster and more agile but, springing to his feet, he knew he wouldn't let himself catch her.

Happy just to hear Shammy's shrieks of excitement, he gave chase, happy as long as they were together. And Shammy, her eyes lingering on Sol just a second longer than her sandalled feet lingered on the boardwalk, did indeed shriek. Rounding a corner into another narrow, Sol heard her yelp again. A nasty scrap and thud vibrated through the boardwalk. A deeper voice joined in the exclamation.

"Shammy?" Sol fiddled inside his pocket for the cut-throat razor he always carried 'just in case.' Bursting round the corner, face screwed-up with put-on viciousness... only to find the potato smeared across the boardwalk, as if the victim of a vegetable massacre. And there was Victor, helping Shammy up off the ground,

The Hymn Whisperer wore his inside-out robes but also clutched a cloth rag in his grubby hands. Fidgeting on the spot as if dying for a piss, Victor's eyes shone wildness. Most oddly of all, his face glittered with specks of green.

"I saw him." Victor's voice was a rapid staccato instead of the usual drawn-out monotone. "Artos is back. He came back.

Alone though. I don't know what happened to the others. He said he knows what we got to do. Gave me a new, better job. A wood warrior or something."

Rarely hearing Victor speak more than a few sentences in one go, Sol eyed him with suspicion. "Promotion, you say? Soon you'll be the mayor of London then."

Shammy looked back and forth between Sol and Victor. Her face alight with mischief, she smiled a mix between joy and confusion.

"Have a sniff. It makes you feel good." Victor's large hand trembled as he shoved the cloth toward Sol. "Artos said it's good." A ringing endorsement. The magic words. *If Artos said it was okay, then why not?*

Playfully, Shammy snatched at the cloth. Victor scowled, his wild eyes growing hard. When Shammy unwrapped the bag, sticking her face into the bundle and taking a big, comically exaggerated whiff, Victor's frown melted into a dopey smile.

A second later, the outline of Shammy's loose silk dress buckled as if her bones had turned into jelly. Lunging forward to catch her, Sol drew back when Shammy regained her balance and removed her face, now covered with a glittering green powder, from the cloth. Her brown eye twinkled with the same wildness as Victor's

"Oh, I can hear music." Her voice drifted to somewhere far away. Tapping her sandalled feet on the boardwalk while dipping fingers back into the cloth bag, she started to sway with bawdy grace. In imitation of how a Lady might gesture, Shammy rolled out a hand, fingertips green, in Sol's direction. "Dance with me, good sir. I dare you."

"Double dare!" yelled Victor.

The expectant eyes of Sol's friends felt oppressive. Uncertainty coiled tightly in his stomach. *Bloody Victor. Shouldn't he be at the bloody bridge earning his payment of freebies, favours, and respect?* The Hymn Whisperers let the gangs run a regular riot on the streets, as long as nobody indulged in dangerous magic, but here was Victor playing with some...magical powder! If Victor could do it, Sol certainly could. No problem.

Taking Shammy's hand in his own, just like he had a moment before with the potato, he half-inhaled and half-sucked in the green powder. An itch surged through whatever was behind his face. His ears crackled. Bright spots danced in front of his eyes.

Everything rippled like looking up at the world through water, waves magnifying and spiralling the planks and bricks of the warehouses and his friends' faces. The pure echo of a rising choir called to him in glorious melody, but with words he didn't understand. Surging in all directions at once, the choir rumbled the ground, easing into a rhythm like the beating of a heart.

From beyond the ether flickered another world, of half-transparent images behind and above the outline of the docks. Ghosts of vast knobbly oaks stood silent and proud while willows lashed across the sky to knit a sudden canopy, passing in and out of existence a dozen times every minute. Oblivious or simply lost to it all, Victor and Shammy locked elbows and danced and span in ever-faster circles.

Rubbing his eyes, Sol peered beyond his friends, beyond the ground which flashed between grass and boardwalk, to where faint tree ghosts framed an enclosed view of a real-world cobbled street, with the usual back-and-forth throng of colourful and shady dock characters. He noticed something else, that same shimmer he knew so well whenever he called on 'Luck.' This time the shimmer *thickened*, congealed into a transparent haze, now a bright green that formed into a definitive figure, the air picking up a needle and thread to stitch a new thing into existence. Two things, in fact, squat-midget things with big ears and beak-like noses.

Traders, patrons, and malingerers carried on with their casual everyday disregard. No one else seemed to notice, even though one of the creatures sat on a pub sign kicking its little legs over the edge while the other leant against a fruit stall where an old maid was perusing the recent crop of unseasonably ripe apples. The creature's bulbous, yellow eyes flared like gas lamps at every passer-by.

Swaying like a drunk, Sol stumbled away from his two friends, still spinning in their mad dance. He squinted and forced himself to concentrate on the street, on a gentleman dressed in a straight black suit, strolling toward the fruit stall. Poised and somewhat stiff with his movements, delving one hand into his jacket probably for his wallet, the man looked to be completely balanced. Then, as if time had condensed the air into treacle, the man turned with laboured slowness to look at Sol. The creature at the stall stuck out a bright green leg, and the gentleman jerked forward. Time sped up as he tripped, so inelegantly, into a flat-capped man in front of him.

The commotion pulled at the attention of those nearby. A Peeler, his towering top hat plain for all to see, came rushing over to the gentleman's side, hoping to catch him as he rebounded off the flat-capped man. But he never cleared the final few feet of distance. Instead, the gentleman finished his dance of misfortune, hitting the cobbles hard, splaying out like the loser of a prize fight. And the Peeler stood completely still, one hand covering a splat of liquid that drooled from his forehead. Sol had seen the midget creature on the pub sign, now gleefully swinging back and forth, spit in the man's face, although the man himself seemed to lack any clue as to who, or what had done it.

"My God," whispered Sol. "Is this what hides behind my good luck? Are they...boggarts?" Nobody he knew had ever actually seen a real-life boggart, though many had claimed they had felt their presence.

But that wasn't the end of the mischief. The old maid started to scream and choke; she had taken a mouthful of bright red apple, only inside it teemed with maggots.

An ugly sneer on its pinched face, the little creature on the pub sign turned its head, its eyes blazing at Sol like a house fire. Then the thing leapt up to balance on the sign and performed a most gracious, right-angled, bow. With a stubby clawed finger, it pointed at Sol and then started to caw like a raven. It flicked its wiry body, swung from the sign, and landed, with feline agility, on all fours. Still sneering, eyes still glowing, it stood upright and waved its broomstick arms at Sol as if beckoning.

"Follow me, I swear I found a way to make a man rich in this world." Grabbing Victor's robe and giving it a good yank to distract him from his dance with Shammy, Sol sprinted up the boardwalk and into the cobblestoned street. Shammy and Victor, their eyes wild and twinkling, shared a glance of excitement before running after him.

⋄⊰⊱⊰⎯⎯⎯⎯⎯⊱⊰⊱⋄

Barely keeping pace with the sprightly green things, Sol ran flat out. The boggarts bounded from floor to window-ledge to roof and back again like squirrels. Every once in a while, the city flashed, a candle snuffed and instantly re-lit, and seared green light ghosts of the forest into Sol's eyes. Though the boggarts leapt and swung onto those magic ghost branches, the trees passed right through Sol's fingers if he tried to grab them. Skipping over whole streets, the creatures peeked back and waited just long enough, as if playing a game, for Sol to momentarily catch up.

Before long, the dockside smells of fish, salt and spice gave way to the earthier stink of the Marsh Worm Mile. Crowded squares and tight streets choked into higgledy-piggledy narrows. Wooden warehouses and proud, white-washed, classically columned government buildings collapsed into a riotous drunken blush of colour.

Market stalls made from a myriad of human and faerie stuffs, wood adorned with runes and amethyst, pearlescent stone, luminous moss, and lily pads, fought for every inch of trading space. Cheesemongers and bakers touted their wares; Elf mushroom-larks brewed slop in cauldrons; tiny sprite girls flitted and sparkled to draw in customers for a snort of faerie tobacco or a shot of Absinthe. Through the tunnel alleys rang the omnipresent clangs of knocker hammers, shaping metal fresh from their forge. But nobody noticed the creatures that led Sol on a frantic chase.

"What you pinched, Sol? Is Rozzer Jim on your back? Lose 'em in the Dark Alley," yelled a knocker, his stringy beard ruffling into a smile. Instinctively, the stout fellow wiggled a few protection signs in the air as if it would deter whoever gave chase.

Ducking through flapping bed sheets soaking on lines criss-crossing an alley and squeezing between rough-faced men with tattoos of moving eyes, Sol scattered most of the coin he and Shammy had made behind him. His usual charity. Money didn't matter much to him; a man of good luck needn't keep his purse full for tomorrow. Sewer grates scraped open, cat-flaps sprung ajar, and grubby rushes of orphan and Fey hands shot out and grabbed all they could.

"A banshee's trying to kiss Sol," shouted someone lost in the bustle of bodies.

A little sprite, buzzing high above the crowds, spied Shammy joyfully rough-housing through the shove of people. "Not a banshee. Shammy's trying to kiss him."

"Worse than that, Victor's trying to kiss him," said a lithe elf lad puffing blue smoke on his pipe. But his voice trailed off, and he ducked back inside his doorway when Victor appeared, looming in his Hymn Whisperer robes and tingling with anti-magic charms. Victor barged the crowds out of his way, the smaller faerie folk almost panicking to find safety.

Out the street-tunnels Sol popped, like a cork from a bottle, into a small space called Old Well Square. A place of curses and blessings, an altar for the Fey and the superstitious. Above the square stood the clock-spire of a rarely used, priest-less church, the tallest building in Marsh Worm Mile.

The golden clock face brought Sol to a jolting stop. Folks in the square mumbled, their faces locked in worry when looking up at the church spire. Some threw coins into the nearby well and drew signs on their chests, others scratched chalk symbols on any bit of paving stone sticking out from its mud-coating. Something had shaken their superstitious assurances.

It was the church clock face. Vandalised. The hands and the Roman numerals were pulled off; something to jar the spirits of pagan and Christian alike. All that was left was a smooth disc of light-reflecting gold. It looked like the sun.

Giggling with delight at the adventure of the chase, Shammy bumped into Sol while trying to bring herself to a stop. "Who are we getting?" she gasped, hugging Sol by his shoulders and steering him around the lingerers with a friendly push-this-way or pull-that-way.

Sol went with the flow, suspecting to see a green flicker any moment: there, a blink of green at his vision's edge, by a wattle and daub shack in the corner of the square. A place he had never noticed before, slumping and wretched, for which the word 'hovel' would be too kind. "Got them, I got them," he said, nodding his way forward while Shammy pushed his shoulders.

The shit and rot of Marsh Worm Mile rolled away. Something alive and vibrant filled Sol's nostrils. Wet grass and sky soared into his lungs. Instead of the ghost trees he had seen while he chased the creature, ghost grass suddenly appeared. And an after-taste, or after smell, that reminded Sol of the books kept by the most wizened human shopkeepers of the Mile.

A drape of moth-eaten cloth served as the door to the shack. It flapped open as if tugged by a phantom breeze, making way for a shrouded figure hobbling through, a hunchback in a swishing robe voluminous enough to shame Victor's Hymn Whisperer uniform. Obscured by a hood, only the bottom half on an ancient face could be seen, a maw of gaping emptiness above an unsightly chin, which sprouted the odd grey twines of an old lady's 'beard.' Around the woman's feet huddled the two green creatures, their gas lamp eyes wide and watching. Shammy gasped; her arms dropped from around Sol's shoulders. "Who the 'ell are you?"

But the woman ignored her, looking only at Sol. "The girl only sees me. She can't see the little bleeders. These are Fate's weavers, my personal, well-trained boggarts. But I see *you* see them."

Grass rustled against Sol's trousers, damp and chilly blades seemed to tickle the bottoms of his feet through his battered shoes. For a moment, he was in a field, stretching far and wide, with only the old woman and her shack for company.

"I know you, Sol. A novel little Fey you are, guarded by these spiteful spirits. They like novelty. You see, a thing like you hasn't existed for a while. Come inside and learn, if you will." Old Well Square flickered behind the image of the great grassland. A gathering crowd stared at Sol while tossing coin after coin into the church well or drawing cross after cross over their chests.

"Quick, now. Every weave of fate brings us closer to the frayed hem of the garment. It never pays for short-lived things to waste a stitch," the woman said, creaking her old bones as she hobbled back into her shack.

# CHAPTER FOUR

## FATE'S BURDEN

### *Marsh Worm Mile, 1861 A.D.*

Sol took a single step toward the elderly lady. Instantly, the church yard, with its lingering crowd, as well as Victor and Shammy disappeared. The hovel rushed around him like a closing fist, plunging him into a wooden room of omens and magic. Each wooden plank in the walls, floor, and ceiling began neatly slotted into place, polished, and worked to a fine finish. However, the further into the room Sol went, the rougher the planks became. Bulging into bark-shaved logs, then moss-addled tree trunks, the once-planks finally sprouted sturdy roots and sunk into a back wall made from the blackest soil.

Shelves stuck out from the wooden walls, densely loaded with charms and totems, bear and wolf sculptures half-finished, soft lines and fine detail on one side but smooth and unworked on the other. Tapestries hung from the upper walls, embroidered with daytime scenes of fishermen and hunters, dairy maids and cows, and star-laden night-time scenes of dancing Fey constellations. These hangings remained uncompleted too, the threads gradually loosening until they dangled freely at the bottom.

"Visions of more hospitable times, they are. Times when all could see the boggarts." The crone carefully watched Sol, examining his reactions to his every word. "Times when boggarts visited hearth and home. They entered the kitchens of both Lords and common folks, to be fed on thick fresh milk and just-baked bread in exchange for good luck. But the inhospitality of history has twisted them into nasty little things, vengeful things." The hairs on Sol's skin bristled.

"The boggarts have been protecting you, although usually, they don't like having a master. Maybe you've been chosen? We'll have to get to the bottom of it." With the cracking of tight joints, she beckoned, with a wave, to a single stool beside a crackling fireplace. Apart from chewing his lip while considering his options, Sol didn't move. Finally, the awkward silence urged him to speak.

"I'm just a common lad, minding my own business, and would like to be on my way. Sorry for chasing those...boggarts. You can have 'em back." Sol slipped a hand into a pocket and fingered his cut-throat razor. *It's the bloody green powder. Victor... next time you want a bit of luck for a game of pitch and toss, I'll bounce your coin down the deepest drain in the blackest part of the Dark Alley.*

"No, not *common* at all." The old lady's voice caught between a gargle and a scrape. "Some might say closer to *unique.* Closer to *royalty.*" She let the words hang. Her ugly smile mocking. Sol found he couldn't focus, as if every object shimmied back and forth by the tiniest degree as if every thought only allowed him to prick the flesh of an idea but deprived him of the meat of its meaning. *That green powder, worse than elf- mushrooms for clogging your mind, for sure.*

"You'd be best to know me," the woman said. "You could call me the 'Patron Saint of Unfinished Things,' though it wouldn't be completely true."

Sol tightened his grip on the cut-throat razor, easing out the blade by a few degrees. He squinted at the Crone. "Have I went and gone mad?"

Hunching over, the Crone started to sway from side to side, as if on a sailing ship in rough seas. *Better to sit,* Sol thought. Stepping over to the fireplace, which flickered without smoke nor heat in a constant cycle of ember-to-roaring blaze and back again, he slumped onto the stool. The old lady seemed to smile at that, though to call it such would be to define 'smile' as something that would surely make babies cry and turn milk sour.

"I know what poisons simmer inside you. You have been cursed. To humans, the ashes of forgotten gods merely heighten their sensations, but to a Fey, it binds them to the Old Ways and allows them to see the way things once were. You are the first Fey born in a long, long time. A Fey gone too human. A sickly thing, your instinct for magic rotted before the root took hold. Unstable, torn between worlds, indeed, I fear madness certainly awaits..." Watching and waiting, the crone continued to sway.

Sol thought about the gutter witches who read pigeon entrails for a few coins, or burnt herbs to enchant any who would listen. But *this witch* was clearly more powerful than any tinkerer of magic. *Well, that's it. Madness. I've gone and lost my mind, just as she said. Gods, this must be some nightmare. Head down, shut up, and wake up.*

"But all is not lost," the old lady continued. "Fate has obeyed me for the first time in an age by bringing you here, gifting me a moment loaded with possibilities and potentialities."

Slowly inhaling, holding it until his ribs strained to contain the trembling need for breath, Sol exhaled with a long, great calm to settle the nerves in his stomach. *What was there to fear of a dream? And if she was really some magic hag, maybe she had a use?* After all, with all that nonsense she was spouting on about, she seemed to like him. What was that she called him? Royalty! Why not run with it?

Suddenly, fixing his eyes to where hers should have rested within that hood, Sol spoke with put-on confidence. "I have a question, old lady. Can you make the orphans of the Mile rich? Can you magic us clean streets and good doctors, magic away the stink of tanners' and tobacco factories, and stop the Peelers whacking us with their sticks?"

"Listen," she spat, with such sudden venom that Sol immediately shut up. "I am the last, but two, of the old gods. One is lost to the world and rotting away, the other is the murderer you call Artos. He is a failed god who wishes nothing but ill. I do not want to give him the reins of the boggarts who once doted on him. I have hidden them from his control for centuries."

"Wait a minute. No. I don't understand. I am an orphan, like so many around here. Artos found me by the well, protected me, and brought me up. I won't have you calling him no murderer even if you are just a bad dream." Holding the sides of the stool, Sol prepared to spring up and jolt himself awake.

The old lady waved a hand dismissively. "I have lived here longer than you, young Fey. Lived here even before people called this land England, right under the noses of those who love or hate the old gods. I hid by the old well and church, sustaining myself on the manna of all races. Together, a well and a church made this a place of prayers in a pitiless city, the target of both curses and blessings. And the well was a place where once desperate women threw guilty new-born secrets. Nowadays, people leave their unwanted swaddling as 'gifts' to Artos to grow and bind to his will. Like those two you run with."

Leaning forward on his stool, Sol butted in, "I only have memories of him, from when I was a kid. But everyone talks highly about Artos. They say how he made the Marsh Worm a place for all. Say how he saved all us orphans."

"No, he didn't. Such power here, it made this place a beacon to faerie and God alike, regardless of Artos. And in that well, which leads to the graveyard of a great victory, now just a black emptiness, the shadows turned sticky with sentiment and magic. I felt it grow, a clot of power and emotion, like from which gods and Fey were once born. The well became an artefact. A growing force."

"Old lady, with respect, I've my friends outside and have surely knocked my head too hard. I best be off." Sol made to stand; his mind prickly with the spell that had surely been woven around him.

"Friends, yes. And something more. I know of your heart's desire, Xiao Mei."

Standing up straight and sharp, the jolt failed to wake Sol from the dream. "Who you on about? I know a girl, but her name is Shammy,"

"Her true name, in the tongue of her father, is Xiao Mei. I heard it; I was there. It was the first time I intervened in the wishes and prayers of men for over a hundred years." The lady paused. From behind her hood, Sol felt like she was dissecting him with her eyes.

"Go on..."

"Yes, you are fond of Xiao Mei, an intriguing girl. Her father was a sailor from the East, unable and unwilling to stay in this land. His companion was an Irish girl who had grown up around here but long since fallen to one of the many sicknesses which plague the poor. They placed the fruit of their coupling, baby Xiao Mei, wrapped in layers upon layers of dirty silk, by the well. I heard her father pray with foreign words. I felt the energy of gods and creatures at the far end of the eastern land-sea. And magic crawled from inside that well, as old things awoke from ancient death for a single moment, like salt of hartshorn to a groggy prize fighter. The magic was a vicious shock to Albion.

'The guilty sailor prayed for fate to grant his baby girl a protector, someone to always love and care for her. I know, because I sent the boggarts to the woken heartbeat of ancient magic and found you in the well, a Fey-thing-baby buoyed on wishes. You became an anchor, fused with life in the old faerie way, born again on emotion and a wish. But not pure faerie, not birthed from the forests but the corruption of the city. An unfinished broken thing, made only to protect and accompany little Xiao Mei."

Sol brushed his hands over his face and rubbed vigorously. "Wake up, wake up."

"On that day, when Artos came to collect his newest orphans, he found you next to the little celestial girl, a boy-baby hugging Xiao Mei. Unknown to him, it was a Fey-thing, not that he would have minded in those days, as long as it wasn't a boggart."

Slumping back down on the stool, Sol said "So, you are saying I'm not human?"

"You are more, and less. A guardian to a girl of no special significance, but to you, she is more than the world. However, fate conspires to make you something more, a boggart prince, dare I say, to balance against Artos."

"I don't understand, I just don't understand. Oh Jesus, is this hell? I'll start going to church, I swear!"

"Artos is a monster, perhaps a demon, but not *the* devil. His need for revenge has heated again. First, he wanted revenge against foreign invaders, then against the old gods. Next, he chose revenge against magic he deemed a curse. This time he wages war against all the old world, not just gods but Fey too. It is worrying. For the first time in centuries, Artos has claimed land and taken power from the magic of that claim. Now, far from hating magic, he plans to use *his* magic to enslave or murder his enemies. But he is a failed god, blind to the boggarts he once controlled. You must…" Suddenly, she hushed and peered up through the leafy ceiling of the cabin, exposing a throat of stringy sinew and tendon. "I did not see this. He is powerful enough to intervene with fate. The knot hangs loose, and events remain undecided."

"What's happening? What must I do? Wake me up!"

As quick as a lightning strike, the crone snapped out her walking stick and pointed at Sol. "He is here. You! Get out!"

***

Winking away, the room of omens left Sol, with the old lady and two boggarts, exposed in the church square. Evening now cast a veil over the Mile, and the square bustled with curious onlookers.

A waiting Fey congregation shone torches, candles, and curious stares Sol's way. Shammy, grim with worry, burst into a smile at his reappearance. Victor was there too, with a dozen Hymn Whisperers, water tanks on their backs, ready for action. *But no, they are not needed!* He caught the eyes of his hated, gibface rival, Shiv, who sneered before mouthing cusses that would surely shame the devil. Then Sol noticed a spindly man dressed in a blue jacket, top hat on his head, orange bristles on his face, skin darkened by some form of make-up. But the man didn't acknowledge Sol.

"So, evil magic has reclaimed the Mile while I was gone. The Crone's been hiding right under my very nose. Go ahead, my bears," said the man, "Cleanse this place of filth."

Face unflinching, Victor, along with his fellow Whisperers, levelled his hose. As one they started to hum a melody of Christian faith, a rising drone to ward against evil. Then they sprayed Sol and everywhere around him with blessed waters. The wash steamed against the vague outlines of grass and the wattle and daub shack.

Curling like prawns as they wailed, the two boggarts bloated like salted slugs. Onlookers covered their ears, but the way they glanced about the square suggested they couldn't see the boggarts.

*Can nobody else see how horrible this is?* Sol tried to grab and pull one of the creatures away from the spray, but his fingers only passed through its dying form. Their squeals of agony ceased when the Hymn Whisperer's tanks clunked on empty, leaving only a drenched Sol and the old lady in dripping robes.

No longer could she hide.

"Hello, Crone, it has been a while," said the blue jacketed man. "Time to end the evil of petty prophecies and magic. You once tricked me, now you belong to me, weak and vulnerable as you are. I will wipe you from the face of Britain once and for all."

Her open maw turned down at the sides. The Crone croaked, "I watched you cower for centuries. Nobody can fight forever, Artos, God of Impotent Vengeance."

Artos roared. "I fought Roman, Saxon, Viking, and Norman. It is the insidious, sick centre of faerie and ancient gods who lack heart. I will remake Albion the way it should have been. For the men, women, and children of Albion!" Out shot a hand, grasping under the Crone's hood and snatching the hag stones which hung around her neck. Artos tugged with force enough to break the necklace strings.

The watching audience started to gossip and look among themselves. A couple of knockers spat and glared at Artos. Sol returned their glances. Something was wrong with the man they all looked up to. *Artos...what did he mean 'remake Albion?'*

"Only when I saw the great golden clock did I start to understand how we must entirely sever the fate of the old world from the new. You are an anchor in a dried-up sea."

"Do you not see what you have become?" said the Crone. "Perhaps I will call you Caesar."

Eyes bulging, Artos' face twisted. A sheen of pink coloured his cheeks. The fist which held the hag stones trembled. "Lads, wrap up the old hag before I kill her. I may be a foreigner in my own lands, but I know my purpose now. One more corrupt echo of a diseased past dealt with. The last problem left."

"Do what you must, Caesar." Then the Crone was silenced. As if rehearsed, the Hymn Whisperers rolled open a sheet of sackcloth, making sure the seams faced outward and held up ropes of many knots. Descending upon the Crone, who didn't raise even a finger or curse in protest, they dragged her to the ground. Wrapping her up, they imprisoned her in a fortress of impregnable seams and knots. Artos didn't even watch. Instead, he held the hag stones by their strings, up above his head, and stared at them intently. Mouthing single words again and again, he looked to be chanting. By reading his lips, Sol could have sworn Artos was speaking the names of everyone in the church square.

Eventually, looking up from the stones and turning to the congregation of Marsh Worm locals, Artos pointed at Sol. "You, take a stone and learn your future, know the Crone is full of lies. Then, come and see me, Sol, when it gets too much. You have big problems, lad." He threw a single hag stone. Sol deftly plucked it from the air.

The stone vibrated, the neat hole at the centre warping, swelling like a puddle under a running drip. From within that hole grew a void of nothingness, a claustrophobic black which caressed the minute hairs on his face, brushed against Sol's eyeballs, and crawled into his mind, lashing through his senses. And in the background, he heard Artos' voice. "Your future and death are empty because you are like all Fey, soulless maggots chewing on all that is courageous and worthwhile."

Hot tears brimmed in Sol's eyes. His stomach lurched like he was falling down an insatiable pit. With all his might, Sol flung the stone away and watched it glimmering with surrounding torch light as it sailed over rooftops. With the whole square watching, and knocker-dwarves eyeing Artos with increasing menace, Sol sprang off to the side buildings, jumped up onto a window ledge, and pulled himself higher onto the rooftops where he disappeared into the night. The last thing he heard was Shammy calling for him. "Sol, the carnival starts tomorrow. Wait for me!"

But he was quicker, and this time he wouldn't let her catch him.

# CHAPTER FIVE

# REKINDLING HOPE

*Wales, 1080 A.D.*

I *am just a joke, a cautionary tale. Just another fool tricked into becoming a tool for gods!* Suspicion had worried away at Artos for a thousand years. His heart finally cracked in two while he wandered the valleys of Wales. On a rugged hillside, a couple of children were chasing each other, red-faced and wide-eyed with pure, carefree happiness. A young girl and boy, stopped playing and stared at Artos with sensible caution and natural curiosity.

"Don't fear. You will have heard of me. I am the God of Victory."

The children shared a look. The boy shook his head slowly. The girl's brow furrowed, and she pointed an accusing finger at Artos. "I know who you are. A trickster! You don't bring victory. You want to curse us with your sad eyes." The children's own eyes were filled with scorn and fear. Before Artos could reply, they ran off. He had no wish to follow them. Instead, he would dwell on the feeling of defeat that had become his constant companion and use it to urge his rage into force enough to break the battle-lines of his enemies. *One last chance...*

⊷⊶═══════⊷⊶

Striking down into the dirty rush of chain-mail and broadswords, Artos screamed damnation on the ever-absent gods. A blade tore through his shoulder, his wooden shield dropped to the sodden grass. It was hot agony; something he relished! Roaring as if possessed by the giants of old, Artos stabbed the forearm of his would-be killer, gouging his spear point into the wound, brutality ripping muscle from bone. The thrill of battle surged through his blood.

But one man was not an army. To his left and right crowded the warriors of his shield wall. Concern animated their spirits, not rage.

"Now, for your homes and families, fight them!" The shields of Artos' line pushed against the Norman enemy. But the old magic failed to spark. There was too much hopelessness in hearts and circumstances.

A man down the line fell forward and was dragged into the Norman ranks. His brothers-of-the-liner, on either side, stepped back and abandoned their shields. Encouraged by the breach, the Normans surged forward. Horses whinnied, the rhythm of a calvary charge thundered from the right flank. The huddled warriors of the shield wall broke. The Norman push-back felled many and sent others scrambling to the ground.

Artos was left among a heap of bodies, instinctively stabbing at the Norman corpse on top of him. Yet, when he got to his feet again, even more Normans, and their allies, took up positions and unloaded a storm of crossbow bolts into the fleeing mob. It was this weapon of dishonour that peppered Artos across the ground, leaving a pulpy smear trailing his way.

Muttering curses, clenching at muddy grass, the power of the land washed like a balm through his fingers, as it always had before. But Artos was too damaged this time. Perhaps his heart was too heavy for the magic to pull him back up into the fray. His last thoughts sent a spear of spite up into the sky, to the trio of circling ravens mocking him. His final message would be one of damnation to that degenerate Crone…

⟡⟡⟡

Among hilltops, a young knocker-dwarf warrior called Blunt led a band of several humans into a campsite. All had their faces painted woad-blue and had hair of shock-white spikes. The knocker's expression lay mostly hidden behind a great auburn beard, but the dead set of his eyes exposed a rising concern. Bitter healing poultices and spicy magic flavoured the air. Several goats wandered freely, bleating their song of valleys and mountains.

"They said the god has been wounded? I've seen axe and sword rake his body in dozens of battles, only for him to get up stronger and angrier than before. This does not bode well."

With a once beautiful allure, now tainted and sunken, an elven healer attended to the bloody body of Artos. His chest barely rose with each rattling breath. The healer's wet and reddened eyes spoke more than words ever could.

"But what does it mean? We must keep him safe." Pinching at the sky, the knocker drew a summoning sign against the grey shroud of clouds.

The familiar shimmer of air bade all to step back. Five boggarts leaked from the Fey world into being. One, quite ostentatiously the leader, wore an over-sized Norman helmet and went by the name of Gobba. Sniffing the air, Gobba immediately scuttled between the healers, brushing obnoxiously against the females.

"Shoo, pest. Take your master away to the tunnels, keep him safe," Blunt said. Behind him, the hilltop began to fill with the silhouettes of more and more warriors slinking away from the battle raging over the hills. Humming a melody, their voices emotionally delicate and scratched thin, eleven healers tempted the aid of increasingly unsympathetic magic. At least their tune gave heart to the injured and defeated, spurring them onward towards the camp.

The sound also beckoned a very large nanny goat towards Blunt. An animal of majesty, her coat was the deepest black and her eyes sparkled with gold. Gold too were her four horns, two curled backward, two branched out on either side of her head. It playfully butted against the knocker, who patted its side in affection. "You've got a perilous and important task, Lady," Blunt whispered into the goat's ear. "Only you are brave enough to do it."

The knocker warrior helped the boggarts to lift Artos' cold, damp body. Awkwardly, they slumped the dead weight across the shoulders of the goat, who protested with a bleat.

"Appeal to all that is left and heal him," said Blunt. "We have to regroup and pummel those invaders back across to the land-sea, or relish glorious death in Avalon."

⊙≍╫═══════╫≍⊙

Stirred by the juddering motion of the goat, Artos watched a world of grassy hills rattle by, a shifting vision of yet another conquered land. *Why was it all going so wrong?*

When he propelled his thoughts into the ether, searching for the pulse of leylines through which to call for help, he found nothing but terrifying silence. Not even the mere spark of an afterlife could be found to provide a beacon for the souls of slain warriors, souls he could summon to fight anew. What was left? Black oblivion? Strange how, when he was fully mortal, he never feared hurt or death. But could Avalon continue to exist when fewer and fewer warriors dedicated their souls to its ancient fields of glory?

Crunching against his ribs, the harsh jerk of goat hooves on hillsides sent him coughing a manic fit to expel what felt like pine cones from his lungs. Artos spat blood and gasped. *At least I can rest under the hills. Gods, let me sleep for a millennium or two in the deepest mines.*

⊙≍╫═══════╫≍⊙

Gobba snorted and flicked a lid from one of the thimbles around his rope belt. "Sniff it deep. Will push you on because it stinks so bad." The creature shoved the thimble under Artos' nose. Indeed, the stink thrust up into his very soul.

Coughing at the invading stench, alertness buzzed through his mind...

Flint shards raked across Artos' body. Mud clung and pulled at the spear holstered to his back. Yet, the cold and greasy mud also eased Artos' passage through the earth. Wales, the land of Cymru, was once thought to be safer than England. Yet Time, that constant betrayer, had brought something deadlier than Saxons.

The Normans from across the sea, slaughterers of Saxon Kings, conquerors of England and now Wales, had undermined the deepest depths of these knocker mines, which Artos had planned to use as a refuge until he was healed. These invaders proved almost as capable as the dwarves with their engineering and building.

Behind Artos, dozens of Fey lay dead and dying in the collapsed tunnels. And Artos felt utterly weak, all too vulnerable in these once-home soils, now conquered and made foreign. If not for the boggarts shielding him from collapsing timbers and earth, Artos would have died on land that provided no manna to the old gods.

Endless invasions forever weakened the leylines, forever pushed Albion into the recesses of memory. But Cymru had still pulsed with magic enough to call Artos, even while Saxon and then Viking warlords sunk their teeth into the soil of what came to be known as 'England.' Artos, always on the periphery between what was defined as 'free' or 'conquered' land, had fled to Wales for another new start.

Sustained by the abundance of Fey power on those once-free lands, he anointed tribesmen with a jab of his spear, called them 'brothers to the cause,' and pledged his immortality to the struggle. But now, his faithful Woad Warriors lay dead. The faeries and demons of Cymru, beaten and forgotten, left behind a thousand myths and a single broken god trapped in a collapsed mine.

Fingers digging into the earth, Artos dragged himself toward a current of fresh air, following the trail towards the ruined entrance. Finally, he punched through dirt to emerge onto a hillside in the northern Welsh valleys. Crawling into the open, rolling onto his back, he felt weaker than ever. Lost on the edge of the world, he glazed into the brilliant starry night, to the miserable mouth of the waning crescent moon. It illuminated the craggy silhouette of hills and mountains, the ancient bones of giants stretching to the horizon. There, on a precarious outcropping perhaps a mile away, stood *the* Norman stamp of authority; the crenelated outline of a castle. An imposing, permanent mark of conquest and subjugation, it was not just a giant-bone breaker but also a hope breaker.

*How old have I become?* It seemed an age ago now when Artos had last relished the youthful sensations of practically immortal godhood. Passion and energy had faded into fatigue and boredom. Memories flashed through his mind in a golden haze, yet the future was imagined with stark, threatening sharpness. *So tired.* Rather than a God of Victory, leading old-world armies to success, defeat had followed Artos: a hundred last stands, the annihilation of a hundred tribes.

Immortality cursed him to see the ghosts of whimpering old men in youthful red-haired warriors. The Romans may have gone, but Artos' revenge had little power in the world their Emperors had forged and even less in what came after.

———◦▸┃◂▸━━━━━━◂┃◂◦———

Artos was cursed. He knew it. Tribesmen, his people, had increasingly turned against him, bit by bit, over the centuries. *Artos, the sign that forewarned the coming of a helpless struggle.* No matter how he tried, binding others to him with woad rituals, his name had become twisted up into in the legends of his peoples as something...*despairing.* It must be the insidious, vile machinations of the Crone! Empowering new symbols on Coats of Arms, trapping the destiny of Kings and peasants alike in webs of deceit, her only wish was to keep all indebted to Fate.

*Heart breaking.* Only a few months previous, when Artos had hidden under a hood and cloak while walking among the tribes during a great feast, he listened to the idle chat and heard the most disparaging remarks. Casual conversations always revealed unvarnished truth. Gossip whittled away others' belief in his powers.

It started and ended with the oldest and youngest, the stories of grandparents nurtured the imaginations and hopes of children, perpetuating and creating legends by adding embellishments for every new generation. These embellishments gave birth to heroic legends, villainous myths, or worse, made things into... *irrelevance.* This was how stories died.

Elders routinely whispered to naughty brats, 'the God of Defeat will look upon you and curse you.' *How this sapped at his strength.* Words like this depressed Artos and eroded his ability to fight. He grew insecure, his pride was increasingly built around a failure of victory.

"Not a bad looker, a certain charm, strong and lean. But I bet he can't rise to the occasion no more," gaggled a group of women around an evening fire. Nowadays, there was always pity in the women's voices, although often mixed with cruelty. Artos even found it hard to hold the women's gazes, to hold anyone's gaze. Because of this, their lies turned into truths.

Even as his people turned their back on him, even as only the Fey proved loyal, Artos tried to hold on to his power, to his place in the scheme of Avalon and Albion. History must have written him a greater part than this? However low this point might be, if he persisted, it must get better, even if time stretched until there was nothing left to say. Somehow, until everything ended, until the world became an empty, great 'nothingness,' he would survive and be the last. *Outlasting everyone, wasn't that a victory of sorts?*

<hr />

Under the haughty, conquering gaze of castles, Artos unsheathed his spear and leaned on it to get to his feet. Perhaps he was a God of Defeat after all? Maybe that was how the machinations of the Crone worked, fitting retribution on one who slaughtered her fellow god. *Is fighting the only way? What else is there?* He longed for the night sky to wrap him up and swallow him whole. Even the infinity of stars judged him, condemned him with their pitying twinkle.

Patches of the night grew hazy. Around Artos the air rippled a shallow green; boggarts, though transparent and fading with every passing year, still aided him. "Where will I go now?"

There was only silence, except for the wind carrying the whisper of waves. That was enough of an answer.

"To the coast, to the Final Country. There we shall gather the remains of the Fey." On Artos went, letting the spear take his weight, his body aching and stinging as if a single living wound. Aware of how dimly the boggarts appeared compared to when he first claimed the mantle of godhood, Artos strained to keep sight of them when they ran too far ahead. Every defeat had lessened his power, another curse of fate, of the Crone.

In his dreams, when magic surged through his soul, he saw that great golden circle from her hag stone, an image of prophesied death. He could feel her constant tinkering at the edges of his perception, a nagging itch he couldn't reach, loosening and tightening strands of fate in a frantic attempt to repair the holes left by the deaths of so many gods over the last millennia.

*Just let me sleep for a thousand thousand years...* Nevertheless, Artos continued his journey through the moonlit hills. Just like a thousand years ago, when Rome was the enemy, he followed the shimmer of boggarts. Back then, he was part of the great rebellion. Now though, Artos was the loneliest man in the new Norman Kingdom

A midday sun beamed across the cliff, high above the froth and brine of a maddened sea. Such a sight buoyed Artos, stirred his spirit. He stood tall, chest out, embracing the bitter breeze. Boggarts huddled around his knees, cowed by the lashing, salty winds as the infinity of ocean raged against the rocks below, as if rage animated the very sea itself, driving it to break the land and swallow it up. The sea shone like a glowing liquid emerald.

When locals spoke of the sea, they often called it the 'green meadow.' Fishing villages dotted the coast, and their inhabitants would gather for festivals. Artos had joined fishermen and their wives dozens of times, on this very cliff, to watch the faerie isles rise from the sea mist. Schools of porpoises, ridden by sea-elves and nymphs, decked in shells and pearls, would gift good fortunes for the coming season. For now, though, the sea whipped ferociously and empty.

*After a thousand years of fighting, the ocean remains free. The sea still holds Albion and fights back, wrecking what it can, protecting these isles the only way it knows how.*

The hush-shush of waves began to heighten. Other distinct sounds trilled and beckoned too. Something was calling Artos.

First only one, then two, then a whole brigade of frothy plunges dotted the water. Out of these plunges rose porpoises, smooth and graceful, ridden by blue and green sea nymphs. They held their tridents high, the water cascading off their naked torsos.

*Do they salute me?* Artos looked to the horizon, across the vast unconquered green meadow. He knew what he had to do.

Suddenly, pain lit up his left thigh. A boggart had sunk its razor teeth in, deeply. It was Gobba, eyes yellow and full of spite. Artos stamped at the boggarts and shooed them from his ankles. Gobba scowled back.

*What was this?* The wind picked up. On the cliff, long grasses rippled in mimic of the sea.

Behind the boggarts, shadows formed and hardened. A voluminous cloak and hooded face whispered, "Weak. Irrelevant. You are no longer welcome on these islands, God of Defeat. No longer will the boggarts heed you."

The Crone had come to gloat. That didn't matter now. Artos looked out across the sea as the wind shoved against his back; a not-so-subtle gesture to finally rid Albion of his unwanted presence. He took a few steps away from the cliff edge before sketching the sign of 'oblivion' in the air. Then, Artos sprinted to the precipice and leapt into the sky. Racing past his ears, buffeting his face, the wind blinded him. Salt spray flecked his skin and invigorated his soul. That terrible itching and burning of earth from conquered lands ceased. Oh, it felt wonderful.

The cold wash opened and swallowed him whole.

---

Life went on as a dream, one of those all-consuming dreams that can never be wholly remembered. Upon waking, the only evidence of dreaming was sweat and confusion. Artos' life on the Fairy Isle of the Green Meadow passed like this; haze built on haze, a place of golden light without time. A place of emotions, a jumble of celebratory events mashed together like broken pieces of vibrant mosaics.

More so, this was the home of some of the loveliest nymphs Artos had ever set eyes upon. Oh yes, lovely enough for a few memories to linger and, for that, Artos would forever be thankful.

Occasionally, Artos let his thoughts, and his thoughts alone, wander outside of the Fairy Isles, sending appeals to the leylines to search for old Fey and ancient gods. He spoke in the ring of blacksmith's hammers, the whisper of branches lashed aside by galloping riders. He left signs in falling shadows, minor wounds, and, of course, dreams. Artos searched for anything which still lived from the times of his mortality and could share his memories. He even prayed, offering his devotion to any ancient, lost thing which would have him and guide him. But the prayers echoed unsuccessfully across empty leylines, finding nothing but a dark smudge where Avalon used to be.

Always returning to the Fairy Isles though, to that constant flicker of happy times, eternal feasting, and lovemaking, Artos was occasionally haunted by the sickening plunge of *destiny*. Something momentous waited, like a Kraken in the depths, and bade Artos to pay attention to the passing of history back on the mainland. His presence may have been like a mere breeze, a ripple on lake, a cracking of branch, but he was there in spirit when the world turned upside-down and the English killed their king. Britannia embarked upon a Puritanical purging of everything seen as frivolous and pagan.

The Puritans hunted the sources of the few remaining leylines, waging a new kind of war, of smoke and thunder-gods that could tumble down the walls of any castle. They dug up and desecrated ancient groves, and executed any they suspected of being druids or witches.

Like whip lashes across his mind, Artos felt the burning of old manuscripts, the melting to slag of relics, swords, cauldrons, totems; a tangible hurt stripped away more and more of his godhood. At the height of the Puritan purge, the dying screams of other ancient gods regularly cut through his bones. An eternity of beautiful daydreams on the Green Meadows had been replaced by nightmares. He couldn't even escape the Crone's curse by sleeping. There was nothing else left to do...

---

### Cornwall, England, 1672 A.D.

Artos woke up.

Gasping for air in the cold, salty wash of the sea, he knew instantly that the Fairy Isle had faded to oblivion. He had been spat out into a cursed sea. Instinctively, he knew that no boggart would come and aid. Whatever claim to land he had once possessed, whatever power he once wielded, was all but snuffed out. Artos had proved unworthy of the mantle 'God of Victory,' or God of anything else.

---

Early dawn, on a small beach outcropping of the Cornish coast, three ruddy-faced men pointed out at sea. Excitedly, they shouted at the shape rising from the water. Wine skins lay scattered around their campfire. The men's imaginations interpreted light and shadow under the fog of drink and sleeplessness. They could be forgiven for dreaming.

Various gear was spread across the beach around them; parchment, coins, ripped tatters of fine cloth. Two bodies were slumped lifelessly on the sand. Nearby, tied to a makeshift driftwood jetty, horses balked and whinnied.

The approaching shape focused into the form of a man with straggly white hair, his body and face smudged with the lightest blue. "It is a devil. Nothing holy, that's for sure. A Cromwellian demon!" The men drew their swords and looked alternatively at each other and the figure. With groggy uncertainty, they fanned out and prepared for a fight.

*Pathetic,* thought the ancient Briton, checking that his spear still held firm in the sheath on his back. Highwaymen or murderers? Artos found a hardened numbness inside him, the tastes and smells of this land no longer buoyed memories of battle and romance. With every step, the sea frothed shallower and shallower

These reprobates would pose no threat to him. Millennia of war had forged instincts of lightning-quick attack and defence. Something did pique his curiosity, however. One of the drunk men grabbed at a little cross around his neck and appealed to virgins and ghosts. Why, what with all the ritual and criminal hypocrisy, Artos would have suspected a return to the 'old ways.' But hadn't the Puritans purged all old relics, pagan or catholic?

Substituting courage with a loud voice, "Faith and King, protect me," yelled one of the men, running with drunken swagger, his sword held high. Artos side-stepped, turned slightly, swung out a foot, and tripped his attacker onto the sand. He stamped down into the man's armpit, twisting against soft muscle until something harder cracked and the man let go of his long, curved blade with a roar of agony.

With another stamping heel to silence the screaming fool, Artos caved in the man's skull. The remaining two, faces pale with sickening shock, circled to either side of Artos and tried to corner him against the surf. They held their swords at arm's length, their faces betraying a desire to do nothing more than run for their lives. Artos had seen this a thousand times in battle.

"He called on a king, didn't he," said the warrior. "King Cromwell? Surely not?" However, Artos didn't wait for a response. Snatching his spear from his back, he let loose in a smooth arcing motion, spear whistling towards the man on his right. The fellow had no chance. Barely catching a blink of the black shaft speeding his way, the spear sunk through an eye socket and dropped him like a sack.

Only one opponent left now, and Artos watched his prey's resolve crumple. Looking for an escape, the remaining man's eyes darted around the beach, his alcohol-fuelled bravery burnt out as suddenly as it sparked. Under his breath, he whispered more prayers to virgins and ghosts.

"I have been away a long time. Leave me a horse and answer my questions, if you value your wretched life. Tell me of the Puritans. Who rules this land?" said Artos.

"It is King Charles," said the man, with a trembling voice. His sword arm shook. He swallowed and tried to wet his lips. "Not the executed king, I mean, but his son, King Charles

II. Please sir, wherever you have been, know that we are all allowed to make merry again. I meant no ill. Please, take my horse and everything, just don't kill me. I don't want no quarrel with demons."

*The king had come back and ended this talk of Cromwell. Surely this was good news?* "Piss off then and tell no one, or I'll haunt your dreams until your dying day."

Dropping his blade, the man hurriedly engaged in a series of bows as he edged away. "Yes sir, thank you, sir." Spinning around, staggering on clumsy feet, he broke into a sprint and ran like the beach had turned into hot coals, sand puffing a trail behind him. Artos couldn't help but smile.

*Now, this is a strange sensation,* the sputtering rekindling of Hope.

⬦⬥═══════════════⬥⬦

Artos followed the roads on horseback, a gentle trot across a changed land. A bountiful but rigid land, it was neat, divided with dry stone walls, regimented, and obeying orders. Yellow and green fields slotted together perfectly.

Occasionally, a field worker or farmer would call to Artos, but he rode on, jaw and fists clenched. The instinct for violence ran through his very being, and this was something he had to control. If he was to find a place in this strange Albion, now called England, he needed to let go of everything which defined him. *But only if he wanted to find a place...*

So much had changed. Change had built on his memories; towns over wilds, rivers through marshes, forests cut back to nothing. These changes pinched viciously at his soul. Beyond this, it actually caused him physical pain, an aching deep in the pit of his stomach to see his lived existence dissolved by time.

At a place near the Welsh border, where he swore, he had once dallied with a host of nymphs among a vast, impassable knot of trees and voyeuristic will-o-the-wisps and boggarts, he found only a mule, attached to a harvesting-contraption of sorts, in a field. The creature eyed him curiously before huffing and looking away in disinterest. *Gods, everything is so empty, so underwhelming...* The land now ceased to emanate even the faintest magical pulse. It was barren.

Everywhere Artos went, he saw similar things. The once untamed freedom of wilds no longer shaped valley and glen. Men drained bogs, cut back forests, and stuck huge wooden wheels on rivers to mill and labour. *Unrecognizable.* So much of the land was harvested and shackled to the whims of mankind. Never had Artos felt more detached from the earth beneath his feet.

An oppressive melancholy dragged at his soul as he trudged onward. *How could anyone fight against this?* War hadn't finished his old ideal of Albion, but peace seemed to have proved the greatest, most insidious weapon at removing all trace of the Old Ways. The fattening of the land had done a better job than Roman Legion or Norman Castle. Fewer adventures and more comforts had made people soft. Although, it was not as if this... *England* was paradise.

Misery still presented itself in every isolated farmstead and backwater hamlet. In-country taverns, poverty and desperation walked hand in hand with beer and rosy cheeks. Huddled on stools near the fireside, patrons listened to minstrels sing stories of old battles and magic swords to take people away from short lives of hard work. More so, some of those stories Artos had lived through, yet, to these people, the minstrels sung only of myth.

⊶⊱══════⊰⊷

After months of travelling the roads, Artos found himself in another region once thick with forests and teeming with wildlife, but now cleared and worked. In a weary daze, he took it all in, humming to himself, lost in thoughts of battles and pleasure. Suddenly his nonchalance was disturbed; a pulse of magic sparked his mind's eye. Something stirred in his chest, a subtle tingling warmth, like the edge of heat beyond the candle flame.

*Unmistakable!* Inadvertently, he had touched the periphery of a leyline, an isolated ripple. It resonated from a distance though and was very weak. Perhaps the death of an already sickly god had energized it? Perhaps, somewhere out there, a faerie grove persisted? Perhaps the Crone taunted him, still? There was nothing to lose now. Artos turned his horse towards that throb of power and rode on.

Eventually, the faint sensation of magic led him to a stream, a green and frothy thing full of, what he first thought, was river weed. But there was a glittering about it that bade him get off his horse, to kneel on the bank and have a drink. Yes, this stream wallowed with the faintest film of a leyline. The very one-and-the-same path he had followed two thousand years ago, on the day when his people had, for the briefest moment, rewrote their history and future. This was the Marsh River, leading to the source of that magic sparkle he had seen in his mind's eye.

Gods, what a fool he must look, gulping water with a great smile across his face. He couldn't stop smiling. He knew that he *must* follow it to the site of Albion's ancient victory, to the junction of two rivers, the place once called Londinium.

Now called London, a city dense and spreading like the sepsis in a wound, Artos had heard talk about it across the country. A place where the wealth of many lands met, before being re-made into status and luxury. A good place to make a future. *Perhaps?*

⊙⊷⊷⊷ ⊶⊶⊙

Snaking along grassland and fields, the leyline river led to a festering sore of a village about a mile from London, a scab of wattle and daub on sodden earth, the exact site of victory over Rome, all those years ago. Glorious victory.

Now, it was distinctly... *inglorious.* Weasel-faced men and women eyed Artos with suspicion. They sneered and muttered curses through brown teeth. But all were too timid, and superstitious to approach the wild-eyed, faintly-painted-faced man.

Magic still clung on to this place, though. A nasty, spiteful sort, never leashed or tutored by capable Fey or gods. It, along with everything from the balmy days of Albion, had degraded.

Artos snatched a glance at an emaciated, back-bent Fey-thing scurrying behind some haystacks; a grey-skinned rat of an elf, but still the first Fey he had seen since he arrived back on the mainland. Like him, a survivor nibbling on the remnant of magic.

It was here, not quite London, on the final stop of the last leyline, where Artos decided to make a new life among wretched elves sashaying their wares to red-faced drunks. Where knockers, stomped on and kicked by the villagers, lived in rain flooded burrows, often emerging to hack at groups of ruffians with crude, rusted picks.

Constantly sick, pale, sneezing, and coughing, the local humans blamed the Fey for all misfortunes. Both communities, human and Fey, traded wares and insults with the same breath. Fear and ignorance kept the nameless village humid, forever stewing in malevolent magic and disharmony.

<hr />

Keeping his distance Artos watched in fascination for the next few days. He noted village routines, the constant prayers at a run-down church run by a round-faced priest, Father Gamaliel, the fattest man in the village. Only when uplifted by the Priests' holy presence did the villagers gather courage enough to return Artos' stare while their warty hands rubbed small wooden crucifixes. Still, superstition held sway enough that the congregation would leave the church after their daily services and make great pains to avoid the attentions of a nearby well, daring not even to cut a glance at it.

Every Sunday, after mass, Father Gamaliel would go to that well, watched by an audience that never got too close, and chant damnation against the blasphemy of ancient creatures, his performance rising to a fever pitch of spasms and tongues. All that ritual gave Artos a strange sense of familiarity.

An ill omen in the peripheral vision of the locals, Artos could only bear to remain a passive observer for a short time. Curses and misfortune sweated from the very stones and pores of the village and infected every deed.

Sleep was troubled by night terrors. Tending pathetic strips of land, the villagers always failed to grow anything other than the grayest and withered sprigs. The cloth they wove rarely held its stitching for more than a few days. Mothers feverishly combed their daughter's hair to get rid of unnatural tangles, elf-knots that put Gordion's to shame. Hens laid eggs full of nothing but maggots, and milk curdled within the hour.

Greater curses afflicted this place too. On a day when a huge, black dog prowled through the village, scaring children inside, Artos skulked passed the local tannery. Even he had to hold back his bile at what he saw. With unflinching calm, and speaking the idlest of gossip to a patron, the tanner proceeded to skin his arm without even a flinch, until the patron fought him to the ground to awaken him from his 'possession.' *Yes, the place reeks of corruption,* but the magic was enough to set the dormant energies inside Artos to a slow smoulder.

Across the way from the Tannery, an elderly couple struggled to repair a chicken coop. Dirty hens strutted a trial of footprints in the mud. One of them bobbed Artos' way.

On noticing the Woad Warrior, the couple's eyes followed the hen's path suspiciously. *Now is the time to test if Albion still grants me power of any sort...*

Nimble as a spooked deer, Artos pounced then scooped the hen up with ease. With as big a smile as he could manage, a full set of strong teeth on a blueish face, he offered it back to the couple. They both clucked like their hens before scurrying into their shack to peek through cracks in the door. Artos needed practice in ingratiating himself with humans.

He tried another tact. "Good people," he said to the rickety door, "I will bless you, in the name of all gods, and stop this spread of evil." With that, Artos tickled the belly of the hen before tossing it into the air and sending it flapping in the direction of the coop.

That night, a high-pitched whopping scraped abrasively against the slumbering calm of the village. Sleeping amid a scavenged hay pile, the sounds shook Artos awake. He smiled. Curiosity got the better of him though, and he wandered back to the elderly couple's shack, their front door ajar to welcome a small crowd.

The small crowd mumbled and parted for Artos. He peered into a room lit with both flickering candle flames and laughter. Despite their creaking bones, the elderly couple danced a jig around a basket of eggs. One of the eggs had broken spilling not maggots, but slimy egg white and golden yoke.

'Hallelujah,' they sang, raising their hands and faces to where they imagined heaven might be. The woman noticed Artos at their door, instead of recoiling in fear, she waved him in. "God listened to you, he did. Sent us a blessing. It was the hen that you touched. Miserable thing laid more eggs in one day than in all her life."

A spark of the purpose which had once gifted Artos courage for battle ignited his soul and uplifted his heart. "You keep me close and spread the good news," he told them. "I'll fix this place; you mark my words." He spoke loud enough for the curious crowd to hear. *Perhaps all is not lost? A finger-hold to cling onto with all my strength.*

From that day, from household to household, he passed to give his blessing, touching warts which shrivelled and dropped off, or stirring prematurely aged milk until it unfolded and the curdles dissipated. Anything infected by malicious magic healed and the curse-reeking air thinned. Everything, but the most insidious of Fey curses, seemed to right itself. But the worst was yet to come.

When crying mothers came to him, with swaddling of babes in their arms, they begged the Woad Warrior for help. "Only yesterday my little one was cooing and as lovely as a summer's day, but now look at him!"

Cursed with the tissue skin of great grandparents, and the pointed teeth and pinched features of rats, whatever malignant magic was at work had decided to strike back against Artos by replacing infants with imps. It was a challenge, brazen in how it mocked his intentions. To stop this vendetta between humans and Fey once and for all, Artos knew he had to root out the source. If he took too long, the villagers ' blame would turn on him.

Quick to respond to the laments of his congregation, Father Gamaliel left his church swinging a censer of incense.

Preaching damnation, he proclaimed to the women that their babes were possessed by devils. He condemned the grieving mothers to return their hellspawn to 'from whence they came,' or else all would suffer eternal damnation. To the wails of mothers, menfolk snatched and dumped the cursed infants into the well under bucketfuls of holy water. Tensions tightened. The knockers and elves kept to their hovels and holes, out of sight.

One night, when the women took up their pitchforks, rabid like dogs, the village looked set to engulf itself in civil war. Those who called for calm were pushed aside. Only when the Priest bellowed, with his great baritone voice unleashing all the fire and brimstone platitudes he knew, did the situation cool for but a moment.

"We rest on the cusp of hell here. It is a test, and we have been chosen. It is time to cast out the blasphemies among us once and for all. We must..." The words caught in his throat when his eyes met Artos.' With voice quietened, the Priest continued nonetheless. "Follow me, good Christians, and send the demons back to the abyss!"

Torches raised and hate stiffening their nerve, the villagers applauded Father Gamaliel before heading towards the knocker holes to enact their crusade against all those they saw as responsible for curses. With relish, they burnt and killed, venting all their frustrations with the world against unholy Fey.

Insides coiling and clenching tight, Artos absorbed it all into his very centre, compressing his anger into warrior rage, letting every inhumanity strengthen him. Hoping beyond hope, Artos cultivated fury enough to light the embers of the god he once was.

When the time was right, he silently stepped over the corpses of knockers and into the crowd of rampaging men. Keeping his spear holstered, Artos used his bare hands, relishing the sick sound of fists against flesh. He beat men bloody, beat them until they flopped limply into the mud.

Like a beast, he roared to cower all around. The whole world seemed to freeze in time.

Tentative, like deer taking food from a stranger's hand, Fey slowly emerged from their burrows. They clustered toward Artos, holding knives, picks, and expressions of terror. The human mob started to back away, uncertain, until the Priest pushed through them and glared at Artos. "And what are you? A devil-man who loves things perverse of God?" The holy man's voice shook.

With a low growl, barely heard, Artos spoke through his teeth. "I will bring us peace in the name of your crucified god. Watch me." Then louder. "Watch me!" Turning to the Fey, who looked up at him with imploring eyes, he said, "Lead me to your most sacred place of magic. Do what I say, in the name of Andraste's successor."

Shuffling anxiously, the knockers and elves kept their eyes to the ground. Despite those most full of hatred chomping at the bit and glowering with palpable violence, Father Gamaliel held his mob back.

Speaking ever so quietly now, Artos continued, "Either you do this for me, a friend-to-be-made, or else I'll be unable to stop the Priest from sacrificing you to his own God. You, your children, everyone."

And like bashful children the Fey nudged each other. They whispered, the whispering rising to a murmur. A few young elves stepped forward; one raised his hand as if asking for permission to speak. "You are a god?"

Thumping his chest, Artos said, "Do I look like a mere man to you? Believe me, I am the God of Victory, the God of Whatever-You-May-Like..." The elves looked back at their Fey brethren. They argued with stares until the sterner glares of elderly Fey caused the young elves to look away.

At that very moment, the pale light of the moon pulsed with a strength that drew Artos and the mobs' attention. It was so bright, all wondered why they hadn't noticed that the moon was full. Yesterday, it was a waning half-moon. *It is an omen.* A second later all turned to Artos.

"Please, follow us, to the moonlit fields," said one of the younger elves, twitchy with excitement, cheek bones sharp like razors on his gaunt face.

Accompanied by the villagers and their forest of torches and pitchforks, Artos followed three young elves away from the trodden paths. Only a short distance into grotty fields of withered crops, the elves stopped and scraped a circle into the dirt, crude but effective enough for a ritual. Then they skipped around the circle in silence, faces sombre, stopping exactly at the end of the third circuit.

Dishonest shadows stripped away from the fields in long flakes, like giant potato peelings, revealing the truth under a spell of concealment. Now, other shadows appeared and flirted with moonbeams, shades of women, perfect sensuous silhouettes pirouetted and preened. Once irresistible forest beauties, but now corrupted by the decline of Albion, they were surely the remains of some of the last nymphs. Artos felt his face break into a brief, half-smile. *Oh, the good times...*

Silent rituals of dance spun moonbeams into beautiful spirals around their shapely shadow bodies, accentuating all that man could find desirable, but lacking detail and fragrance. The magic merely teased Artos, a cheap giddy thrill that was easy to ignore. However, his stomach clenched at the other shades crawling around the nymph's feet, a parade of infants, the spirits of the new-borns thrown down the well.

Artos turned to face the watching village folk. "The last nymphs have fallen this far, feeding on the manna of the young to sustain spiteful curses against the villagers." The warrior sighed and again faced the nymphs. In his life of nearly two thousand years, he had at least a thousand stories of lusty nymphs. Memories he could enjoy when fighting and revenge had been pushed out of his mind for just a little while. *Such transcendental beauty. I cannot let them fester in this state, a shameful existence that deserves nothing but oblivion.*

"I carry the hope and future of this village against you. May you feed the worms and marshes and one day, again, give birth to something beautiful." Freeing his spear, Artos felt it thrum with power. His palms heated under the pulse of ancestral spirits. Strength returned, lacing through his blood, his sinews. Balancing the spear, he moved closer to the nymphs and took firm footing. Then he struck.

The shaft hooked into light-less flesh. For an instant, the moon glowed with such intensity that Artos could make out the shadow nymphs' faces. Like dough kneaded and shaped, their features rolled and twisted. Silent beauty gave way to hideous noise. Shrieking away from existence, the once-nymphs shattered among the moonbeams into a rain of white crystals. The moon turned dull again as shards of light and screeches of agony swept around all who watched.

"Banshees, they've turned into banshees," yelled Artos, through the storm of light and sound. Long subdued by intolerance and suffering, the elves watched without emotion, with hands covering their ears. Slower on the uptake, many villagers screamed against the storm as if to drown out the sound which made their ears bleed.

The nymphs were no more, and in their place remained a large gaping pit, an abyss replacing the vanquished magic. A place to be guarded and sealed until needed, a hole through the worlds of men and Fey.

When the moonlight settled, like glowing snowdrops across the field, the night descended into stillness and the air lifted. The heady stew of curse-laden air seemed lighter against the skin.

Artos stood tall and shouted to all who would listen. "Look, all of you, and see the final sentence of a guilty verdict. Utter just one curse and I'll throw you into eternal darkness. You may as well call it Hell. Does anyone disagree?" Nobody said a word. It was a hopeful start.

# CHAPTER SIX

# NEW TRICKS FOR OLD GODS

*A mile from London, England, 1672 A.D.*

Artos inhaled the air; *earthier, with a touch of sap and the barest notes of oak and mistletoe.* It tasted like Albion. *A new Albion.* He looked again to the dwarves, elves, and villagers who followed him, a smile turning the corners of his mouth and eyes.

"Welcome to my new kingdom. We all have new ways to learn. Mark my words, you follow me, and we will not just survive, but thrive."

For the rest of that night, the usually sparse knocker tunnels heaved with Fey and villagers, all listening to the stories of their strange visitor. Artos told of his life, how he had fought for the Fey across the British Isles for more than a millennium, and how he had fought invaders to protect all who called Britannia home.

He bullied and cajoled those who would listen, and he made a thousand promises of better lives ahead. Though many Fey had devolved into simple-minded fools, a few of their seniors hung onto every word. Their eyes lit with old glories and future hopes, and they nodded and mumbled agreement. Artos pondered their ancientness. *Could some of them have lived during the Roman invasion? Maybe some existed in the Fairy Times before the world became enamoured with empires and nations?*

"Things cannot go on the way they have been," said a middle-aged knocker, through an impressive greying-auburn beard. "I'm called Blunt. I followed you once, in Wales. I'm prepared to follow you again. But we must look to the future now, not the past." With what must have taken tremendous bravery, the knocker approached Artos and did the most unfamiliar thing a Fey could do. He offered his hand to the Woad Warrior, and Artos shook it. Then, despite a hangover of resentment and sorrow, the villagers and Fey *all* started shaking hands.

These handshakes carried implications Artos understood. No longer a hidden thing of imagination, the Fey would endeavour to emerge into the full light of day again, something that could be touched, treated, and traded with without animosity. The handshake was a dozen rituals in one, a promise that hinged on fulfilled expectations. The deal had been made.

When the villagers started returning to their homes, Artos bade Father Gamaliel stay and talk about his plans for the Fey. "You see, I have great ideas, and I need to teach them a few things. Something I have heard in the church during every service, 'Our father who art in heaven...'" said Artos. The fat priest started to chuckle, that chuckle soon turning to the booming drums of laughter.

The following morning, Artos strode out ahead of the Fey, leading them like the champion of an army. At every household, he would stop and the Fey would beg forgiveness for any malady they had afflicted on the villagers, be it real or imagined. With Artos overlooking it all, scowling and holding his spear, even the most vehemently hostile humans stayed their hands and listened. Some villagers even invited the knockers and elves into their homes.

Elves unwrapped pungent poultices and demonstrated how to crush and mix local plants to treat casual illness. Knockers showed villagers how to engrave simple good-luck symbols on wooden chips or pebbles. Even though the most cynical and world-weary Fey resisted grovelling before their oppressors, gritting their teeth as they watched, they couldn't help the gradual softening of their frowns at the rising merriment and camaraderie.

To appease the loudest dissenters, Artos paraded the Fey before the church. The menagerie of lithe elves, stout knockers, and tiny sprites all grasped wooden crucifixes. Artos grunted and clasped his hands together in the form of a prayer; the signal was given.

Unanimously, but with diverse disparities in pitch and tone, the Fey belted out a cacophony of The Lord's Prayer. Artos had taught them enough of it, though they thought of it as gobbledygook, to please Father Gamaliel. When the Fey called out for baptism, the congregation, led by the Priest, cheered 'Hallelujah.'

One by one, the Fey genuflected before the Priest as he flicked them with water and anointed them in the name of his one God. Many of the more mischievous elves and knockers shook while holding back their snickers, aware of Artos' watching eyes.

Finally, at a moment that silenced all onlookers, Artos knelt before the priest for his baptism and first communion. When he got to his feet, the taste of bloody red wine in his mouth, his head spun. He staggered as if the ground was uneven. Taking a deep breath, Artos steadied himself and faced the village. Father Gamaliel stood next to him.

"Now, all gods are one, all are joined together. One God, yes, that is what we believe... Say 'amen' then brothers and sisters. Amen!" A slow trickle of 'amens' turned into a flood when the Priest raised his hands to declare 'Amen' to the heavens.

Yelling through the chorus, Artos declared, "In this place of marsh and worms, we now realise that corrupting magic is our enemy. We must defend against the curses of those who wish to harm us, all of us. Don't you agree, Priest?" Artos rested a hand on the priest's shoulder. He gripped hard, and he smiled wide.

Red-faced; Gamaliel nodded. "Yes, yes. Amen, amen to that." Again, the villagers joined in, but this time with a single, rising cry of 'Amen.'

"A mile from here, in London, they will hear our voices, Man and Fey together against evil. This village...this Marsh

Worm Mile will be a place of unity and happiness." The Woad Warrior held his spear aloft. Everyone, Fey and human alike raised their hands. The chants of 'Amen' sounded almost exactly like 'Artos.'

---

Rumour spread like wildfire to the outlying farms, villages, and taverns. Rumours of the Fey of Marsh Worm Village, a once dirty and ill-kept secret now out in the open. A village where men built houses next to Fey burrows and traded neighbourly gossip. Curious wanderers came to see, later telling their friends and families. Soon, tourists of all stripes came for a glimpse. More than just curiosity to see the Fey though, people came to meet the blue-faced man, the man as old as the mountains. In that weird village called Marsh Worm Mile, it almost seemed natural, like something not to question but marvel at, a place of observable, touchable myths. The village market swelled, its produce of magical mixtures and trinkets on their way to becoming *'fashionable.'*

Superstitions of the benevolent kind, of the old beliefs sunk into the timbers and mud of that village, had once been proclaimed blasphemous by priests and God-fearing men. Not now. Indeed, visiting men of the cloth interpreted every blessing as a gift from their one God, whether the source was Fey, man, or nature. Enlightened times indeed.

However, the presence of 'corrupt magic' lingered. It threatened the delicate entente that allowed humans to tolerate the magic in their midst. Families facing hard times were always liable to look harder for a scapegoat than for a solution to their problems.

One day, at the old well, Artos stopped a disgruntled farmer from casting a baby into its depths. "A demon-boggart got at my wife," the farmer said, his eyes red and tearful. "It is true, I tell you. I haven't touched her in years and yet she gave birth to a bleeding screaming imp." The man's hands were thick with calluses, his skin tanned and rough like bark, from a life of hard work. His pride was hard too, but Artos saw the shame in his eyes; the look of the unmanned resorting to lies. Wrinkled and pink like all babies, the infant cooed happily.

*How cheaply these people valued the living.* The offspring of infidelity, or those born out of wedlock, or born to the desperately poor, or simply unwanted were cast aside into the pagan well, a place they believed, perhaps, beyond the sight of their omnipresent God. Those vengeful spirits of tossed-aside lives prickled Artos' sensibilities, evoked his godhood as much as it evoked bad luck and curses. But Artos fought the rage that burbled under and spoke with soft, measured words.

"I will take the child. From now on, bring your unwanted to me. Pass the word, I will raise them, I will build them a home and give them a place in Marsh Worm Mile. This well will not become a symbol of darkness. It is holy too, like your church."

Startling both the farmer and Artos, the eavesdropping Father Gamaliel shuffled into their conversation. Still fat, but older, a sheen of sweat glistening across his face, he spoke to the farmer through heavy breaths tainted with alcohol. "Listen to this brave man of the old world, for surely God speaks through him." Then, taking Artos' large hands in his own smaller, moist hands, his voice softened. "A philanthropist too! You really are a blessing. I have learnt from you, and together we will make this place pure, a heaven on earth."

Instinctively Artos tightened his wrist to pull away but then relaxed. The sweaty Priests' words warmed him, an honest offer of a place in society, a welcome, a chance to change things from the inside; perhaps no longer as an outcast, no longer as a rebel fighting a conquering invader. How could he ever choose life in hiding again?

"Yes, Gamaliel. We will sing your songs together and forge a holy order, with all the panoply of warriors who fight against evil magic."

The drunk Priest swung his arms to heaven and bellowed Artos' praises. Passing folks joined, praising God, singing their dirges. *Gods, what awful sounds they made.* Artos could barely stand to hear such a noise. "Yes," he shouted over them, "but we will be discrete, no need to make such a noise. We will be a brotherhood of 'Hymn Whisperers.'" From that day, any man or woman, lost to their purpose in life, could volunteer to serve Artos as a crusader in the devil-land outskirts of Marsh Worm.

Eventually, as all mortals must, Father Gamaliel passed away to the laments of the population of Marsh Worm Mile. Even Artos felt the plunge of mourning in his chest. Leadership fully passed to him, and he empowered his Hymn Whisperers. The Hymn Whisperers, a Christian mask on the old ways, warriors who despised the curses and evil doings of man or Fey. Devils and boggarts would be their prime targets, creatures that relished cursing others for their amusements.

*Boggarts...*The word sent a shiver down Artos' spine. He had waited long enough. Did those subservient weavers of ill fortune still follow the Crone, after they had abandoned him? He had felt the presence of boggarts more with every passing year, felt their *intentions,* but never caught a glimpse. Perhaps, with his relinquishing of the old ways, his eyes could no longer see them at all? But he knew they would be watching him, plotting. As his power had returned, the Crone would have surely felt his presence, a chaotic disturbance on the last of the leylines. For now, though, Artos would make sure that anything which threatened the sanctity of Marsh Worm would be pulled out before it could take root.

Gloriously, the Hymn Whisperers proved their worth, stamping on every sign of magical malevolence. Evil eyes scratched on walls would be removed as soon as possible. Improbable periods of misfortune, be it a prolonged bout of rotten gambler's luck or areas suffering a proclivity of clumsy 'accidents,' felt the wrath of righteous superstition.

Many times, a certain, stubborn grassy mound, forever growing back by the bank of the Marsh River, caused the tripping of merchants, tipping of carts, and the lamming of horses. The Hymn-Whisperers dug out the cursed land with rune-engraved spades, all while whispering church dirges. It was an abandoned boggart hole! When banditry increased, due to a prevalence of misfiring militia guns and gout (even on the sober), the Hymn-Whisperers took up the slack with silver-tipped crossbow bolts.

With trinkets, both Christian and pagan, the Hymn Whisperers would form battle lines. They scoured fields with hoses and tanks of holy water. With silver-edged daggers and swords, or bladed pikes, they fought against boggart apparitions whenever they became visible under the steaming streams of righteousness. Almost comical to those who watched, brown-robed men swatted the air, and the cries of the creatures confirmed the kill.

Intermittently, the purges continued, flaring up during periods of misfortune but misfortune in ever-decreasing circles, until only the occasional magical malady assaulted the village-turned-town. By the end of the 18th century, man and knocker shared tankard, and woman and elf prayed together. The Marsh Worm Mile stretched along the banks of the Marsh River, mingling with the edge of the great city of London.

It was at this time when rumours set London ablaze. Beset by puritanical nightmares, Artos awoke one day with a new fire raging in his warrior heart. Now, the French had killed their king and declared war on the whole world! This time Artos was determined to fight and finally lay old ghosts to rest for good.

# CHAPTER SEVEN

# ARTOS, KING OF BRITANNIA

## *Marsh Worm Mile, London, 1815 A.D.*

When Napoleon held sway over Europe, Britain was wrung dry of volunteers for the army and navy. But recruiters avoided the Marsh Worm Mile. Superstition and distrust flavoured the army's opinion of Fey and, what were considered, Fey-touched humans. What rankled Artos more was the refusal for him to join the ranks, even after he presented himself to the recruitment offices in the very centre of London. *Too important for keeping local order,* was the usual excuse. But some jumped-up ministers dared to say he was 'too old.'

However, the great armies of European resistance eventually prevailed. Napoleon, once conqueror of a continent was beaten and dismissed to an island Artos had never heard of. Yet Fate often allowed men of destiny a final roll of the dice. As if by magic, Napoleon escaped his island prison to France. In 1815, he led an army bent on repeating old glories. Only then did the recruiters brave the Marsh Worm Mile to request help, finding Artos marvelling at the new parade of gas lamps outside the One Tun pub. Artos, a man of destiny himself, already had a plan. *Time to put a little of my own magic to use,* he thought. *Time to breathe new life into distant legends.*

⊶╫⫿╢⎯⎯⎯⎯⎯⎯⎯⫿╟⊷

'I've got you now,' thought Blunt, the knocker lamplighter, squinting at a gas lamp from the alley beside the One Tun pub. The lamp cast a yellow halo in the fog, illuminating a figure perched on the ladder bar next to the casing which harboured the flame. Reaching across the lamp, its long hair flapping and flailing in the wind, it opened the casing with a 'click.' The flame flared; the halo skipped out of shape. 'Yes, I've got you now.'

For weeks some ne'er do well had been snuffing the gas-lit stars studded throughout the streets, and always during the blackest part of the night. Blunt feared it was boggarts, or Frenchmen, or, worst of all, French Boggarts with some insidious Bonaparte plan to keep London in the dark. The great governor, Artos, had already reprimanded him thrice about 'unfortunate incidents,' when awkward gentleman and bashful ladies, fresh from their flurries of apologies after bumping into each other, let off steam with complaints both written and in person. They accused Blunt of doing a 'poor job!' Well, not any more.

Sneaking through the fog until just below the suspected boggart, Blunt watched, eyes wide, as a green, transparent hand reached out and snuffed the glow without even a whimper of hurt. Caught red-handed as they say! Jumping to grab a foot, "Got you, you conniving sneak," yelled the lamplighter. But the foot collapsed on itself, fog puffing from underneath. Blunt fell. Flopping over his cloak, rolling a little until it wrapped him like a mummy.

For a minute, all went dark. A bizarrely pleasant smell, like grass after rain, replaced the usual nightly funk of rotten vegetables and excrement. Fearful of a coshing, Blunt waved his arms in a maniac fit and flung the damned cloak away, only to find the surrounding fog thrumming with an odd luminescence.

It rolled up around him like some will-o the wisp from the old times. But creatures of the dark had never scared Blunt. After all, many had thought *him* a ghost, a strange glow in the night hovering mid-air on his ladder and appearing quite frightful from a distance. Even when the fog closed in tight like a blanket, Blunt didn't scream. Even when it pressed tighter still, until it held him in a fog-straitjacket, Blunt's only concern was with re-lighting the snuffed lamp, which now freely hissed gas into the night.

"Who are you?" the hiss seemed to say, curling around Blunt's ear and causing the hairs on his neck to prickle.

With pride, Blunt declared, "A lamplighter. I keep the roads well-lit, shooing off robbers, boggarts, and other Marsh Mile midnight maladies." He smiled at his alliteration. *Must be learning from all the newspapers I read in the One Tun*, he thought.

"You make the ever-burning fire? You command the dragon?" said the fog-wisp, in an accent that squashed and stretched words in ways Blunt found familiar but unsettling.

"If you put it like that, and I do like the sound of it, yes. I command the dragon!"

"Merlin! It is me, carried on old Britannia's druid breath, unable to reach Avalon. Forced to learn new ways and new words, I can no longer separate fact from fiction."

Blunt sighed. Yet again, the dark had conjured one of those superstitious things for him, and just his luck, he gets sent a mad one. "Merlin, am I? Well, Blunt will do. Who might you be?" *Better to humour the thing, before Hymn Whisperer's cleanse the One Tun and all around it.*

"Your friend, Arthur, King of the Britons."

"Who is this playing a trick on me?" said Blunt. The luminescent fog swirled into a face. Nothing sinister to it though. Fog brows formed over a bearded fog-mouth, solidifying into the dandily dressed form of Artos.

Beaming with mirth, Artos said, "Every day my magic strengthens. Tell you what, Blunt, it's given me a plan. After this, all in the Mile will be free to do as they wish. Put your cloak back on and let's talk about it over a drink."

"Convenient is that Artos, sir. The One Tun serves the loveliest, warmest beer. Just here, behind us. I've been dying for a drop." Blunt grimaced and clenched his lips before opening them again and trying to draw the faintest trace of moisture into his mouth.

<hr />

The One Tun pub was a model of after-hours grit, with everything from the floorboards to the tables made from an indistinct 'dark wood'. Burnt bits here and there, puddles of something or other congealing, never completely mopped up, in myriad ill-set dips. Lit by only a dozen or so candles, the corners swelled with shadows, ready to vomit darkness over the whole pub. But Blunt loved the place, his nightly stopover between lighting and snuffing 'shifts.'

Everyone knew him well here, and he always read the newspapers left discarded or donated on the counter while nestled directly under one of the struggling candles. Only a smattering of people propped up the bar during the weekday witching hours though. Presently, the pub was uncharacteristically full, patrons crowding around Blunt's stumpy table, marvelling at his companion, who seemed to glow with something alluring, inspiring, even as he drank great gulps of beer from a tankard.

Between swallows, Artos explained his problem. "You know, legends and myths are a burden. They give you hope, which, if not used, makes people lazy and liable to put up with ill-treatment. But, if acted upon, myths and legends can deal with real, observable good in the world. You've heard the prophecy, 'King Arthur and the Knights of Camelot will rise again when Britannia is in great need.'" Blunt swayed along to Artos' words, to the giddy rhythm of alcohol. Entranced by every turn of phrase, it was as if Artos' tankard contained the very 'spirit' of the age.

"So, I said to myself, why don't I, and my brave Marsh Worm warriors, use the magic left in this legend, when we really need it. Find a war and save Britannia. I just need you to gather all the magic of the Mile, to recall ancient knights, and then we'll find a battle for a send-off to remember. What's more, we can prove to the superstitious that magic has a *good* side."

A man in a battered army coat, once red but long since faded to a sort of brown, one sleeve buttoned-up over the elbow, tipped his patchy busby. "Beg your pardon, Artos. All England is humming with the news that Boney is back. Making his nuisance felt among the foreigners on the continent, he has the cheek to call himself 'Emperor' again. I heard, from my sources, Wellesley's the man to put an end to him for good. When those two meet, that'll be the battle you'll want to find. Get our lads in that, bring a bit of renown to this place."

Artos' beaming smile flared brighter. "A fine brother of the shield wall you'd make."

Flushed with drink, and the embers of patriotic fervour, Blunt raised his tankard, "Any Fey, man or woman who hates Napoleon, who knows even just a pinch of magic, I'll bring them down to the One Tun. Cheers." Draining his dregs, he slammed the tankard down. After, he fumbled under the stumpy table where he kept all his lamplighter tools and withdrew his stick-lighter, a fresh wick at the tip. "So, *King Artos of Britannia*, I'll make your dragon fire. Tomorrow evening, we shall gather over maps and pull at the strings of legends!"

"First, I would say, we better move to the centre of this room, to that likely looking round table." Artos' eyes gleamed.

"Of course, the round table," said Blunt.

<hr />

Against the round table, wobbling on ill-set legs, the patrons of the One Tun leaned with tipsy imbalance. Chatter, speculation, and excitement fit to burst, filled the room like clogged-up manure pits and a struck flame. All were there, human and Fey, to eke out as much magic as they could. While outside stood the finest of Artos' Hymn Whisperers, dressed in military red coats, dancing a jig to fife and drum.

Covering the round table inside was a map of Europe. A dozen ink blotches marked points of interest. People pointed here and there, reading the funny-sounding names of European places while magic coalesced around them.

All noise hushed the moment an elf lady, Valeria, squeaked in embarrassment and surprise, flinging her cloak aside to reveal a foggy, ghostly will-o-the wisp in all its cloudy glory. Every pair of eyes followed her stare, transfixing on the single flame of the stick lighter held aloft in Blunt's hand.

The stick trembled with Blunt's excitement, the flame juddering on the end. Suddenly, the will-o-the-wisp bunched into a muscular puff of smoke before dissipating into a faint veil of grey, stretching and thinning until every space billowed with the mist. Thickening afterward into a fog as opaque as grey cement, only the wick was visible, shining a yellow pool like a lighthouse in a storm.

Other lights blinked to life in the haze, swirling orbs called from far off nether places by the swelling magic of the room. Slowly, the lights grew in intensity as they rubbed away the fog. Blunt listened closely, his knocker ears catching a distant clanging of metal on metal, echoes of men shouting and the whinnying of horses, as if battle raged beyond the fog.

As suddenly as it had bloomed the fog receded, recoiling into a concentrated puff around the wick of Blunt's stick-lighter. Like dough, the puff flattened and clumped around Artos, whispering over and over, 'King Arthur, King Arthur.' But the magic didn't just call on the fabled cause of Arthur alone. Outside, the fog wafted and moulded around the Hymn Whisperers, around any nearby horses, bestowing mere mortals with the gumption and courage of a mythical phantom army. Then everything returned to stillness, to that tension-filled moment on the brink of bursting.

Blunt just couldn't contain himself. "God save the King! To Arthur and the fall of Napoleon." That set everyone off. A rowdy hoorah of jingoism burst from the One Tun. Such an ungentlemanly ruckus at such an early hour.

"But where are we headed?" said Artos

The lamplighter's eye flashed as he turned to the map. "I guess to France, Boney will be somewhere around there."

The old soldier, with the war wound, joined in. "Find Wellington and his red-coated army in the north of that country, maybe even in the Netherlands." He pointed to a blotch on the map. "His cannons are the true dragons of our age. This old myth would get a grand sending off, just as you want."

"Cannons, you say? France, you say? Boney, you say?" said Artos, seemingly drunk on magic. Blunt was indeed drunk on something, though. *Now was not the time for such petty matters. Now was the time for dreams of glory,* and Artos' words helped him to conjure images of that dream.

"We will march under a rising storm of ravens to show us the way. Just you make sure to keep scrying and wishing us magic. Never luck. Luck is for fools." Again, the patrons of the One Tun cheered as Artos took a bow.

Blunt sat back on his stool and swallowed another gulp of beer, the excitement being all too much. The first rays of sun oozed shyly through the outside fog and the grease-smeared windows of the One Tun. It made him rather giddy. Not just from the booze. It was as if the sun somehow felt fresher, younger, mysterious. A sun of legends.

<hr/>

A fleet of ravens, cutting through a half-fluffy, half-wispy cloud, streaked ahead of Artos' troop once they had landed on the Dutch coast. Swirling vigil north of France, near a place called Brussels, the raven swarm sighted a moving mass of an army on the march. The great flock came to rest in the skies above an indistinct town named Waterloo. It was only two weeks since the summoning at the One Tun pub.

The mighty raven-formation had been the focus of farmers' exclamations and comments for several days. More than a few newspaper inches had been given over to the bizarre phenomena, a huge sky tower of flapping and cawing, forever maintaining its size and composition on its journey to wherever.

Following the ravens, and the vast kicked-up trails of armies on the march, Artos and his Hymn Whisperers came to rest around a farmhouse in, what must assuredly, pass for a modern age battle. Raven scouts trailed back on themselves, like a slowed-down whip-crack, disappearing into cloud cover once farmers, hunters, or even soldiers started taking pot shots at them. The avian retreat went mostly unnoticed to people on the ground though, since on that day the sky heaved with miserable rain clouds, having freshly burst once already and threatening to do so again.

On sodden fields, where men stretched for miles, the battle raged. Artos and his Hymn Whisperers were set to bolster the ranks of the farmhouse defence, although they had yet to make themselves known. Aided by the sight of circling ravens, Artos' band had scattered through the hills and forests on the approach. Magic, smoke, and rain concealed them from other soldiers' eyes. Artos' sixty-odd warriors and a dozen horses would be seen as shadows, blown grass, or puddles in the mud. Only when close enough to taste the blood on the wind would he unleash the full potential of his ritual of myth.

Hazed with smoke and brick dust, the air choked those caught within and near the farmhouse. It was dangerous work to find a suitable place to form up. *This is as appropriate a place as any for a grand sending-off of legend.*

Despite the pressing circumstance, Artos couldn't help but marvel at these modern soldiers' as he examined them through the eyes of his ravens; bright red and dark blue uniforms with peculiar hats: furry things and three-cornered things. Vast swathes of men stood aside and watched others fight. Some even formed great square shapes, a fancily fangled shield wall no doubt, but without a shield in sight. As for their spears, well he knew of these, muskets snapping at their foe from a distance, gushing fire and smoke.

"Battlefield? There are more soldiers here than all the people of Old Albion. Little honour in this type of thing. Look how they stand around watching, like wooden toys in a princeling's game." But Artos didn't allow himself to dwell, too distracted by the things the old soldier at the One Tun had called 'cannons.' He had never seen one fired in war. Large tubes of metal, belching with the thunder of old gods after too much mead, unleashing torrents of smoke into the distance and scattering blue and red dressed men alike.

"Britannia expects victory and prophecies need to be put to rest."

By the farmhouse, a British square of soldiers held their composure like statues despite the barrage of noise and mud. Some started to twitch with agitation, disturbed by the sudden chill. Men whispered to each other of voices. Other men just nodded because they too heard them. When Artos and the Hymn Whisperers threw off their magical concealment just a short way from the square, behind the back wall of the farmhouse, the shaken British lines had worse to worry about than a motley-looking crew of street urchins wearing red coats over monkish robes.

The increasing disquiet didn't go unnoticed by the enemy. Seeing the confusion in the British ranks, the once tight square seemingly unravelled into a sloppy indistinct shape. Commands filtered through the French lines via beating drums, flag signals, and screams. Horses whinnied as they were repositioned, sabres flashed from artillery and gunfire. From a trot, the French cavalry picked up into a gallop towards a British howitzer battery, exposed as vulnerable while the square lacked cohesion.

All fell into chaos. Bluecoats swarmed the farmhouse directly. The red coat defenders presented bayonets and clashed. Further out, a line of blue uniforms took withering aim at the disintegrating red-coat square. And the howitzer battery-men, engulfed with smoke from the local battlefield, heard fighting all around. Worse than that, some heard an ever-nearing rhythm of galloping horses. Artillerymen whispered prayers.

Looking on, Artos said, "By gods of Albion or Christ, the moment is ripe. We will do it like the old days, frontal charge. On the breath of a dragon." Drawing his spear, couching it under an arm, beside him the few mounted Hymn Whisperers drew ringing blades. A call to arms louder than any church bells. The smoke of battle thickened into blind-grey smog.

<hr />

The artillerymen despaired. The battlefield haze seemed to choke like a malevolent entity. And now all of them heard the thunder of hooves. Men huddled together, drew their swords, and waited for death. They took the weird lights, sparkling within the fog, to be nothing but gunshot. When these singular points bloomed into dozens, and then into constellations worth of light, some thought they had died and woken in purgatory. Then their abandoned howitzer's roared...

Great puffs of smoke belched from the cannon dragons, sweeping through the fog and washing the air as clear as polished glass. Like ocean waves, the fog surged forward, taking on other shapes. Knights, dressed in the full panoply of the ancient Britons, spurred on their ghostly steeds. Behind them, the fog formed a shield wall of valiant warriors, charging with spears thrust forward. Just as the French cavalry stormed through the smoke, about to fall upon the artillerymen, Knights clashed. French sabres cut harmlessly, as if through the air.

At the farmhouse, soldiers from both sides held their bayonets mid-thrust, watching the ghost-army swarm around the cavalry to a chorus of, "Mon Dieu!" Spooked horses, neighing with distress, bolted and threw their riders off. Mud kicked up everywhere as man and horse fled from the phantoms. Still, Artos' army continued to swarm through battle-torn fields. Onward and onward they went. Above, a circle of the most brilliant blue winked open in an overcast sky. The ghost army rode and charged on, across the battlefield with supernatural alacrity. On and on to the horizon, leaving a swathe of dead and routed soldiers on a small section of the vast battlefield behind them.

⊙❈⇒═══════════⇐❈⊙

Blunt had heard the news before he read the newspaper. People had been cheering about it all day long. Still, he liked to read during his break at the One Tun, between his first lamplighter run and his second, at sunrise, when he would snuff the lamps.

Struggling over the words, with a little help from a tankard of ale and Valeria, he caught the gist. 'The nearest run thing you ever saw in your life,' that was how Wellesley, the Iron

Duke, the Duke of Wellington described the battle. 'The nearest run thing,' Blunt mused, imagining how Artos might have tipped the balance at the most opportune moment, on a surge of magic. But, of the foggy miracle, the newspaper was silent. He would have to wait a few more days to hear the story from Artos.

The sun was about to embark on its daily conquest of the night when Artos finally returned with his Hymn-Whisperer's to the streets of the Marsh Worm Mile. Glowing points, like little gas-lit flames, emanating from each warrior's centre gradually dimmed, blinking before winking out. Artos' was the last to dim.

In droves, Marsh Worm locals had come to celebrate. They knew what had happened. Scrying magic-wielders had kept track of the whole thing. Many threw flowers at the Hymn Whisperers. All roared at the triumphant few. It was like something out of history. Something from long, long ago.

That long-lost feeling of victory!

After the victory, when Hymn Whisperers had joined the ranks of British soldiers, when rumours circulated of Artos sending magic to aid the victory at Waterloo, the Marsh Worm Mile became known as an official borough of London. Such was its fame and the fame of its main patron, it attracted industrial philanthropists, creaking grey-haired generals, delicate women hiding under umbrellas in fear of the lightest ray of tanning sunshine.

The Marsh Worm Mile was *de rigueur,* a local yet exotic hot-spot, a place to acquire what even the clipper ships couldn't carry. *After all,* the British Empire now stretched over the horizon and came back around the other side of the world to pat itself on the back. It yearned for more, to taste and absorb everything the world had to offer.

It was with satisfaction that Artos stood at the Marsh Worm Gate, looking across the Marsh River Bridge. He had come so far; a woad warrior bedecked in monk-like robes, a hero of the Napoleonic Wars, stronger than he had been for centuries.

Serenity gilded the landscape of water and forest before it sputtered into the spires and chimneys of smog-filled London; an image to freeze in his mind. But, like a fly disturbing a peaceful sleep, something nagged from beyond that landscape. A perverse feeling that gnawed instead of scintillated. If Artos concentrated on it, it made him grind his teeth in irritation. This hidden thing had gone unnoticed. Artos was now powerful enough to sense it.

It was the call of faerie, a muted call from a grove still perpetuating outside of his influence. One day he would have to deal with them, bring them into the embrace of Marsh Worm Mile before they fell into corruption, curses, and spread tainted evils. One day, but not today. Today he would enjoy calling the land he stood on his 'own.'

## Marsh Worm Mile, London 1855 A.D.

Chatter-filled pubs, tea houses and drawing rooms gossiped over new technology, faraway places, small wars, and tall tales about Queen Victoria, victory, and glory. However, no good brandy-cigar ritual would be complete without a story alluding to the Marsh Worm Mile. While London busied itself with celebrations for the never-ending imperial conquests and subjugations, Marsh Worm Mile bulged with magical commodities and superstitions. The borough grew from the home-grown 'crafts' of its inhabitants, instead of imports brought and bought via trading companies, sails and redcoats.

Newspapers applauded Artos' "little amusement park" on the edge of the greatest city in the world. It teased the burgeoning business classes with a hunger for profit and, in this day and age, all that mattered was profit. Artos fed their hunger with magical oddities crafted by knockers and elves; things only a little less satisfying to the money-minded than diamonds, rubber, or tea.

It didn't take long for lordly patrons to invest in the place to curry Artos' favour. Human craftsmen joined knocker craftsmen to refurbish the old village church, to embellish it with symbols of both Fey and Christian. It was a unique place, serving as a centre of worship and as the local town hall. But the Marsh Worm Mile was also a place of secrets and discreet alleys; one such place being the Dark Alley, which hid the abyss created on the Last Night of the Nymphs.

Many called Artos 'Mayor' now. Public officials from London had initiated the ceremony of his investiture around the old well, and the whole borough came to cheer in a celebration that lasted nearly a week. Whizzing sprite fireworks, bottles of absinthe, knocker-made clockwork dancing-nymphs, and all the little orphans Artos set up on Chavver Street, chanted his name. Artos, for his part, knew the names of every one of them.

Alongside the sale of faerie wares, Artos encouraged a 'good favour' economy; foodstuffs and laundry were donated by would-be benefactors in exchange for his approving wink. Protector of the weak, the last of the druids, a magician to some and holy man to others, Artos' words carried weight.

Just when Artos had freed his emotions from the heavy pull of history, found his place in the world, and relished the prospect of immortality as a god-man of 'the Buried Hatchet,' Time itself intruded into his comfort zone. It happened at the unveiling of the new church clock, on the day Artos had decided to track down that final faerie grove and bring it into the embrace of his borough. It was to be a trade mission, full of the Mile's finest spell-weavers and charm-makers, in hope that they could learn the ancient skills of the wild faerie to make the Mile even wealthier.

Crowds cooed at the great, gleaming dial of the clock. Made from hoards of knocker gold, on that bright morning, the disc shone with reflected light like a second sun. All seemed well, but as the minute hand encroached toward 12 o'clock unease simmered inside Artos' stomach. When the clock struck its first-ever hour, chiming twelve dainty jingles of faerie bells, burning bile rose in Artos' throat. *That golden disc! Those Roman numerals...! My prophesied last moment in this world.* As his 'subjects' made merry around him, he could only think of the Crone and her hag-stones on that day in the forest nearly two thousand years ago.

Anxiety fought with memories of cherished times. The Crone had cursed him. Was his life to end under that clock? But the old ways were almost extinct. Ties of fate surely did not apply anymore?

Looking at the clock, Artos imagined which weapon might end him. He found less fear in imaginings of those new-fangled rifles, a bullet more palatable than the fearsome edge of an axe or point of a spear. But a warrior should relish the eye-to-eye clash of the ancients. *Have I become soft?*

But time would wait for no man.

Shoving the thought into a recess of his mind, Artos mounted a horse and made ready to lead the trade mission. Under the centuries of woad-staining, the crowd would not be able to see the paleness of his skin, his dry mouth could be hidden behind his beard, his voice behind stoicism. In this way, he ignored the raving mob and pushed on across Marsh Worm Bridge, followed by a gala of the borough's best.

On the other side, the mission passed a rank of droning Hymn Whisperers, accompanied by dancing orphan apprentices. Artos knew them all, in fact, most he had known since finding them abandoned as babes by the well. All smiled at him, looked up worshipfully, one of them a great big lad. *I should say something...*

"You, the big bear of a boy, Victor. Guard us in my absence. Keep the faith." His voice was hollow, but it proved good enough for the lad to suddenly straighten his back, army-like, ushering the Hymn-Whisperers to do the same.

Trotting on, Artos passed a clutch of Fey-things spilled over from the festival on the other side of the Marsh River, making merry magic in a carnival of light and sound. Quite unexpectedly, Artos clenched his jaw at such a scene. The first thoughts which came into his mind were damning. *Look at them, pathetic and ignorant as they dance around my horse, the leftovers of ancient power all because no one had stood beside my people.*

And what now, Artos was supposed to die because a hag-stone showed him a picture? Old religion had used and abandoned him, hadn't it? The same way it had used his tribe, his people. Instead of fighting with the old world against the new, perhaps he should have remade it the way he remade the Goddess of Victory? Kill it first, rip it asunder before laying new foundations.

*No, don't let poisonous thoughts sour such a day...*

It was slow progress away from the urban sprawl. Sucking in the pollen thick air, Artos let his dangerous pondering drift away into the ether unanswered. He would lose these doubts on the journey. Yes, this journey, with his trader-Fey friends. They would enjoy the adventure of getting lost in civilised lands. Properly, hopelessly lost with no awareness of the way back; a rare thing in these isles of criss-crossing railways found after every few miles of field or thrusting through every range of hills.

That thought ignited something hopeful. To get lost like men used to do whenever they wanted to go beyond the veil of daub and wattle communities and ancient tribal squabbles. To go where the wind thrummed with song and temptation, curses and myths. To get properly lost, so he could find the wild Fey once more and remake the past world in *his* Marsh Worm Mile.

# CHAPTER EIGHT

# DOUBLE DARED SOL AND
# THE SEA NYMPH CARNIVAL

*Marsh Worm Mile, 1861 A.D.*

Slinking away, across the rooftops, Sol kicked off ledges, grabbed edges, and swung on the odd flagpole, taking a route long ingrained in memory. He held back tears, as he rushed away from the Old Well. A mixture of confusion, shame, and anger bit at his nerves. Before going back to his digs on Chavver Street, he needed time alone. He needed to calm down.

Even the heavens shared the cold spell that had just been woven across his emotions. Bursting open with icy, sputtering rain, heavy, grey clouds darkened the sky. Sol shivered, his footing becoming less sure as roof tiles became slick with water. Eventually, he bounded back down to street level, hiding in a shadow-black nook between two shambolic houses. Relatively sheltered, in the tight grip of urban decay, Sol decided to wait out the rain. He would just listen to its shatter-like pelleting of the streets. The rhythm of the wet, drab chill lulled him into some form of numbness.

The streets were now empty of people, replaced by shadows and echoes muffled by the rain. Only the odd gas lamp flickered against the gloom, providing its wind-shield was present and tightly fixed. In a way, there was a charm to the starkness of the weather. Something he needed.

For at least an hour, maybe two, Sol waited. The shower passed, leaving the world glistening, though not clean. *Time to move, to get some kip,* thought Sol, slipping back out into the street. But he stopped immediately and ensured he was still in shadow.

There was a commotion, just up the street. He spied a figure and squinted against the flicker of gas lamps to draw out facial features. *Not to fear.* It was only Small Paul, an elf lad, swinging up on a clothesline that hung between two dilapidated windows. *Hold on, there's something else there.* That green shimmer, increasingly familiar to Sol now, alerted him to mischief. Sure enough, a boggart was perching on a window ledge. The spiteful thing gnawed on the clothesline, threads fraying, timing it perfectly...It snapped!

That was not all, however. A second boggart sneaked low across the pavement. With fingers and claws, the creature teased a golden coin through damp, muddy streets. To anyone watching, the coin rolled as if on its own accord, a flashy speck taunting instant one-night wealth. Scrabbling after the coin was a group of drunks, flat caps pulled tight and casting their faces completely in darkness. Sol knew one of them was Shiv, his loud, bragging voice rang out above the others. Sol's muscles tensed, his heart quickened, as Small Paul fell in the prime moment to spark an artfully created drama.

Small Paul dropped to earth, a dead weight onto the pack of drunks, sending one and all sprawling into grime-sodden puddles. Shiv, and his mob, kicked about in the mud and tried to find the coin but, of course, the boggart had scurried it away. *The bastard will blame Paul.*

"Give it here, you little bleeder," snarled one of the drunks, staggering to his feet and kicking the elf. Booted feet rained blows, Shiv and his mates, on the prowl after events in the church square, determined to create their own entertainment for the night. *Brutal. Not fair play at all.*

Bursting from his nook, Sol screamed, "Stop! Get out, this is Guinea Dreadful turf, and you know it!"

Turning to face him, Shiv's shoulders rose and fell with an agitated viciousness. "No fear, it's only *Double-Dared Sol,*" he spat the words like an insult. "You want some, do ya?" Shiv looked different. His flat cap had been knocked off his straggly-haired head, revealing a face painted nightmarish-blue. Next to him, another lad cracked his knuckles to make a show of slipping on his brass dusters. Gas lamps licked the thug's approach into silhouette, a dark, looming force padding around Sol. He was to be their new entertainment.

Sol flicked out his cut-throat razor and shook it in front of him. That only angered the mob. *Gods, I wish Victor was here. He would show them all what's what.*

"I said, you want some, do ya? I dare ya!" roared Shiv. "Time we finish old business. Let's get it sorted before the Carnival. Comes with Artos' blessing, it does." Sol felt sick. In the darkness, he could see little room for escape. He had no time to plan for anything. *I swear, I'll cut Shiv, even if they take me down. I'll cut him, leave him with a scar for life.*

Suddenly, the thug with the knuckle dusters surged at Sol, his eyes white popping balls of rage on his shadowed face. Flimsily, Sol flailed his arms and razor, certain he was about to die...

Like a puppet on a string, the raging drunkard's head jerked back, eyes bulging even larger than before. Wheezing nastily, as froth boiled from his mouth, he clutched at his throat. This invisible assault caused Shiv and his mates to stop dead in their tracks. "Damn me. Artos was right. You some evil-magic Fey filth," said Shiv.

Sol glared back. Remembering how Shammy pretended to cast spells at the docks, he raised his hands and wriggled his fingers as if playing an invisible forte piano. Unnerved by this witchery, Shiv and his mate continued to back away. One step, two steps, the shadows wrapped around them. Both turned at the same time, scampering off into the darkness.

All Sol could do was watch as the little green creatures crawled over the remaining thug and choked him. Many little clawed hands ripped over his skin; other claws eased behind those popping eyes. And Sol kept watching and watching... Until he doubled over and vomited onto the street. What made it even worse was knowing that, apparently, only he could see those green demons. It was something he couldn't even share; the burden was his alone.

In an attic-floor room hideaway, away from Chavver street, Sol tugged at tattered sheets as he wrestled to sleep. It became an endless blank stare at worm-eaten walls, broken up by blinking. Sleepless hour after sleepless hour eventually fuzzed into morning. Sun rays sludged through the window before choking on dust-thickened air. Shadows bloomed over here or waned over there. Everywhere became highlights and lowlights.

Guilt rankled at something in Sol's chest, twisted his mind into insomniac meaninglessness. Eventually, Sol gave up trying to sleep for good and slumped on a stool by the small window. He looked over the streets of Marsh Worm Mile and watched locals pass by in stops and starts. Shammy went by once, calling his name. Others too, the old knocker Blunt and his constant companion, Valeria. Even Victor. But Sol remained hidden from them all.

Now and then a green light flickered in the shadows. For every flicker, the streets filled with an ever-greater vacuum of unease. Sol sensed it but received it passively. Blinking to points of interest, he saw things as a series of still-frame pictures. That was until his eyes came to rest on a menacing group of painted men. Painted, like Shiv's face from yesterday.

Some were from the Guinea Dreadfuls, his own lads! *Only a few though, perhaps the yellow-streaked ones?* Most were from all the other Marsh Worm gangs, all eyeing each other uneasily. And there, just as he might suspect, was Shiv. Even in his sleepless state, the sight of that bullying bastard caused Sol's numbness to recoil and spiked his chest with anger. *My mates...have chosen Artos over me?*

More Peelers than ever patrolled the streets too, along with Rozzer Jim, their local constable. Every one of them was jittery, making too much of a show with loud but empty chatter. However, when confronted by the painted men, the Peelers nodded and moved on. *Spineless.*

Damn them! Everyone so admired Artos. No one dared speak against him. Definitely not the authorities. *What did they fear?* That the riotous mobs of the Mile would boil over into civil unrest. Angry magic-users. To those unfamiliar with the borough, it seemed as if every Fey must be armed by virtue of their 'superstitious pagan powers.'

Outside, the streets flickered again, the green light returning. Sol almost missed it, mistaking it for a blink of his heavy eyelids. This was followed by a nasty crack. In the streets, the painted men were scuffling with knockers. Should Sol go and join the Guinea Dreadful lads down there? Or even, help the knockers?

But why? Gods, yesterday he tried to help Small Paul, and it resulted in... murder! No, not that. Never that! It was self-defence.

*Let them all go to hell. Damn this wretched Marsh Worm Mile. Damn the magic. Damn Artos!* But others still showed courage. Sol watched Rozzer Jim yelling at the brawlers, waving his arms, and trying to calm the situation down. With his waddling bravery, he looked ridiculous. Nonetheless, he stood his ground.

*Shame on me.* How could Sol sit idly by, when a *constable* dared to face such odds? The day when even the Law made a show of 'protecting' rather than 'oppressing,' and he moped like a child, like a spoiled son of Lord Muck!

Slipping on his trousers and falling-apart shoes, Sol unlatched his door and stumbled a malnourished stupor down the stairway. Buoyed by purpose, he pushed through the lingering crowd with relished discourtesy. "Jim," he called, catching the fat constable's eyes between a wink of green light. "I know how to do it, how to make things better!"

*The Carnival! It was Carnival time. Sol's time!* The Sea Nymph Carnival was the reason for Sol's fame in the borough. No matter what, he would be there this year. And he would remember to stick two fingers up in Artos' face.

Four years ago, in the year of our Lord 1857, on a bitter morning in nearly spring, Sol and Victor answered the call of gossip and witnessed the event which would give birth to the yearly Sea Nymph Carnival. Shammy lazily wallowed in her bed and reprimanded them. "You must think I belong in Bedlam to get up this early."

Sol remembered having a cold that day, his face wrapped in a recently pinched, dandy-red, woollen scarf. Despite that, he led Victor through the peasouper smog choking the city. Curiosity pulled them towards the Marsh River. They must be quick before others got there and there was nothing left.

The boys scurried up drainpipes and leapt between ledges to get as high as they could. As always, Sol helped Victor keep his balance on the half a dozen times the bigger boy's footing slipped. He couldn't help but snicker. "What would you do without me, you foozler."

Spreading the gossip, the buzzing sprites were out early too. Speaking quickly, they told how a melted and ripped bulkhead, from a gunboat-loser in some unknown foreign battle, had washed up from the coast and clogged the flow of water in the Marsh River. Already the mudlarks had scooped grenades from the riverbanks, making a show of their 'treasures' at impromptu market stalls. Well, it was their patch for first dibs. However, others came to claim the spoils soon after. Lucky treasure hunters boasted of kegs full of soggy black powder, muskets, and, best of all, medals encrusted with precious stones.

When Sol and Victor arrived, they watched from the rooftops as larger lads, ratbags most of them, calling themselves the 'Marsh Mob Boys,' clawed through river mud. It looked like Victor and Sol would go back to Shammy empty-handed. It wasn't worth thinking about, how much she would 'take the piss' for their failed adventure.

Tooting pipes sounded from scribble-scrawled alleys. Another gang, the 'Guinea Dreadfuls!' That was Sol and Victor's crew. Bitterest enemies of the 'Marsh Mob ' in the turf wars of Marsh Worm Mile. Immediately, without even a thrown insult, both sides rushed to face each other and clashed over the scraps.

Smoke and razors, knives and knuckledusters, claws and teeth. Knocker gangsters flung dung, teeming with razor-maggots. Sprites pricked human skin with poisonous needles. Both sides cast spells, but only derisory puffs. The corrupting toll of urban magic restricted the arcane arsenal down to fire-pebble spells and dizziness chants.

Victor crouched at Sol's side with glinting eyes. He smiled wider than Sol had ever seen. "A proper ruckus." Nudging with an elbow, Victor said, "I've got your back."

From behind his scarf, Sol remained quiet. His shadowed eyes blinked and twitched with worry. Neither he nor Victor, has been in a *proper* big dust-up before. They left that to the older Dreadfuls. But he knew Victor *longed* for his chance. He thought it was the best way to become a 'face.'

Energized by boy-fearlessness, Victor bounded off the roofs into the, weirdly, salt-smelling smog-turned-an-eerie-green. Compelled to follow, Sol found himself crawling through the legs of a particularly brutish ogre as he tried to avoid undue attention. The sight of Victor, viciously brawling into whatever came into his path, cold-flipped his stomach. *I ain't cut out for this... pulava.*

He sneaked away, to a nearby doorway set into a sad-looking two-story house with rotten timbers, glad to hide for the remainder of the fight. Victor was bellowing, for all to hear, "This is me! What I was born for, Sol."

Something more interesting grabbed Sol's attention. From behind the twisted bulkhead, in the river, came an invigorated gust of sea breeze, lashing salt stink across the area. Sol peeked at the bulkhead from his doorway. A silhouette emerged, trailing tangles of seaweed. The water seemed to part around her, make way as if for royalty. *Oh, gods,* it took Sol's breath away.

A Sea Nymph rippling with ocean magic, on the edge of urban decay, ethereal in her beauty. Her skin was of the deepest blue, catching the light and throwing it off at a hundred different angles. Seashells were woven into her slick green hair. Her bright-green eyes pulsed with passion, perhaps lust, perhaps violence, shining with a promise of something more if you were brave enough to tempt the waters. The sight was...*enchanting*.

Distracted, Sol turned around to confront the thud of heavy, running feet too late. A lumbering lad, known to him only as 'Shiv' put the boot in, hard and firm, knocking the air from Sol. Sol collapsed and covered up. Shiv rained down punches and kicks. Through the gaps of shielding arms and fingers, Sol saw the manic, even joyous look on his attacker's face.

First, Sol's flat cap was tossed aside, then his scarf ripped away before Shiv pulled him up by his lapels and tossed him backward, as if he was nothing, into a wet puddle of nearby muck. "Runt," spat Shiv. "This is how the big boys play."

After swatting away an older lad with a haymaker, Victor rushed in, barging Shiv aside. Effortlessly, he pulled Sol to his feet. "I'll grab him, hold him down, and you belt the daylights out of him." Eyes wide and wild, his lips thinned, Victor bared the top row of his crooked teeth.

There was a click. Shiv flicked open his knife. "Fancy yourself, do ya?" He stepped forward. Victor raised his fists and posed as a pugilist.

A note rang the air and billowed the green, salty smog into something hypnotic. Like rats that nipped and cats that scratched and hissed, the Sea Nymph defended herself. Though this was not through teeth and claws, but through the only means at her disposal. Magic.

Magic burst forth as she sang her siren song. A chord, struck with force, shattered through urban drabness, exposing something brilliant yet formless underneath. The only way Sol could describe the feeling was 'awe.' And the awed gangs stopped fighting as that voice took hold, a gloriousness rising laced through all sensation. Better than the poppy, absinthe, or gin.

Energy pulsed through Sol's limbs. Warm, invigorating. He understood the ways of the world now. Everything was just wanting to be... *good*. What a beautiful world, how lucky they all were to be here, together!

Along with some other lads, Sol pulled out a harmonica and started to play. Faerie and human danced a jig, beat a rhythm with their feet and weapons, and sang songs of happy idleness. Perhaps the moment lasted mere minutes. Perhaps it lasted hours. Eventually, though, the Sea Nymph's magic, borne of nature, seemed to corrupt under the oppressive aura of the sludge-filled Marsh River. Drying cracks puffed up dust from all over her face. Her eyes dimmed. With supernatural speed, she ran, almost seeming to float, as she followed the embankment deeper into Marsh Worm Mile.

No one gave chase though. Everyone remained stupefied, happy. Drunk on something, which even spared them a hangover the next morning. Sol's last memory of the day was of Victor's eyes, oddly wet. Later, back at Chavver street, he told Sol how he had dreamed he was an ancient warrior, covered with markings, celebrated as the strongest of all! Only when it was all over, on the cusp of the evening, did an annoyed Shammy show up. "I heard all about it. I missed it! Next time wake me up, even if I make a fuss."

"Hark, Lady Muck. I'll tell you all about it over a good dinner. We can still make a night of it," said Sol.

"What about Dares first?" said Victor, looking at Sol.

"Dares!" Shammy clapped and nodded gleefully.

Sol shrugged. "I'm going to get stuck with it, ain't I?"

"I dare ya to...piss in the face of Lady Justice." With a twinkle in her eye, Shammy skipped over and nudged Victor.

"Yeah, right. I double-dare you to do...that."

Feigning hurt with mock earnestness; Sol placed his hands over his heart. "Why d'you always pick on me?" Nonetheless, he sprang off into the Mile, Victor and Shammy following.

⊙≫❬═══════════❭≪⊙

Gas lamps cut stark and solid shadows in the night. For the past few nights, in places where others saw only blackness, Sol's eyes saw every ember of light glare like a tiny sun. It was the curse of that green powder, of those boggarts their green light taunting him. Sol had reasoned to never call on them again. Nothing had changed really, had it? He wasn't corrupt, wasn't evil. *Damn Artos!*

Arriving at the embankment early, Sol passed the time polishing his cut-throat razor to a mirror finish and waited for the gangs to arrive. Curiously, he took note of the graffiti murals colouring the wall of the embankment. Engraved, or written in charcoal and chalk, they depicted the origins of the Sea Nymph Carnival, the life and times of Marsh Worm Mile laid bare. The graffiti murals didn't do the Nymph justice though. Four years ago, on that special morning, she had looked...well, stunning.

Four years ago, when life was normal. Before he was a faerie thing. Before being a faerie thing was even bad! And he wasn't even a proper faerie at that. Proper faerie, it was said, were birthed from the forest dreams of great old trees. Slumbering peacefully under the warm wash of sunshine through the canopy, the trees soaked up all the joy, health, and love and birthed the most beautiful faerie. But, according to the Crone, those dreams were not responsible for conjuring Sol into the world. If tree dreams were to have borne him, it would have been the dreams of the sad, greying trees, dwarfed by nearby smoke-churning funnels, fed on city air full of poverty and despair. Yes, Sol was not a proper faerie. Just a shadow-thing born from an urban nightmare. *No, nothing had changed!*

*I won't give in to you, Artos.* He would play the Carnival game to show all he was still the same Sol, the King of Dares.

⬧⊪▦▦▦═══ ═ ═ ═ ▦▦⧫

With a finger, he idly traced the tags on the wall, charcoal scrawls and knife scratches of addresses, cusses, and, most importantly, names. The name 'SHIV' stood out larger than the rest, a crude crown sketched over the 'S.' Hot anger suddenly burbled up through Sol's anxiety.

He dug into the tag with the corner point of his cut-throat razor. "I hate you; I hate you," Sol hissed, gouges turning into hacks. But then a rising tide of approaching voices signalled that he was no longer alone. Events would soon start. Sol held his breath to calm down.

Knots of knockers swooned from nooks and crannies, bumping into each other, still groggy from the opium they brewed dreams with. Sprites buzzed beside them, green absinthe sloshing in the little bottles some of them carried. Finally, a few ogres, big, stony, and never discreet, thundered from their cement hovels.

Most of the faerie folk appeared withered, tissue-skinned. More so with every passing year. The city had taken its toll, twisting them with its unhealthy industry and greed. Yet, they all came to support Sol. Some waved banners while others rhymed:

'Sol, Sol, The King of Dares,

Escapes the snares and avoids the stares,

Sol, Sol, We all declare,

Sol, Sol, The King of Dares.'

*Yes, the King of Dares.* Dares made orphan kids into men, made freaks into heroes, and gave them big names to carve on walls for all to see. And The Double Dare was the most important event of the Sea Nymph Carnival, at least to the behind-the-scenes gangs of Marsh Worm Mile. More than child's play, more than fantastic feats of free-running or theft. It was all about bragging rights. And Sol had won every year. Humans appeared from numerous alleys, swaggering along in corduroys and flat caps. *No Victor?* Something was...wrong.

Broader than the rest, Shiv marched at their head, blue-faced and spiked-haired now. Behind him was...Artos. Again, anxiety snapped in Sol's stomach, but his moment to emerge into plain sight had come.

Clambering the brickwork embankment, he vaulted over rusty iron safety rails. Gas lamps exposed him. He raised his hands into the air. Clapping and cheering, the faerie folk welcomed Sol, as did many of the humans. Shammy was there, yelling her head off, giving him a thumbs up.

"I missed you, Sol. Are you okay?" He wanted to run over and hug her, but he had to play the game. *Look hard.* So, instead, he nodded slightly, almost imperceptibly.

Buoyed with support, Sol walked with purpose to the human mob. Smirking Shiv, in woad with a rough zigzag of scars grasping his left cheek, immediately pushed straight in his face. Only the pride of the faerie kept Sol from running back into the shadows. Coating his nerves with bravado, Sol hissed. Bouncing up onto tiptoes, he prepared to announce his welcome with faerie-pleasing theatrics. "You're calling the dares for the Mob Boys this year? There's nothing I can't do, and you know it."

"Faerie freak," spat Shiv, momentarily looking back to Artos, who subtly, shook his head. "I told everyone about what you did. Attacked us, you did. Murdered one of us, you did. You're gonna get yours now."

Sol winked, "A few years back, I was dared to piss in the face of justice, so I climbed above the courts and relieved myself on the statue of that madam holding the scales. Then, I was dared to stop the wind, so I stole the weather vane from atop City Hall." Excited faerie cheered, a mixture of pitches from sprite-squeak to ogre-rumble.

"Last year, you Marsh Mob Boys all got cleverer, dared me to make the day longer. So, I climbed the clock tower, hung off the minute hand, and pulled the time back a quarter of an hour. Everywhere, you'll find the name 'Sol' scratched in the hardest to get to corners. I *am* the King of Dares."

Breath chugging from his nose, eyes wide and wild, a palpable urge for violence throbbed from Shiv. "We ain't no Marsh Mob no more. Woad Warriors, we are. If it turns out that you're too scared, this year, we can settle it good and proper. Like *men*." Tiny twitches broke out over Shiv's face. He *itched* for a fight. Behind him, a group of tearaways cracked knuckles in a show of support.

"Whoops, Shiv, you called him a man," said another of the gang, poking his tongue crudely at the inside of his cheek, racking his throat then spitting onto the floor. Sol felt lucky that the Carnival tradition of peace held. They seemed to really want to do him in. Shiv's response had him unsettled. *What is a Woad Warrior?*

"Using imagination, mate?" Defiantly, Sol held Shiv's stare. "Trying to be *ingenious?* That must have hurt. I wondered why you looked so pale. Thinking … never your thing. Neither were dares, come to that, what with your clumsy lumbering feet and all. And you call me a *freak*, what with my graceful tippy-toes." Shiv's smirk contorted into a rage mask. Like lightning, he lunged forward, jabbing a flick knife. Instinctively, Sol skipped back faster than lightning.

Eager not to be disrespected in front of his gang, Shiv hissed his next words. "Victor ain't turned up, has he? Been having second thoughts about being all matey with a freak, he has. And I got something for you. We all thought of it together. Might mean visiting Miss Nymph in her tunnel. Might mean asking her to sing. And it ain't nothing I wouldn't do. I went there already. Carved my name there too."

*Bullshit. No one goes to those tunnels.* Sol shook his head in disbelief.

"Does it hurt, little freak? Scratched my name under the river a hundred times I reckon, even when I heard her gargle. And I didn't see your name nowhere." A few of the lads behind Shiv flicked blades between fingers and nodded.

"Easy, for me," Sol said. "What you want me to do? Just tell me."

"I dare you to make the city *dream*. The *whole* city." And so, the formalities started. "In fact, I double dare you. And if you got the balls, or whatever passes for them with freaks, the spoils ain't just pride this year. The spoils is the Marsh Worm Mile. You win, we leave you alone. You lose, you piss off to one of those London slums."

Sol grew pale.

Pushing his large frame forward, Shiv puffed his chest. "Piss your pants, did ya? Tell you what, let's just fight it out." But Artos grabbed Shiv's shoulder and pulled him back.

"Can you show us what you're made of, lad?" said Artos, his stare forcing Sol to look away.

Faerie chants crashed against human shouts. Both sides exchanged evil eyes and curses. In the corner of his field of view, Sol noticed a few sprites dab needles into thimbles of something. Poison. They were preparing for a ruckus.

*Just run,* Sol thought. But this was his niche, a victory expected by his mates. More so now, by all the faerie. "Piece of cake. I'll do it right now. I'll get the Sea Nymph to sing the whole city to sleep."

Turning his back, he slunk ahead, heading to the tunnel which ran under the river. He knew Shiv was smiling behind him, as he followed. The swagger of his shadow made it obvious.

◦●━━━━━━━━●◦

In tight streets, ringing with bells and shaking with drums, the mob of Marsh Worm gangs squeezed through a throng of well-to-do types. Tourists, mostly, these folk enjoyed the risqué celebrations and cheap-side colour of the Sea Nymph's Carnival.

Weaving around the narrows, the mob soon approached an alley, one which led to the tunnel. This was the place the Nymph had fled, four years ago to the day. A dangerous place, unremembered except by those daring mudlarks and urban explorers of the Marsh Worm Mile.

Trailed with slime and cluttered with molluscs, the damp concrete belched fishy odours. To Sol, this was one of those rare unvisited places, a source of terrifying rumours about magic and corruption, almost as bad as The Dark Alley. As far as he knew, *no one* went down here. Only an idiot would... But then again, it *was* Shiv who set the dare.

Many of the mob lit lanterns, shining the light over the rough-carved stairs at the alley's dead end. At the bottom, a rusty iron gate guarded access to the tunnel. It should've been locked, not that it would have been a barrier to those determined to enter. Now, though, it stood ajar.

Sol was shoved forward. "Sol, Sol, the King of Dares," the faerie still sang. *I'm the best pickpocket, free-runner, diver, and skiver of all*

*Marsh Worm Mile. I can do this.* Cold against his palm, Sol pushed the gate open. It creaked, loudly. *So much for sneaking.* Lantern light washed into the tunnel, flickering over slick concrete and slime, catching on patches of furry green moss. Shells crunched underfoot and darkness throbbed from nooks.

As he crept inside, ever so slowly on shadow tiptoes, Sol flicked open his cut-throat razor. A few of Shiv's gang followed but kept a distance.

A thud echoed through the tunnel. Sol turned. Someone behind him had slipped on the wet stone floor, a human on a congealed splat of slime. The poor man screamed as the slime steamed his hands. Under him, a puddle swelled, and the water from his body drained into grated sidings. Trying to stand, to get away, his skin withered into leather, dried into ash. A second later, he puffed away in an explosion of white powder. It was horrible.

Everyone jumped back. Some screamed. Except for Shiv, who acted the big man, reached into his pocket and took out a hip-flask. Spilling a drizzle to the memory of the fallen lad, he looked down the tunnel at Sol and smiled long and cruel. "I've been down there. I told you. Look out for my name."

Whatever happened to the nymph had turned her into something deadly. *No matter how deadly, I hope she can still hold a tune.*

⊸≍──────≍⊷

Not far off, at the entrance, dozens waited for him. Even so, Sol felt alone. Cold silver flipped in his stomach. The steadily strengthening rasping noise only made matters worse. From somewhere around the constant gentle bend of the tunnel, it came. Getting nearer with each step. It sounded like troubled breathing. With the rapid knocking of his heart, Sol dared himself *not* to breathe.

It didn't help that Shiv kept coughing and spluttering behind him, deliberately breaking the silence and willing the Sea Nymph to emerge. "How is it down there, Sol? That nymph, she the jammiest bit of jam going. I imagine you'll make a great couple." *The idiot.*

Forewarning magic, pins and needles crept through Sol's every limb. Odd piles of powder were scattered around the place, many indented with footprints. Sol tightened his grip on the cut-throat razor as if his life depended on it.

Deeper he went. More and more piles of powder covered the ground. Here, there were names scrawled on the walls. Sol examined them as much as he dared while keeping one eye on the tunnel bend.

It wasn't many names at all. Just the one name, scrawled over and over on the damp brick walls. 'SHIV.' It was all a setup. Different handwriting, different spelling, the name SHIV never appeared the same way twice. 'SHEEV,' 'SHIEVE' and even a 'SHEEF.' None of them were drawn with the crown above the 'S.' None of them looked like the name Sol had seen on the embankment. Even though Shiv was not the brightest, Sol knew he could at least spell and write his name. *Probably...*

*Cowardly bastard.!* But that was not all. On the wall, immediately in front of Sol's face, came a familiar green shimmer. A disembodied clawed finger hovered there, curling up and beckoning Sol to watch. It turned over and proceeded to scratch a single word into the crumbly, wet brick. 'Mirror.'

*Be calm...* Sighing for composure, Sols's ears pricked at a slither coming from just around the curve of the tunnel. No use sneaking or hiding now. "Miss Sea Nymph, I mean no harm. Please, don't be afraid," Sol whispered, sounding as gentle, as non-threatening as he could.

Two green glowing points appeared, with a slithering sound, in magical-tainted darkness that even Sol's eyes found hard to penetrate. The Sea Nymph spoke, her voice bubbling mucus. "I feel you, in the shadows, watching me. I feel your disgust and fear."

All was still, except for the rasping huff of breath. Sol's heart ran like a train, yet he felt stuck, daring not to move, not to provoke this thing in any way at all. Salt stink suddenly cut fierce; the air gasped a vacuum. The Sea Nymph pushed back the darkness in a spray of green light. Sol was exposed against the pockmarked brick of the tunnel walls. However, the green glare also revealed the full horror of the nymph. Sol swallowed a scream at what he saw. Swallowed again to keep the bile down.

No longer was the Sea Nymph a creature of beauty, but a Sea Hag *thing,* a giant-sized mollusc with eyes drooling trails of slime. The city's utilitarian squalor had warped something birthed from the romantic dreams of oceans. No dream for dirty rivers or sewers, it seemed, only nightmares.

Almost undulating, under a man-sized shell, her slug-like body sweated grey ooze. For the second time in his life, Sol listened to her song. It wasn't as wonderful as the first time. But she was trying.

*Oh gods, no!* A hellish screech ripped at his soul. Warm liquid ran from his ears.

Trembling in time to the jackhammering of his heart, Sol remembered the cut-throat razor in his hand, all polished like a mirror. *Mirror...* He clenched his eyes shut. Damn it, he even felt sadness for this thing. Once, for just a moment it had inspired peace and joy throughout the Marsh Worm Mile. Now, though, this creature would never sing dreams again.

Opening his eyes, just a slither, he held out the cut-throat, exposing the mirror-polished blade to her gaze. "I'm sorry," said Sol, as the Nymph witnessed, perhaps for the first time, the extent of her corruption. "And... I understand."

With a slick grey hand, the sea nymph touched her face, and traced the lines, finding no semblance to the thing she once was. Fresh goo welled up from her eyes, spilling green over cracking cheeks.

The air energized and heated. The tunnel started to shake. Invisible surges of force buffeted Sol as he watched. Warped like dough, the hag's flesh rolled and reshaped, sculpturing something else, transforming the ugliness of her present into the beauty of her past. Into the Sea Nymph of four years past. For an instant, her beauty was restored. Sol opened his eyes and stared, concentrating to take in every detail. He would have gladly traded his heart and soul to look upon her forever.

Yet, things are never solved so simply. The cost of such magic was tremendous. The Sea Nymph's face reverted to the polluted caricature of urban under-works before she tried to recast it again. Again, and again her skin writhed, steam belching from the hag nymph's body as magic ultimately aged it and ate away. Cracks webbed over her form. A chalky mist puffed up all around her.

Still holding the razor blade, Sol couldn't help but watch until the Sea Nymph disintegrated into powder, dried up, and dead. Just a human-sized mollusc shell, delicate and in slow decay, remained.

⊶≫≒═════════════≒≪⊷

After poking the shell to test it was no longer dangerous, Sol touched his face. *A wretched faerie thing too. But I'm built for the city, not the forest, not the ocean. I am something...unique.*

With his razor, he etched a zigzagging 'SOL' into the shell. Then he dragged it through the tunnel, no longer damp but utterly bone dry. Edges broke off the shell as it rubbed on the concrete, and he had to take care hoofing it along. Ahead, lights glared from the entrance. A sprite, all glitter and butterfly wings, squeaked, "Sol, I see Sol!" Others rushed to see. On spying him, many ran into the tunnel to help. Big grey ogre hands, and even a few pairs of pink and brown human hands, pulled the shell up the stairs and into the alley.

"Well done, Sol." Shammy cheered herself hoarse. Human and faerie voices shouted praise, in recognition of such derring-do.

Even Artos had a few words to share. "You are brave, lad. But what was it like? A twisted, evil thing, yes?" Breath chugging hot from his nostrils, Shiv, however, didn't share the sentiment.

"What we cheering for? The dare weren't to kill her. He ain't asked her to sing. He ain't made the city dream. He failed."

Sol had a bone to pick with Shiv and pick it raw. "I saw the piles of powder down there," Sol said, the air wet and warm against his clammy face. The few lads closest to Shiv prickled, looked up at the big man. Shiv looked back at Artos.

Sol continued, "You're too big, too clumsy to make it that far and get away. You just sent others in to do your dirty work, just so you could challenge me. But most of them didn't make it back."

"No, I didn't." In an instant, Shiv thrust a palmed flick knife. Springing back, Sol swung the shell around for protection. It caught against the wind and a gentle melody thrummed out. Something far-away, a lingering resonance from another world passing by in the night. It was simply beautiful.

Everyone froze like statues as the notes urged calm. To some, a faint memory rekindled of the wonderful song they had heard four years ago.

Breaking the moment, Shiv kicked out and shattered part of the shell into dust. "You failed." He made to grab Sol.

With all his breath, Sol blew into the remains of the shell, a frame of crumbling gaps twisting the air, carrying it around the whirls inside, sending it out as music: magical and wonderful. It came out as a brilliant cascade of sound and light as a Sea Nymph's voice should. The world slowed. Everyone's movements were muffled as though they were underwater, except for Sol's. The music maker had full control.

Hissing, Sol flicked out his cut-throat razor again. He swiped at Shiv, the big man now dopey and exposed. Without a sound, the blade cut into cheek, bit into bone, and sent out an arc of blood. Everyone continued to smile in a clueless stupor. Sol clicked his razor closed and stepped back.

"I won't do you in," he said to the enchanted Shiv. "I just want you to know, I'm proud of what I am. I'm gifted. I'm magical. I'm about to make the city dream."

Sol turned to Artos next, frozen too in old-faerie magic, and glared into his grey-blue eyes. "But maybe I should do you in..." All of a sudden, those grey eyes blinked. Sol jerked back as a smile drew across Artos' face.

"A goblin-cursed rat like you can't touch me, not in my Mile. Nothing can hurt me in my own land. But you are a danger to your friends, lad. Know that you will cause them to..."

Sol thrust his middle finger up at Artos. "Just shut up, you blow-hard. You won't ever catch me."

Pushing his arms through the corroded holes in the shell, Sol fitted it to his back and leapt high onto a window ledge. He climbed onto slate roofs. He scrambled across edges and chimneys, to the clock tower where the clock tolled a quarter of an hour slow. Sol's silhouette danced away into the moonlight, leaving Artos standing still and watching, his breath steaming into the cold night.

Climbing past the clock tower into the business district, where glass and steel-reinforced new-builds breached the clouds, Sol bounded up higher and higher. Blending with corners and blind spots, winding around ledges, he kicked off onto the Cathedral-level highest of heights.

Far above the city, he hung the shell on a spire, a place where the wind caught and bellowed through it. It was as if the city itself played the instrument. Music rained over Marsh Worm Mile and beyond, louder even than carnival drums, flowing into both pauper-filled rookeries and uptown mansions. Everywhere, humans and faeries got lost in a melody of dreams.

Wind battered the shell, gradually blowing it through to dust, the song only temporary. But it didn't matter now. A thought drifted through Sol's mind, an assurance that made him feel, perhaps for the first time in his life, complete.

*Whatever may come, tonight and evermore, I am faerie.*

# CHAPTER NINE

# BREAKING OF THE WAYS

*Marsh Worm Mile, 1861 A.D.*

Sleep didn't visit Sol that night, his mind wouldn't stop dwelling on recent events. A few stolen minutes of shut-eye were all the mercy given to him. Green ghosts of boggarts imposed themselves constantly over his eyes. The creatures' malicious energy became ever more tangible, ever more powerful. Nasty things, responsible for so much inhumanity. But now, Sol had the power to do something, to make things better. *I must embrace my nature and lead the boggarts to improve the Mile.* No longer would he allow them to engage in petty mischief for their own entertainment. Circumstances in the Marsh Worm Mile had made it ripe for manipulation.

More and more gentlemen seemed to linger in the markets, perusing curiosities and running their moneyed hands over items of intrigue. Swanning around like Lords of the Manor, many winced whenever a Fey got a bit too close. Woad Warriors protected them though, they let the Mile know that Artos was watching.

Everywhere in the Mile, Sol saw Woad Warriors congealed on corners and glaring at him. "Artos wants to see you," they'd say. But nothing was further from Sol's mind than meeting that...*monster.*

So, a sleepless Sol decided to keep out of sight, befriend dark corners, and make his home under bridges so he could observe the suffering. First thing, though, he would deal with that pang of guilt he felt when the boggarts had tricked Paul and Shiv.

Sol spent his time following Small Paul. A smart elf, Paul used his new limp to squeeze ever more coin from the sympathetic ladies in the tea houses in the finer squares of London. Even so, Sol would bless him with more than just a touch of luck.

Under the arch of Marsh Worm Bridge, a prime mud-larking site where trinkets and even the occasional magical oddity washed up, Sol watched as Small Paul scavenged through the muck and rubbish. Now and then green lights flashed in Sol's periphery. He concentrated on those lights. He concentrated so hard, clenching his jaw until he started to tremble and black spots joined the green flashes until he flitted on the edge of consciousness. Only then could he visualize his thoughts as arrows, sending them into the ether, urging his will to become that of the boggarts.

Sending his arrows of design like a magical telegraph, Sol summoned the boggarts his way, pulling towards him those who attacked Small Paul. The pinched face little things came crawling with mocking pleas for forgiveness, just the way boggarts liked to play. "We will all make amends," Sol whispered.

Away the boggarts went, chattering to themselves as they slunk into the mud of the riverbanks. Suddenly, all around Small Paul, the mud started to burp and fart. Sol smiled, glowing inside with satisfaction when a dozen gold sovereigns flipped from the bursting bubbles. To Small Paul, it was as if a mere natural occurrence sent riches spluttering out of the mud.

After that, it became an obsession to Sol, a compulsion to right every misdeed. All he had to do was concentrate. Without this pinpoint focus, he feared his mind would snap into insanity. So, he twisted every blighted bit of chance to help those he had grown up with. He made prey of the curious gentleman and ladies; pocket watches, purses, necklaces, and earrings were snatched and pilfered with ease by invisible boggart hands and passed along to the poorest. More than just that though.

From lucky punches in bare-knuckle brawls, when boggarts chucked a handy bit of fairy dust in an opponent's eye, to fortuitous dice roles, the gambling obsession sweeping through impoverished communities started to pay up. For the next few weeks, a myriad of distractions helped the dippers to hone their art of picking pockets. A crime wave even washed over the wealthy boroughs, where boggarts would tear out slates from mansion roofs for quick entry, and then drain every shiny thing into the dirty fingers of street urchins.

When the peelers started to get tough, barging through groups of Mile youth mob-handed, they fell under boggart-sent curses of uselessness and misfortune. Sick horses, rickety carriage wheels, misinformation whispered in fetid air, and a growing tednancy toward dizziness and confusion in the winding London streets meant that the Law floundered. Delayed, lost, and embarrassed, hapless police officers were left wanting to ever catch anyone 'red-handed.'

It became a game to work out how Sol could spread himself as far as possible. Eyelids heavy and blue, eyes straining under a red web of lines, sleep became just a memory. His mind began to falter from the strain. Anxiety bit into his well-being. Gods, what if he lost concentration, would the boggarts slip back into their petty evils? When Sol dared to close his eyes, he still saw the outlines of the green things. Perhaps now they toyed with him? Had he become *their* game now? One day bled into another...

Exhaustion gripped his spirits. It was as if he was permanently lost from...real life. Dragging himself into an alleyway, huddling into a protective ball, for the first time in days, Sol's mind and body collapsed, utterly, into an unresponsive waking dream.

<hr />

Rudely shoved awake, the light stung his eyes. Sol peeked at the disturbance for only a second, confused, before raising his hand against the intruding sun and clenching his eyes shut. His head ached; his mouth was gummy. Gods, he felt thirsty. Rubbing his eyes, he dared to peek again and saw Shammy standing over him.

Smiling with her mouth but not her eyes, Shammy dared not hold Sol's stare. "Where have you been? You ain't been home to me in weeks. Rumours say you took to the opium or the drink." Still, Sol remained laying on his back, blankly looking at her through eyes that felt like red welts.

"The Mile's all gone to Bedlam, Sol. It don't seem right." Now, Shammy held Sol's stare, her eyes wide with worry. "The kids are nicking from the faerie. Elf lads are getting robbed and Artos ain't doing a thing."

Screwing up his face, Sol sighed as deeply as he could. Shammy's face, once the sunshine of his every moment, looked like just another grubby thing in this grubby city. Another thing to sort out. Another burden to bear.

"I'm fixing it." Sol's words were only breath.

"Come back. I'm so bored without you."

With the movements of a man beset by rickets, Sol pushed himself to sit up against a warehouse wall.

Taking hold of his shoulders and looking into his eyes, Shammy shook him playfully. "Let's 'ave some fun."

She only made Sol's headache throb more painfully. Why was she acting like everything was fun and games? No excuses now, not with all the insane going-ons. They weren't kids anymore.

"You are the most selfish person I have ever met." Sol said in a distant monotone. Words of the slow deadly knife, not the quick surface wounding slash of anger.

"Elfish, I ain't no Elf." Shammy beamed a smile, her eyes still not matching it but imploring Sol to smile back.

*Is nothing serious to you?* Sol just looked at her face, her stupid face. What would she be without him? She never had the discipline to be a Hymn-Whisperer, like Victor. A whore on Chavver Street corner then, like most of the girls when they grew up. A gent's plaything, kept in opium until she turned old before her time. He had seen how other men looked at her, now she had grown. Only he could keep her safe, but she had never... *cared enough*. Her face, made him grind his teeth until he felt sick, made his head throb until his eyes blotted with spots. Sol's finger twitched.

SLAP!

Shammy's face snapped to the side, she stumbled and held her cheek. Eyes wide, Shammy asked a thousand silent questions in that one second of shock, before tears bubbled and streamed as if the Thames had burst its banks.

Sol knew he had broken something priceless. Betrayal reflected in Shammy's eyes. *Damn her though, damn all of them.* He pressed his fingers into his temples and screamed.

---

### Marsh Worm Mile, 1861A.D.

In the broadest street running from Marsh Worm Bridge, Artos led a parade of his Hymn -Whisperers past the busy Fey market. He also carried two buckets of some stinking concoction.

The young men and women who followed him came to a halt at an exact point, where two Whisperers untied bundles of spears and laid them out on the cobblestones. All then proceeded to shed their heavy Hymn Whisperer robes, the clothing puddling around their feet, before stepping out in arrays of lighter garments, trousers, and vests. Artos, smearing his hands in a bucket of powdered and fermented woad, came to each of them in turn and painted the faces of his new warriors. Eventually, he reached Victor, who resisted the urge to wince at the harsh aroma of the applied plant.

Victor was here, as his brothers and sisters, to receive a new baptism. Sort of, anyway, since he had never been baptised in the first place. But Victor also sensed something... *amazing*, a feeling that excited him. Artos had seen the truth and told all the Whisperers that 'in the new way lays the old way.' *Whatever that meant.* Something meaningful though, something to be proud of.

He watched with rapt attention as Artos slaked his hands in the other bucket, full of unpleasant, slimy stuff called lime. Artos ignored Victor's grunts from the shock of cold slime, and Victor shivered as his choppy brown hair was pulled into spikes. Artos proceeded to do the same with every other Whisperer there.

"Lads...and lasses," Artos paused a moment, sighing when he ran his fingers through a young woman whisperer's ginger locks. "I've already remade young Shiv. I long to see you all remade the same way, recast as terrifying Woad Warriors, like our ancient ancestors."

Finally, Artos stepped away and spun around theatrically in the street, in full view of a crowd of curious onlookers browsing the local Fey market. They, like Victor, couldn't take their eyes off the Lord of Marsh Worm Mile.

"Brothers and sisters, ours is not the ancient way nor the modern way. I seek a Britannia reborn, but without malignant forces. I seek an old-world sculptured anew. I will make an

Avalon of the Marsh Worm Mile full of the souls of mighty warriors. First, we will ensure that those who remain are made from the 'right stuff.'" His hand shot out dramatically, pointing at the Fey marketplace.

"Human, remember me?" called a gruff voice from among the Fey stall holders. It was a burly old knocker going by the name of Blunt. "We all knew you before you left to find the last grove. But me, I was there with you a long time before. I saw when you and the fat priest brought us together. This ain't the right way."

Victor furrowed his brow. This was all very confusing. *What does it mean?* Artos suddenly looked his way and caught his questioning frown. He sensed doubt...

Without an effort to keep his voice down, Artos spoke directly to Victor. "You must believe me, Bear. Think, however long we have guarded the bridge, evil still plagued our streets. All of you, think about this, how the Fey fled the great lands of Europe and Asia thousands of years ago, only to cling onto these rocks in the sea, uninvited. Monsters pushed to this broken-off chunk of earth, only stopping here because of the oceans to the west. Why did they not settle elsewhere? Because their true nature came out once they planted their roots, spreading corruption and degeneration. I once blamed the old gods, but they were merely pathetic manifestations attached to the sticky rot of Fey."

Some of the warriors 'hear, hear'd' their assent. Others, like Victor, stood on the cusp of half-understanding. Nearby onlookers shuffled nervously.

"We will make new gods, in a new Avalon. After the, regretfully, dirty work is done, we will make a land of courage, strength, peace, and plenty."

Huddling protectively around their stalls of trinkets and root vegetables, a few knocker merchants started to pack away the precious, unseasonable things they had grown with minor magic. Other Fey glared as Artos paced back and forth in front of his painted troop.

"You went and took the Crone, Artos," said Blunt, his flat cap making his eyes a belt of shadow. "You know it's bad tidings, making the world go mad it is. Release her, give her to us and we will keep her out of your way. Else, the world hangs by a thread."

"And I will cut that thread," roared Artos, his eyes holding that of Victor's. "You, see? They feed on our malady, fester and bloat on our misery, yet scuttle and warp when surrounded by happiness." Raising his spear, Artos turned around and took firm strides towards the market. "Hear me! I am not a Fey. You are not welcome on the land under my feet."

With stunning alacrity, the muscle memory of countless warrior strikes, Artos unleashed his spear at the market, shattering a tower of wooden pallets and spilling their contents to the ground. "Leave, traitors."

A shot cracked through the street, followed by the vacuum of utter stillness and the smell of smoke. The knockers stood in a solid phalanx. Blunt held up a pistol to the sky, a new-fangled thing but engraved with the wishes and charms of old times. In his other hand, the second pistol from his brace was pointed at Artos. "Now, I don't know what's gotten into you, but we won't have any of it. You need exorcising, banishing, or a good night's kip."

With a great sweep, Artos stomped back to his Woad Warriors, punching his fist at the sky, summoning his spear to thrum back through the air into his grasp as the new Woad Warriors readied their weapons. Victor's spear trembled, he relished the rising energy and power. Shaking his ancient weapon, Artos gestured for his warriors to do the same and Victor gladly jabbed his spear a few times, grunting with each thrust

Adrenaline, like the heat of gin, soaked through Victor's chest and arms, the thrill of impending conflict sent his heart beating, like the fists of an imprisoned lunatic breaking through his ribs. His lips thinned, his eyes scowled and focused. Time slowed. Still, though, something nagged at his conscience. A feeling that he was about to commit some great wrongdoing, hovered over his hooligan ire.

"I built this place, warriors," screamed Artos, "And I've seen you all grow from wee little runts into the fine lads and ladies I see now. The Fey plan to kill me, but have faith and raise your spears. Know that you cannot die on my land, warriors of the God of Victory."

Immediately, most of the men and women raised their spears. Some roared, gearing their spirits into motion. Others looked around as if they didn't know whether to charge, or bolt. From the narrows, leading from the river streets, came the curses and whistles of other Fey, reinforcements called via a relay of written messages spontaneously springing up on walls throughout the Mile.

Elves, slightly built, with knives and rapiers, Sprites, like large butterflies, brimmed with sparks charged to unleash spits of fire, and more dwarves, some with handfuls of wriggling razor-maggots, foul things which sliced and burrowed into the hearts of men. Behind them, loomed an ogre, one of the last of its kind, perhaps even the one Victor had fought four years ago, at the birth of the Sea Nymph Carnival. Bloated and drunk, too flabby to fight with old-world glory, but eight-foot tall and intimidating to any mere man. Not to Artos though.

Artos' eyes flashed with something between rage and ecstasy He stepped away from Victor and the Woad Warriors and approached the dwarf with the pistol. Suddenly, a dozen other pistols rested their aim on him, but Artos was unfazed. "The Crone bleeds for me daily, a final sacrifice to victory, to cut the thread of fate ..."

A pistol fired, its shot true, piercing Artos' chest. Blood spouted from the wound, sloshing onto cobblestones. But Artos only smiled his wild smile before speaking over the death rattle of his voice. The croak turned to gravel, skin folding, muscle knitting, body healing. "Kill them."

Even before he said this, though, the warriors had charged, spear-points ready to be forged into artefacts of a new world, ready to soak up their first taste of battle. Victor let the charge carry him into the fray. The time for speaking had broken, whatever the rights and wrongs of it ceased to mean anything. The sky rung with a distant choir and the man Artos dubbed a bear thrust into the nearest Fey. Sprites flicked our fire pellets. The air stank of burnt hair and charred skin. Something damp splatted against Victor's back, a teeming fistful of razor-maggots, which gave way to a feeling of warm and wet slicing

But the pain brought Victor to that other place, that place of primal instinct where thought was unneeded. Agility, speed, and strength combined in one as he stabbed, punched, and bit. Never had he felt fiercer, never had his heart felt the thrill of... *revenge against these foul creatures.* With every crunch of bone under his heaving fist, with every swatted sprite or gutted elf, he felt euphoric victory ever closer.

Trampling through all opposition, Victor stalked the ogre, passing another Hymn-Whisperer-turned-Woad-Warrior slouched against a building at its side. A blood trail smeared a slash over a wall. Still, the warrior breathed but would fight no more today, a casualty to the cause. That didn't scare Victor in the slightest, his wounded brother-in-arms only inspired a desire for violent retribution.

The giant's bone-breaking fist hooked his way. Sidestepping, leaning into a crouch, he launched his spear point under the Ogre's ribs, a deathblow for sure. From behind him, the Woad Warriors roared, the Fey broke and routed into the tunnel alleys. Full of fierce pride, Artos stood tall with his spear held high. Wild eyes locked onto Victor's magnificent, blood and woad-soaked body.

◌┅╬┅━━━━━━┅╬┅◌

Shammy stood in a doorway at the edge of the Old Well Square. Red puffy eyes watched the comings and goings of the inhabitants with intensity. So many people went to the old

Church since Artos' return, stuffy types, real ladies with those clunky dresses all looking like stiff wedding cakes. Strangely, when they re-emerged from church the men and women seemed to sparkle, smiling with enchantment. Shammy caught snippets of gossip, how the talk of gentlemen's clubs and tearooms bristled with topics on the 'new fashion' for magic things and, of course, Marsh Worm Mile was *the* place to go for stuff like that.

But, at present, it all left Shammy feeling numb. She just wanted to go somewhere safe, to talk to someone about Sol, to find someone to reassure her. Never had he left her side for more than a few hours before, but a magic sickness infected his mind. It must be something to do with that green powder…

Artos was another memory. The kind man with the hard face who gave the orphans a home: toys, bathtubs and hot water to wash with, food to eat. Years ago, he used to visit her and the others often, especially in Mid-Winter, around Christmas time, with toy soldiers made from oak and painted with mistletoe oil-mixed colours. Once, he had given Shammy a clockwork dancing girl, though she swapped it for some oak cuirassiers on fine engraved horses. Smiling wistfully at the memories, she refocused on the present.

Someone opened the church doors, a big Fey thing with shocks of white hair and a blue face, a furred cloak fastened around his body. The thing waved at her and smiled with a collection of stained teeth. *Oh, not a Fey at all but Victor dressed all funny. Look at you, Victor!* Yes, Victor. He cared for her too… She just had to get to him.

Weaving her way around the border of the square, avoiding the men who towered over her, avoiding the ever-playful (annoying) sprites who chirped her name, Shammy approached. Unable to help herself, she took one look into that round beaming face and tears blustered out. Throwing her arms around Victor, his furry cloak so cuddly and warm, though itchy in her nose, Shammy sneezed before openly sobbing

It stayed that way for a while, like a painting of a confusing myth, of a woad warrior, church, and celestial outcast with a dribs and drabs street scene of creatures casting curious glances their way. Victor wrapped his arms around her too, although his hug felt awkward as if he feared to hold too tightly. Shammy guessed that Victor might feel a little embarrassed at such sudden gentle intimacy. "Go find Sol. He'll cheer you up."

A lightning bolt of tension, he felt Shammy's body twitch rigid for a second. "He is sick. He hit me," said a small whispering voice.

The tension immediately infected Victor, his body tightened. "Hit?"

It was almost frightening to Shammy, how his body stiffened with immediate anger. Victor had hit many things; she had seen it. Sometimes people didn't get up after he hit them. But hitting girls? Victor hated boys who did stuff like that, a bit of gentleman mixed in with ruffian. For a moment she worried at what she might have unleashed.

"Bring her in, my Bear." Came the gravel of Artos' voice. He emerged at the church door with a finely oiled moustache, dressed like a gentleman, a top hat on his head, a bottle-green frock jacket and a silk scarf marked him out as some sort of dandy. "You'll have to teach the little malignant a lesson. Leave young Shammy to me." With great care he unwrapped one of the girl's arms from Victor's back, daintily taking her hand and bowing, though keeping his eyes raised to Shammy's own.

"Lady of the Marsh Worm, allow me to escort you." He had the same smile she remembered, that same soft-edged manner he put on while with all the children. It wasn't just a memory after all. But she had never noticed how handsome he was before. *Handsome? What am I thinking?* She couldn't stop smiling as she followed Artos into his court.

⊶⊷━━━━━━━━⊶⊷

He led her through an oak interior, heavy with the rainbow rays of stained-glass windows. Yet, this was unlike any church she had ever been in: no benches for the congregation, no sombre droning of psalms. In the aisles, gentlemen and ladies danced and trilled weird melodies, their eyes bright and wide. Plush red cushions, haphazardly strewn all around, eased lounging couples gazing languidly at each other. Some kissed, some undressed, some were involved in other things...Things Shammy had never experienced. Things grown-up girls did. *Grown-up orphan girls...like me?*

Scattered in between the islands of couples were bottles of absinthe, plates of green, silver, and pink sparkling powders too. Hourglass-shaped bottles and pipes, with colourful wisps of smoke holding different scents and flavours, somehow lit the air, and Shammy's tongue, with sweetness.

Artos pulled her forward, keeping her hand in his. He pirouetted around her, a smile on his face, his eyes wild like

Victor's and Sol's after taking that green powder. "Don't be shy." Spinning up close, Artos' free hand stroked her cheek, his fingertips glistening green.

Overwhelmed, Shammy pushed away and Artos let his arms fall from around her. "Look around, see how the good men of the city bring me this land's soul," and he waved his arm, pointing to the altar bedecked with all manner of battered trinkets. Kettle-like things, cauldrons, broken shafts of wood engraved with swirling nonsense, pretty brooches, weapons, helmets, locks of hair. *Hair!* Shammy cringed.

"Artefacts from vaults which once belonged to the Puritans, or from the British Museum, to create my own shrine to ancient Britons. Powerful things, Shammy! Things to remake the Mile just the way I want. With these, I will have the power to control or crush all who threaten us."

*Oh, shut up with all that!* Closing her eyes, composing herself, pushing back the madness of excess, Shammy said, "You must help Sol."

When she opened her eyes, she saw other men dressed like Victor, spike-haired and blue-faced, laying cushions around her and placing bottles of absinthe and plates of fairy dust. "Unburden your soul of all worries," said Artos. "All I ask is for a game of pretend, lass. Let us quiver stiff upper lips, let me gift you with magic unending. Gift you with magic enough to help not just Sol, but all of us." With a quick flick, he grabbed and tossed his top hat across the room. Then he bent slightly, hand scooping a puff of powder. "I will make your wishes come true." He exhaled, blowing a green shock of the stuff her way. "I will make you a nymph, my lass. A thing to twist powerful men's desires, like all my fairer orphans. Only you will be their queen."

Oh, it all made Shammy dizzy. Everything thrummed and vibrated. *I must just rest. I don't think I can stand it any longer.* Weightlessly, she crumpled onto the cushions. *So, so soft. Just like air. Just like a cloud.* Artos lay by her side.

"You should have seen 'im, Artos." Shammy's voice was just breath. "Whenever I got bored, he made me laugh. You should have seen what he could do." Smiling, Shammy yelped a single belly laugh. "I dared him. He told me to watch and went and climbed the Old Bailey and pee'd in the face of the statue of lady justice. The chasing peelers got splattered by a load of pooping pigeons who appeared from nowhere, slipping on it and all that. He's been with me since my first memories of Chavver Street." Again, she laughed, loud, again and again until her ribs ached, and her eyes started to water.

Artos worked himself against her, his lips brushing her ear as he whispered, "You truly care for the Fey-boy? A living curse, a living blight upon Albion. But, little lady, I will help you if you help me."

Fingers traced Shammy's neck; it sent her mind spinning. It felt good. She sighed and closed her eyes.

"I knew your father," Artos whispered. "A good man, a fortune teller, and a sailor. One of the finest cooks a ship ever saw, who travelled between here and the East. He named you 'Xiao Mei,' 'Little Beautiful.' And so good was he at telling the future, your name has come to pass. Those pompous gentlemen, those newspaper reading men from the halls of Westminster, they talk about you, about the beautiful celestial girl. 'Who is she?' they ask. 'Is she a Fey? Is she magical?' They want to dress you, pamper you now that you're more than 'of age', young lady. It is time to grow into a woman, Little Beautiful, for the good of the Mile."

His hands seemed everywhere, gently lifting her old silk dress, fingertips lightly caressing under her small breasts. She had never been touched like that before. It was so confusing… *Time to grow up?* She moaned, letting herself give in to this new feeling.

"I have been a warrior for a long time. But also, a lover, Little Beauty. Tonight, I will make you feel like a goddess. I will teach you about pleasure. Then you can show those powerful men. They will give you an easy life and then, grant me the artefacts I seek." For a second, Shammy's body tightened.

"Shh. Don't be afraid. I would never let anyone hurt you." Artos cupped the back of her head, lifting her forward, pressing a small glass to her lips. A liquid, stark and bitter, seared over Sammy's tongue but she swallowed, feeling the burn turn to tingling pleasure in her veins.

"You like to feel like this, I know. I have the power to make this last forever."

But a last knot of reality remained in Shammy's mind, a delicate thing, loosening quickly into oblivion. She concentrated on it though, before it vanished, and breathed out her last sober thought. "Please, cure Sol. Promise me." The smile dropped from Artos' face.

"You must promise," Shammy said. "A proper promise, on all you hold dear, so that it sticks."

A flicker of something grey contorted Artos' features for an instant. The smile returned, but this time a sober clarity dilated Artos' eyes. "I promise." Then Shammy pulled him close.

⊙≫╠╫═══════════════╫╣╢≪⊙

Sol dragged deeply on a pipe, inhaling a scrounged prick of tobacco, letting it ease, buff, and choke him into a haze. Lost to the world, leaning against a river-stained post at the docks, his red eyes only saw bleeding green light. From everywhere, the world shone green.

A rattling stomp on the boardwalk and a deep roar rudely pulled him back into the present. It was Victor, charging at Sol, scarred and pockmarked, bloating with the huffing, puffing pink of anger. Dressed as one of Artos' 'Woad Warriors,' Victor led a one-man stampede.

Without a grunt, the large man threw a quick, sharp punch that crunched into Sol's left eye. It sent Sol reeling away from the river edge, the world spinning into a place of no ups, downs, lefts, or rights. Another blow thudded sickeningly against his right temple, but Sol didn't see that one coming. Neither did he see the boardwalk rising to greet his falling head.

Sometime later, confused and giddy, with the sun slowly setting behind orange clouds, Sol picked himself up. He limped down the dockside, to a rotten, forgotten wooden corner not wide enough to court the crowds of sailors and merchants. Another place of solitude he knew full well.

So enthralled with tracing the hard-swollen balloon that was his left eye, he didn't hear the creak of the boardwalk behind him. Sol only noticed when Artos hooked an arm over his shoulder, as one might to a lover or best friend. A suited and booted Artos, with only a faint woad stain on his face and hands.

Tensing, nausea rising in his throat, Sol felt Artos' gaze on the side of his face as if it bored into his mind. "Nasty war wounds you got there, lad. The Bear is not one to piss off." There was heavy mocking in his voice. Sol turned away and looked across the Thames for distraction, fear beating alongside his heart. The moment hung, still and awkward. Pulse quickening...

"You cursed me!" Sol screamed, swinging the cut-throat razor from his pocket. Artos caught his wrist, twisted it until Sol gasped in pain, and dropped the razor before falling to his knees. Still twisting, Artos stood over Sol. Sol began to cry.

"All I want is to see the darkness behind my eyelids again. To rid my sight of this terrible green." He looked up into cold stone eyes. "Just kill me if you can't give me sleep."

Artos released Sol's wrist and delved into the pocket of his jacket. "Shammy tells me how you like to watch the docks for hours upon end. I remember looking out across the sea once, knowing that I stood on the edge of the world. It's different now. That world is closing in. This island spreads its influence everywhere these days, ending hundreds of tribes, hundreds of gods. A new, Earth-spanning Rome from where there is nowhere to hide." Sol only looked up pitifully.

"Where can you go for peace, Sol? There is nowhere left in this world. You will be hunted, an unchristian thing, a devil thing. But I have an answer, lad, a place to send all your kind. Look at what I hold, a gift for you."

Clutched in Artos' hand was a hag-stone, the hole in the middle shimmering, threatening to dilate and show Sol his future. Searching to find a nub of clarity in his mind, Sol tried to call the boggarts, perhaps to back-stab Artos or at least help him escape. But the exhaustion, the numbness seemed to have stolen his ability to concentrate, and he felt inexplicably drawn to the hag stone. But instead of an answer, the hole in the middle showed only darkness.

"You go to the Dark Alley, lad. A place where I once banished twisted Fey-things like you. It is a place of eternal sleep and darkness. I don't want to kill you, there is no evil in my heart, lad. I only want to remove the Marsh Worm from this Time and Fate, set it free and let it be the myth it was destined to be. I want this for the good of Albion, for the good of all."

Sol stared, transfixed by the stone.

"To show there are no hard feelings, how about I buy you a farewell drink?"

Blinking away the fug, shakily getting onto his feet, Sol inhaled as deeply as he could. Then he breathed out, imagining he was expelling all the taint inside, a moment's relief. He surveyed the rooftops and spied a dozen green hazes.

"Come on, lad. A beer, a cheeky gin? Maybe a dozen cheeky gins? Then I'll even walk with you, all the way to the Dark Alley, just like a father would."

"Damn you," Sol whispered. A hail of slate and stones suddenly shattered around them. Chips sprayed like shrapnel, lashing across Artos' face. Boggarts chattered in glee, scampering to all manner of roof-born detritus and letting it fly; a storm of architectural odds and ends. Sol watched, a smile creeping across his face.

"For once in your life, be a man!" Artos bellowed, as slabs and sharp ends bruised and gouged him, something heavier smashing against a knee and causing him to momentarily buckle. Away from his *claimed* land, his borough, he was vulnerable, it seemed. He had said as much to Sol during the last Double Dare challenge. Artos' body refused to heal, and the nagging of tiny scratches must prove more than irksome.

Clenching his jaw, Artos nodded slowly a few times. "I tried, lad. Gods know, I tried." An ungentlemanly limp to his gait, he then hurried away from the docks, again leaving Sol alone.

◦◦▸▸⊞▮▭ ▭ ▭ ▬ ▮⊞◂◂◦◦

Deep into the coils of Marsh Worm Mile went Sol, blinking constantly at the bright green lights which continued to sear his mind. Swallowing to hold back bile, his head throbbed at confusing sights. Marsh Worm was filled with gentlemen in well-tailored suits, with flourishing tails and dandy scarves, or demon-looking men with white hair and blue skin. His memory had no frame of reference for this.

*So tired...* Too tired to sleep. It was like his eyes floated as ghosts without a body, an unseen presence weaving around obstructions into the centre of the Faerie Borough.

The Dark Alley was the bogey man of the Mile, the devil, a hell whispered to keep children on the straight and narrow, 'best behave and don't go wandering by yourself at night, else you'll get swallowed by the Dark Alley and never heard from again.'

When Sol was a lad, the Hymn Whisperers guarded the entrance. Those caught and charged with crimes of cursing and evil magic were sent down there and never returned. Christians said it led to Hell, others said it led simply to oblivion. Who knew the truth of it? But oblivion seemed a tonic to the hell of Sol's mind.

The run-down housing, all rotten wood, and cloth-covered windows, narrowed until the roofs of facing houses bowed and kissed their opposite numbers. Here it was, the tunnel maze of the Dark Alleys. But there were no Hymn Whisperers today, instead, Artos' new gang, the Woad Warriors, stood around the narrow street roaring into each other's faces and beating their chests. Their eyes sparkled from faerie dust.

The warriors, away in the drugged periphery of Faerie Land, failed to notice Sol making his way through the narrowing streets. Here, the haunting bright green seemed to fade into a place where darkness blazed like an anti-sun, a balm to Sol's eyes. For the first time, in what felt like an age, the pain in his mind numbed.

About to run into the darkness, to barge through the cluster of Artos' men, Sol was unceremoniously halted. One of the warriors, a broad man standing tall and howling like a wolf to the moon, stepped up, a ball of thread wrapped around his hand. He gave another of the warriors, a sinewy young woman, the loose end. The thread was knotted every inch or so, a thing of superstition and magic in itself. The woman proceeded to tie the thread around her finger, then slapped the man on the back.

Sol watched through a filter of green and black. The large warrior strode between two opposing houses, roofs touching, where the street was at its narrowest and framed the black anti-sun. Then the blackness swallowed him up...

All eyes concentrated on the thread, slowly unravelling somewhere into the dark and pulling on the warrior woman's finger. A slight tension caused the thread to bounce whenever a knot caught against some unknown nick or pebble on the ground. Silence filled the narrow, everyone held their breath.

Suddenly, the thread sprung tight and held for a few seconds, then dropped limp. As the thread was wound back some Woad Warriors, from old habits, drew crosses on their chests. Others gripped totems hanging around their necks. Shuffling along the earth, the loose end appeared frayed and completely un-knotted.

"No." Although spoken softly, Sol's voice echoed in the alley. "Artos means to kill me, kill you all." But only vacant eyes turned back to regard him. *I can't do it, there must be some other way.* Sol backed off, away from the narrowest part of the street, even as the green light blazed its fullness again into his mind.

Swaggering from wall to wall, Sol felt a desperate need to find space, to gasp fresh air. His face shone with sweat. The houses sneered at him. The choked, humid air at the centre of the Marsh Worm Mile whispered 'coward' in his ear.

Then another voice brought him back. *Her* voice. "Sol, I know it was an accident. I'm sorry about Victor. You need help."

Perfume bleached his sinuses and forced his mind to clutch around sobriety. Shammy smelled of spice and sweetness. Her painted face, with pink cheeks, glowed, and her hair was styled and bunched on her head. She looked absolutely beautiful, but not like Shammy.

Knowing his mind hung on the edge of sanity, Sol ignored the thousand questions begging to be asked. Just one thing needed to be said. "Artos. We must kill Artos."

Shammy grabbed his sleeve. "Please, don't say such things. You are ill."

"We must, don't you understand?"

"He will help us. He means well. I care for him, Sol. You must understand."

Something inside of Sol crumpled. Did he really hear her say that? No, surely not... *Care. Love? Doesn't matter, I don't need anything else. What is left for me?*

"Get you stinking hands off me," Sol spat, jerking his sleeve away. He looked back towards the Dark Alley. Even from here, he could feel the balm of darkness. Strength abandoning him at last, he fell to his knees. But he had enough strength, just enough left...

"Sol, stay here. I'll get help, I promise." Sol didn't hear her. *She cares for him? She loves Artos?* Now he was sure of what he must do.

# CHAPTER TEN

# THE FIRST KING
# OF THE BOGGARTS

### *The Dark Alley, Marsh Worm Mile, 1861 A.D.*

Crawling to the black anti-sun, rough and clipped cobblestones haphazardly stuck up from the mud street and grazed Sol's knees. But, as the darkness soothed his eyes and massaged his mind with relief, he found the strength to get on his feet once again. Calling him now, this anti-light harbour in a mind-storm of panic and magic, filled him with strength.

The waiting woad warriors eyed him with silent suspicion. Sol grabbed one by the shoulder and said simply, "My turn. Artos told me too. I know you do whatever he says." When offered to take the end of the twine, Sol ignored it and stared straight into the Dark Alley.

Between the leaning houses, into the narrowest part of the Marsh Worm Mile, he went, black walls oozing up around him. He felt pock-marked brick on either side, leaving his fingers scratched and weirdly greasy. With every step, a greater and greater feeling of peace entered his mind. It felt like a great fist had loosened its grip on his brain and now held it in an open palm. *Freedom.* But not for long.

Blind now, amid the anti-sun, Sol felt corners of opposing walls coming to a 't.' *Which way?* He heard a scraping to his left, a little circle appeared glowing the faintest green. *Follow, follow... Why not?*

The 'faerie eyes' led Sol through the maze, the ground beneath his feet now on a decline. No longer rubbing his fingertips raw, the bricks at every side became smooth, frictionless spaces until finally disappearing into jet-black nothing.

Sol would have considered that every step brought him closer to the middle of an infinity of darkness, except for the fact that it somehow felt claustrophobic, tight. As if darkness was tangible and therefore imprisoned every part of his body starting with his eyeballs. It rubbed with warmth.

Eventually, the ground levelled off under his feet, and in the distance blazed a yellow light. Closer Sol walked and the light focused into a square just hovering there in space. The light flickered, then Sol realized it came from a candle behind a window, illuminating a small room. By that room grew a single, average-sized, silver apple tree, from which a bounty of succulent-looking apples grew. Sol took one, biting into it immediately, the juice a blessing, quenching all that needed quenching. A raspy noise ushered him toward the nearby window. No, not a rasping, a snoring.

"Hello?" His voice muffled as he crunched through another bite of apple. But there was no response.

After taking a few more bites, swallowing core and all, Sol yelled against the darkness. "Oi." The snore caught and become a cough, then a hack as something called up an ungodly amount of phlegm. Up popped a little head from behind the window, pointy ears sticking from either side of a flat cap. A boggart, glowing ever so faintly green. But more so, the oldest, most wizened boggart Sol had ever seen.

"Is this Hell or Purgatory?" said Sol.

The boggart smiled; its eyes flashed their wil-o the wisp yellow. "Why no, my old mate. You're at the end of the last leyline. This is what's left of Avalon, where the warriors rested before going back to battle. Though it ain't like it used to be, I bet. I mean, this place is hardly the stuff of myth now."

Sol shrugged and shook his head.

"Where's me manners? I'm the caretaker, go by the name of Gobba, I do. I used to be King Gobba in fact. Been here for... oooh... a couple of centuries or so. Keep things ticking over. I listen to that great big city above, hear it breathe, feel its heartbeat. Nasty inhospitable place it is, not fit for a decent boggart anymore. I'm here to bequeath me nobility over this one stinking borough to a living successor. It's been well boring of late, but I reckon you're gonna change all that."

⊶┣╫══ ══ ═ ══ ══╫┫⊷

"Come in, take a load off." Gobba picked his teeth with a claw and spat onto filthy floorboards, covered with dust and grease. "I's the littler bastard who led Artos to a forest after the Toga-Wearers kicked his tribe's blue backsides all over the country. I fought with him...Well, tell a lie, I knifed a few shins, put it that way. Nasty battle, that one."

No longer shocked by the insanity that had become his life, Sol merely slumped against a wall and let himself slide to the floor. When his eyelids closed it was black, *proper black*. Darkness, the most beautiful and pure abyss-black darkness.

"See, the Old Lady Fate, she picked me for great things, she did. She's like my mum, birthed me from an apple and set me a special destiny. It all started when she whispered in me ear, 'Bite the blowhard on his bum.' Now, *he* might want you all to believe that it happened some other way, but I tell you, I bit his arse so hard that he started crying and jumped into the sea to play with the fishes and wait for it to get better for a few centuries.

After that, we started dying off. Eventually, folks had trouble even seeing us at all. But you found me! Makes me wish I was alive again." Gobba paused, momentarily, a faint smile on his wrinkled face. He licked his lips before continuing. "The Old Bag left me to wither away with me little tribe. Not long after me death, ugly Cromwell hunted down the Fey, cut off all the leylines, and caused us boggarts to vanish from human eyes."

The only reply was a heaving sigh. Sol felt himself drifting away in a deep sleep, snoring gruffly. A sleep that would repair his mind and body; a sleep in Avalon which would bathe him in warrior spirit enough to recover...perhaps.

"I see you're a little knackered. That's all there is to do around here anyway. Well, just listen to me story while you sleep, and let your dreams form around my words. It's quite a little tale, I call it 'The First (and only) King of the Boggarts."

⊶⊫⫴⊫══ ═ ══ ⫴⊫⊷

### *Somewhere in Staffordshire, England, late 16<sup>th</sup> Century*

Slowly baking in the midday sun, in the hollow of a tree, dozed an ancient creature called Gobba. A knobbly, dribbling thing, grunting and farting through dreams of youth. A miserable, useless thing, everyone said. Once, it had served a god, but then that god turned out to be miserable and useless too. Once, Gobba was looked up to by all of his kind. Now, well, he wasn't.

After a life full of adventure, Gobba was reduced to trailing after boggart tribes and settling in a poxy hovel called Sticky Bark Combe, not far from the town of Ludchurch. All Gobba had left was dreams, lucid shows he always tried to direct towards the... ribald. But on that day, his dreams were not his own. The hideous witch-face of the Crone kept popping up. He tried to push it away, hide it behind more comely images, but then the thoughts merged. *Ugh...Go on then, plague my only respite.*

Blackness at first, then a picture of a little apple tree popped up in Gobba's mind, "grown from a seed of Avalon, just like you," rasped the disembodied voice of Cerridwen. *Daft old bird, but a powerful old bird at that.*

"I have tied fortune and circumstance to your fate, Gobba. My last gambit. You merely have to make the first steps and let your instinct take you on a final adventure. My gift to you, to make you the greatest of all boggarts, in exchange for merely eating just one apple from a very special tree. Do not eat the seeds, they are for me."

*A lot of bother. Easier to lay down and just die.*

"Slovenly creature. Think about it, a chance to lord over others. Enemies like...Chief Nob."

*That greedy, stupid scum! Fair enough,* Gobba thought. *Life is getting pretty boring.*

"Well then...Wake up!" shrieked the Crone, so loudly that Gobba wondered if a dream could deafen him. "Hurry! Events are stirring which will change our course through fate forever."

*Stop your whining, I couldn't hurry if I wanted to.* Groggily, the old boggart stirred from his nap, cursing his clacking joints and aching bones. *Got to get my bits and pieces, me poisons and powders together. I'm due a holiday.*

<hr />

Tangled roots marked a secret path through woods of black trees and high grass, from Sticky Bark Combe to Ludchurch Road. Rising in foot-high knots up to his waist, the roots easily concealed Gobba's scrunched-up frame. It fascinated him, how the branches and roots of the oldest trees resembled his own limbs, gnarled, knobbly, scarred, and dented. What's more, full of nasty stuff too!

Jabbing his stiletto into a root, jelly sap bubbled over the blade and quickly scabbed dry. Gobba ruffled in his rope belt, all lined with threads, needles, pipes, and other mischievous trinkets. He plucked a sealed thimble and flicked open the lid. The contents hissed a ring of steam and spat acrid stench when he mixed toxins together with the point of his stiletto. Dabbing a dozen needles into the concoction, the old boggart brewed deadliness into the tips. Oh, how it filled his little, wretched heart with joy, to think about what big, awkward creatures he could poison to death and rob blind.

The earth trembled a warning. A coach approached along Ludchurch Road. No, more than a tremble, a heavy rumbling of approaching opportunity. Tucking his blade into a belt-loop, Gobba crouched like a wary farmhouse cat on hearing mouse scratches behind walls. Just upwind of his position waited an upturned cart, left bent and broken in the brush and half sticking out across the road. It had been there for years now, a handy distraction often used by clever boggarts like him (and *not* Chief Nob). Quick, Gobba thought, taking the chance to do what he used to do best.

Nerves simmered in his belly, and he had to stifle a burp. He hadn't left Sticky Bark Combe for many years. Happily, mostly, he had waited for the long nap at the end of his life. He was very good at sleeping, maybe the best at it. But his other skills seemed to be...off, somehow. Everything felt slow, stiff. Yet, with every stalking-step closer to the cart, things he thought lost to all but memory awoke. Ghosts of passed trickery visited keenness to his eyes and bounce to his tendons.

*By my warty behind, that's a bit of luck!* It was not a shabby traveller's coach trundling ever closer, but a carriage decorated with the gold and red embellishments of wealth. Perhaps the ghost of some luck god was keeping an eye on him, with orders from the Crone? "My prey," Gobba whispered into the wind.

The coachman pulled at the reins of two whinnying horses, carriage wheels buffeted clouds of dust and shingle. Gobba tensed, pointy ears twitching forward. "Something in the road, your Lordship. I'll see to it."

Soaked in instinct, the boggart padded forward on bandy legs. He relished the grass brushing his earth-smeared body and the 'itch-needing to be scratched' thrill of impending mischief. Closer, closer, closer he came to the carriage's rear. STOP! A sudden panic: the coachman momentarily disappeared from view. Something thumped against the dirt, followed by the metal-screech of a drawn sword. Holding his breath now, Gobba dropped prone and tried to catch a peek at what was going on through the undercarriage. The coachman's boots paced towards the upturned cart. The carriage was left unguarded. *Bless my boggart-luck. Now Gobba, now ...* Feet pattered on the dirt and shingle road. *Had the noise been too much?* When the coachman turned to check the disturbance, only puffs of dust remained.

Holding onto the embellished golden overhang at the back of the carriage, his arms shaking with exertion, Gobba next pulled himself up onto the roof before pressing his body low and tight against the red-painted wood. Sniffing, the sting of new varnish created a miasma all around him. *To business.*

Spare threads dangled from his belt, one of his many tools of mischief. With one hand and five well-rehearsed fingers, he twisted the threads together into quick-thin rope. Knotting it around the gold-decorative vines and flowers framing the roof,

Gobba could now safely hang over the side, if he wished. *Like a great, green spider!*

The carriage rocked. Movements came from inside. Then a voice. "Wilson, what is it?" A man's head poked out the open window. Dressed in a frilly collar, bright red jacket, and a courtly white wig of copious tall curls, he looked fancy and very...*rich*. Buckles and buttons flashed against the late afternoon sunlight. Gobba's eyes swelled wide and wild at the twinkle of shiny things. He knew better than most, the 'shinier the pricier!'

"Helpless peasant? Bastard-born bandits? I have my rapier here," the man waved his sword clumsily, clunking it against the window frame.

From inside the carriage came another voice, higher-pitched than the first. "Darling, I have heard many tales of forests spirits and goblins intent on mischief and murder. Be careful."

*Goblin? Rude, gangly pricks! Who do they think they are?*

"No fear, my Lady Regina, your prince is here. I would give a legion of the filth a fine dusting without so much as a guardsman's support. Goblins are the size of midget children." The unseen lady giggled, and the man dipped his head back in the carriage. Gobba heard fumbling. "Like the children, I will plant in your belly, eh?" This attitude came as quite a shock to Gobba. Grinding his few remaining teeth as an urge to patience, the boggart vowed to show them their place. *Are boggarts just clowns to laugh at? Dogs to kick? We used to be feared, fed, and courted for our luck. How the young have let us down. And all because of the shiny-grubbing ways of those like Chief Nob.*

"Your Lordship," yelled the coachman as he climbed back to his seat. "It's nothing. Just an abandoned cart."

"Yes, well hurry, Wilson. Ludchurch is only a few miles away. I fear the midges are starting to bite," the Lord almost squeaked with annoyance.

In no time at all the carriage continued on its way. Fields and hills of green and yellow rolled by, full of bleating, mooing, and clucking farmyard stock, an accompaniment to the lusty yapping and sighing of the humans in the carriage.

On a lonely stretch of country road, obscured by bushes and trees, Gobba sprang into action. Rolling off the edge of the roof, he dangled like his imagined 'spider on a thread' right outside the open carriage window. There was little danger of being seen since the humans busied themselves with… *other things.* Things which were, once, Gobba's favourite things...

Licking his remaining brown, blunt fangs and green, cracked lips, Gobba watched the young lovers toss their shoes and frilly garments to one side. A waft of cloying perfume stung his eyes. The Lord's face was pressed into the chest of the Lady, her puffed-blue dress pulled up around her waist. Giggling, then tumbling from their cushioned seats, they became a tangled mass of flailing legs.

The needle Gobba took from his belt was one soaked in his 'special brew.' He rested the needle on his tongue. After a long-enough eyeful of the rutting nobles, the boggart took a pipe from his belt too and levelled it to his lips. When a bare human foot kicked into view, Gobba spat his needle with a hollow, unobtrusive breath. "Bloody hell. Something stung me." The Lord slapped a hand to his foot. Pushing himself from Regina, he stumbled on his hands and knees as he tried to stand in the cramped carriage cabin. "My foot…." The poison, quick-acting stupefying, and deadly, smothered his voice into an incoherent slur. A moment later, he slumped against the floor.

"My darling," gasped Regina, as she groped her way back to the seat. She caught sight of the green shadow at the window. About to scream, Gobba spat a second needle straight into Regina's wide-open mouth before swinging, then pouncing inside the carriage to join her. The thud of her dead body went unheard as carriage wheels rattled on cobblestones, the roads improving as the city of Ludchurch neared. Idly whistling along with the birds, the coachman spurred his horses onward.

Mischievous again after all these years, warm pride swelled in Gobba's chest. What with his age, this journey would be his last chance, before time seized his joints and stole his sight. Perhaps time would snap his mind and leave him a lonely wretch living in the hollow of a tree. Mere hours ago, he would have been fine with that. Not now. *Bless you, Crone. I take back all those nasty things I thought and said about you!*

Tired of the new ways, how boggarts had devolved into grovelling creatures barely a shadow of their former nuisance, Gobba thought he now had to make a stand. He would show them the way. He would come back with enough shiny to be chief of Sticky Bark Combe. More so, he would show everyone why his kind should be feared.

For a moment, the ache of age all but disappeared.

Soft as the velvety ear of a fresh-born boggart, Gobba caressed the fabric of his newly acquired red jacket. Far too big but that didn't matter. He reckoned he cut a grand-regal figure for sure. *So, this is what modern-time respect feels like.* The Lord's and Lady's rings covered his fingers, loosely fitting and poised to fall off. But that didn't matter. Gobba already had enough shiny to challenge Chief Nob. But he needed to be sure. He needed enough to make the young boggarts of Sticky Bark Combe listen to a fossil like him. *They must listen to me in awe. I will become a legend!* Just a dash more spangle, something to stun them all. But what? Anyway, he still had that bloody tree to find too, and he was at the mercy of Fate for that.

Struggling with the size and weight of the Lord, Gobba, now panting like a dog, finally managed to shove him under the seat and away from prying eyes. Propping the Lady up against the window next, he noticed that her body still felt warm. Her corset-buffed breasts pressed over her plunging neckline. Almost coyly, Gobba squeezed. Soft, squishy. *Been a while you dastardly old monster! Much squishier than boggart breasts.* Back to business. *One last squeeze.*

The sun spilled late afternoon orange across the sky by the time the carriage passed through Ludchurch's city gates. Gate guards lazily saluted the noble crests painted on the side of the carriage. Gobba covered his face with the Lord's wig and pretended to sleep on his pillow of lovely breasts, although really, he had to stand on the seat to match the woman's sitting height. Of course, the guards dared not impede their superiors. In Gobba's time, he had learned well that guards of all stripes liked to bully only those they saw as weaker, smaller, inferior.

❖❖❘❙❙▬▬▬▬ ▬ ▬ ▬ ❙❙❘❖❖

Through a market square, bustling with chatter, rattled the carriage. Smells of cooked meat, spices and dung wafted through the window. Little had changed since Gobba had last seen Ludchurch. Whitewashed buildings with black wooden beams and sloped thatch roofs framed the square. Some houses stood straight-edged and proud, others leaned to create alleys and gloomy backstreets.

Not like Sticky Bark Combe at all. That little boggart town was just a tuft of makeshift structures, shrinking with every passing year as the young fled for the cities. All too anxiously, the boggart pups made fools of themselves for smirking humans paying only the most trifling amount of shiny. *No ambition. No self-respecting vermin would settle for such a thing. The last pickings of the scraps from the scraps.*

Away from the squeeze of crowds, at a dung-and-straw stinking mews, the coachman pulled inside. In this place, the only watchful eyes belonged to horses. Gobba poised himself behind Regina. There was a creak as a step unfolded, a click as the carriage door unlatched and opened. With his face still buried in lukewarm breasts, Gobba's yellow beady eyes peeked from under his wig. The coachman seemed almost embarrassed at seeing his charges sleep. Reaching out a hesitant hand, he quickly snatched it back afraid to touch his social betters. Gobba wanted to laugh.

"Your Lordship, we have arrived."

Springing like a disturbed squirrel, Gobba's stiletto jabbed, a snake strike, through the coachman's eye and into the satisfyingly squishy centre of things. Like someone had magicked away his bones, the man flopped into a heap on the floor. Jumping out of the carriage, the patchwork of straw and dung soft underfoot, Gobba scurried outside into the bustle, ready to make his fortune. Swaggering like a young boggart in his prime, (a young boggart of *his* generation anyway) he shoved through a forest of knees. Humans eyed him with... *admiration.* Surely, they were intrigued and amazed at seeing a little *goblin* dressed like their lord and superior. *Not everything that changes is bad, hmm?* But, when Gobba caught sight of City Boggarts, he nearly burst with a hot flush of anger.

Dozens of the creatures swarmed, bent-backed around humans, bowing and cleaning boots. Or they carried sacks while humans threw pitiful collections of shiny at them. *Pathetic.* Boggarts of his day used to spit after talking about city dwellers. Now they spit to shine shoes.

Hissing whenever any of his city-kin got close, Gobba found mild entertainment pondering how many of these pups had sprung from the infamous libido of his glory days. Or, if not the pups themselves, maybe their fathers or grandfathers. Those memories of boggart-making were his favourite. Days, long ago, when Gobba's prong was discussed by boggarts girls, blushing the darkest green, the width, and breadth of the leylines. Perhaps hundreds of litters had blossomed from the seed of his loins, all bearing a ring of pocks above their left eyes, a Gobba brand, like how the humans branded cattle. Sure enough, here and there, a few carried such marks. Great, great, great-grandchildren, (or more greats) perhaps?

How Gobba regretted missing the chance to whisper dark secrets to them as he did with the seventy-four sons and daughters he had known. His personal horde of sneaky vermin had all been hunted down, trapped by warriors, farmers, and the rising tide of those who called creatures like him 'blasphemy.' Nonetheless, his brood had been proper boggarts. Proud boggarts. *Real boggarts, undiluted by civil shiny-getting. Better not to dwell on such thoughts...*

Along the edge of the market square, a crowd formed a ring. Curious, Gobba squeezed through their legs to watch a great shame unfold. Two naked-to-the-world boggarts spanked each other's faces and backsides with wooden swords. Deliberately slipping on muck, they amused braying humans. Gobba spat. He couldn't help himself. Waddling into the ring, his oversized jacket flapped, and his over-sized wig slipped over an eye.

"Look at the midget goblin lord," said a voice in the crowd. It started a cascade of laughter and finger-pointing. All of them, adults and children, thought Gobba was the most non-threatening jester, a dog-toy thing. Contempt made it easy for Gobba to ignore them, though. His ire was directed at the performing pups. He spat a glob of well-worked phlegm.

"Slapstick fools. You should be vermin to these people, a pest to hinder. Yet, you beg and play like pets."

Stopping their performance, the two young clowns looked at the fancily dressed old boggart. "You what?" said one, before sharing a conspiratorial glance with his mate. They sneered at each other then bounced up on tiptoes. Spinning in wild pirouettes to either side of Gobba, their wooden swords waved above their heads.

"You're so old. Look like a wrinkled scrotum face." said the pup to his left, grabbing his exposed bollocks.

"Tight-lipped bum-hole face," said the other, slapping his own ass.

With chest puffed, Gobba held his ground, his eyes narrowing into slits. Letting authority and wisdom carry in his words, he sought to reprimand their disobedience. "You should be hunting farmers' stock. You should be poisoning the foxes and laying traps for those who hunt us. If human filth spurs villagers to raise pitchforks and flaming tar against us, you should murder them, hang them up in the tallest branches of the tallest trees. Oh, the banquet you could steal from their cooking pots, better than stale bread. How far you fools have fallen."

Whirling their swords at Gobba, the young boggarts proved to be unmoved. They pulled faces and continued to circle. Suddenly, Gobba squeaked and jumped. He'd been spanked across his backside!

"What a show," a human yelled from the crowd. Others tossed shiny stuff in appreciation.

"Hyah, hyah." One of the young pups jabbed his sword into Gobba's chest, sending the elder tottering backward.

"Shoo. Move with the times. Go on, shoo."

"How dare you!" Gobba screamed. Fighting for balance, he drew his poisoned stiletto. Quick slashes from wooden swords knocked it from his hand.

"Aah, shiny." Grubby-clawed fingers snatched at the fine buttons on Gobba's jacket and ripped them off. Wooden swords spanked him again, the pups too speedy, just dirty green blurs.

Head spinning, body aching, Gobba swayed into the human crowd. Hands came from above and shoved him, feet thudded down to stamp on him; a world of kneecaps, and women's pulled up skirts as they too kicked out. Spurred on by cruel human jollies, soaking up blows, Gobba scrabbled on hands and knees. Squashy horse dung oozed through his clawed fingers; the occasional shingle stuck sharp but ineffectually against hard, withered skin. Dragging himself away from the slapping, kicking mob, Gobba, now all dirt and tatters fell into the tight squeeze of the nearest alley.

<hr />

A battered heap collapsed out from out the narrows into a less gloomy alley, lit by a few lanterns hanging over doorways. Trying to steady himself, vision unfocused, Gobba rubbed the swelling lumps on his face. But, in his near-blind daze, he stumbled against something meaty and hard. It almost sent him sprawling again. Gritting his teeth, the sound of raucous laughter put him instantly on edge. Under a lantern stood three huge figures. They *literally* looked down on Gobba from an even greater height than humans. Ogres, *big, mean, and stupid.* The monsters stood around a foul-smelling barrel, dipping mugs and drinking, rowdy temperaments compounded by booze.

"A filthy boo-gart?" The ogre with the biggest, emptiest head, like a deformed pumpkin with the brains to match, scooped Gobba up by a leg. Thimbles and needles clattering on his rope belt. Reactions too dulled and his tendons too bruised to escape, Gobba still had enough foresight to clutch his lordly wig to his head. Big blood-shot eyes regarded him. Breath, hot with alcohol, rasped against his face. A ham-sized hand pulled Gobba's red jacket away, the cloth hurt as it snagged and tore around his body. Shiny rings were easily slipped from his fingers.

"Take it all, it's not a problem. Please let me go," Gobba said to the smiling brute. Instead, the ogre swung Gobba like a ball and chain, upsetting his nerve-churned stomach. Vomit spewed out, arcing foully around the alleyway. Gobba's wig spun from his head, splattering onto the ground.

"He's not well. Must need a drink," said a gruff voice from somewhere in the spinning alley.

Darkness and wetness came up fast. The ogre dunked Gobba into the barrel. Strong alcohol stung the boggart's eyes and wounds. Bubbles rose in torrents from his nose and his lungs felt fit to burst. *This is my end,* Gobba thought splashing in wild panic. *Damn Crone!*

It all started to go hazy and numb. Gobba barely noticed when they pulled him out, a soggy wretch tossed aside on top of his ruined wig. Then he saw why he was so casually discarded. Two armoured men walked by, their leathers baring the vine and rose emblem of the City Watch.

"Guards," Gobba spluttered from the ground. But they looked at him without sympathy. One pointed, then both laughed at the sot of a boggart sitting in a puddle of vomit. An ogre shoved mugs toward the men like they were old friends. *Typical, useless guards.*

*Never mess with boggarts. Everyone used to know that. Your luck depended on it!* Gobba's shaky hand pulled the wig from under his backside, the thing now nothing more than a puke and booze sponge. Crawling into a pitch-black corner, where the alley narrowed further, the old boggart flicked open the welded lid of a thimble with a blunt yellow claw and savoured a smile. "Flashbang powder, do your worst," he whispered, taking a pinch and snapping his fingers. A spark, then a flame, then a blaze wrapped the wig like some hell barber's joke. From his crumpled state, Gobba tossed it with all his might. The flaming wig plopped into the booze-filled barrel. The stupid ogres laughed. So did the City Guard. Until…

A column of fire shot out from the barrel, blasting the alley apart and throwing Gobba against something hard. A blazing sheet of white winked in his mind before it all went black.

◇⊪⊪━━━━━⊪◇

*The shame, everything a stinking cesspool of shame,* Gobba thought, while weaving around the legs of human servants Under his arm, he carried a freshly refilled jug of wine. Portraits of nobles, sticking their noses in the air, adorned the drawing room. Sparkling chandeliers hung from the ceiling. Apart from a half dozen armoured guards standing to attention, ignored and silent, the drawing room played host to the High Sheriff, the Captain of the Watch, and a visiting Lord of Some-place or Other. The three sat around a table, all dripping with shiny stuff in an attempt to impress. One of the shinies was the shiniest shiny Gobba had ever seen. And, what was more, a large silver platter, with a branch of coiled silver from which the juiciest-looking apples grew, lay in the centre of the room on a table! *Oh, old lady Crone, you clever clever hag.*

It was Gobba's first day on the new job. His bones still ached; his burns still itched. But worse, now he was just a pet like all his kind… *Not for long though.* He steadied his old hands and poured the visiting lord a drink.

"Oh, look at the darling thing. A goblin. I've never bothered to look at one so closely before. This one is…getting on a bit, isn't it?" Tension snapped through Gobba's muscles. Yet he nodded, smiled his mucky, mostly absent teeth, and looked up at the seated man.

The bearded Captain of the Watch grinned, "Yes, your Lordship. I found him by the bodies of the ogres everyone's talking about. The brutes were clutching the charred jacket and jewellery of Lord Derrel and Lady Winnie. "

The visiting lord leaned toward the Captain of the Watch. "I heard they were found dead in their carriage. Sad. I knew Regina well. But exciting news. Why, everyone is going on about it!"

"The ogres surely robbed and killed them. And they killed a couple of my men on the Watch. That little goblin used some forest trickery to cook them alive."

"A heroic goblin? Well, there *is* a first for everything. Or so my father used to say."

Another voice boomed over the table "Well I *would* say, 'well done that man'... creature. Never let it be said that the High Sheriff's office doesn't reward those of meritorious service, even if they are so, plainly, decrepit. Another fine titbit to add to my growing collection of Old Britain, taken from collector's vaults and burial mounds and such, along with all the swords, cauldrons, and the fabled 'apples of Avalon.'"

The Sheriff gestured to the silver branch. No doubt he was out to impress, wearing a silver coronet all encrusted with jewels, with a host of gold medallions and flabby wrinkles around his neck. "This little chap must be the most successful goblin ever, to serve one such as I wearing a Duke's coronet. The Odysseus of Goblins! Maybe it will catch on and we'll all be having the little things grooming our stools."

"Oh, I want one," said the visiting Lord of Wherever. The Captain of the Watch laughed, and a few of the guards chuckled. Even the faux-duke-High Sheriff indulged a smile. Gobba ground his few teeth. *Success? To serve for two shinies a week? Pah. These people should take heed of their fables about putting trust in snakes...* The High Sheriff stood and raised his goblet, followed by the Captain and the visiting noble. Careful not to spill a drop, Gobba hurried around the table and made sure everyone's cup brimmed over, struggling to reach the cups held high. "A toast, to our most heroic little goblin," hailed the sheriff, fat face rosy, lips wine-stained.

"Here, here." More laughter, before they slumped back down to the cosy embrace of good wine.

The fat faux-duke nodded over to Gobba. "Now refill me, little chap. Chop, chop. No, wait. Better yet, let me spoil my company with something stronger. Bring a jug of the very finest from the cellars." Bowing with exaggerated subservience, Gobba's eyes sparkled with something far more sinister.

Suddenly, the windows flashed orange, the courtyard boomed with a rain of shattered glass. Drinks spilled mid-slurp; plates clattered to the stone floor. "What the devil? Go and see what's what." Piggy eyes twitched, and the sheriff's fat rolls wobbled around his neck. Immediately, with a clatter of arms, the guards left the room while the trio of diners hurried to the window. But not Gobba. *Stupid herd of gangly idiots.*

From outside came the sounds of confusion, yells, the ringing of fire bells, the noise so great that the flick of metal tops from thimbles, and the pricking of needles into seat cushions, went completely unnoticed. Flickering candles conspired to help Gobba in his crime. Silent and easy, embracing the darkest dance of shadows, when the deed was done, he slunk into a corner.

"It's the bloody booze cellar. Some ill-bred buffoon must have struck a flame," said the Sheriff, watching the frantic running of people in the courtyard below. Gobba smiled. Of course, it was all down to him. He'd spread flashbang powder over the cellar floor when he last refilled the wine jug. Flashbang powder, just waiting for any little scrape to… FLASH BANG. A boot-step would do it. "I'll flog the whole bloody staff tomorrow. But, no fear, I have several cellars under the East Wing. Come, sit." The Sheriff, anxious not to lose face, gestured towards their former chairs. Drunkenly stumbling back to their seats, the little group smiled, then laughed with the excitement of it all. They fell heavily on their seat cushions, where glinting needles, threaded through the fabric to point at an angle upward, pricked backsides.

"Something stung me…" mumbled the visiting Lord of Such-and-Such-a-place. The others were already too numbed by booze to feel anything. From his nook, Gobba watched the emptiness take hold. A moment later, three bodies sat on cushioned chairs, all unmoving. All smiled a smile of happy-drunken death. Smiling with something very different, Gobba emerged from the shadows.

⋄━━━━━━━⋄

When a midget servant creature, eating a juicy apple, hobbled down the cold stone stairs, no one thought to question it. Guards, running back and forth, simply ignored him. It amazed Gobba how they didn't think him the slightest bit suspicious, despite the chaos. Slung over one shoulder was a bulging sack made from the finest velvet, often used to cut the curtains of landed folk. Inside was a small hoard of treasure, just for him. He had done it all right under their noses! *Don't get cocky. Focus. Slowly, slowly, get out of here.*

Concerned with reporting any minuscule information to dissuade the expected anger of their employer, a menagerie of staff, blind to anything else, frantically shouted messages back and forth. In the fuss, with pained slowness, Gobba made his way into the courtyard. A flurry of servants rushed with buckets of water. Others struggled to calm panicked horses. Then the moment came. Someone shouted from the drawing-room window above. "The Sheriff is…not breathing!"

On hearing this, the *silly old harmless goblin* called Gobba limped away into the night. Swallowing the last of the tastiest apple he had ever eaten, Gobba made sure to work the pips free and keep them safe under his tongue. The night was at its blackest and the sky was moonless and starless when Gobba, head lolling as he walked, first nodded off in exhaustion. It was then when the Crone visited him. All he could remember of it was a great big, hooded cape, a vein-crossed and liver-spotted hand with bony fingers reaching out from it.

"Stay awake, Gobba. Don't delay, your destiny is waiting. Give me the seeds and know, you are bound to what they produce after your dying day." Sure enough, he spat out the seeds, straight into that hand, which made scraping sounds as the fingers closed around them. After that, a second wind buoyed Gobba awake and onward through the dark, an urgency born from knowing he had little time left.

⊶⊢⊩══════════⊪⊣⊷

Never had the ache of age seemed so deep as when he trudged through the countryside, dragging his sack all the way. Red patches of rubbed-raw skin speckled his feet. For more than a day Gobba suffered until, during the early morning, he found and followed the gnarled roots and black trees which led back to Sticky Bark Combe.

Old and irrelevant even among his own kind, his arrival was ignored. Life in Sticky Bark Combe continued just as it had when he left. A group of young boggarts practised gimmicks and sleight of hand, with cups and balls on top of tree stumps, in preparation for shiny-getting missions to the city. *Embarrassing!* Upturned carts or tree hollows posed as homes. A few lopsided huts stood out as comparatively grand. *Never would the vermin tribes of my youth have settled for this.* But Gobba's ingrained weariness had piled up on his recent trip. Perhaps, he thought, a permanent place to rest wasn't *so* bad. Yet he didn't rest, despite the call of soft grasses. Instead, he walked to a little earth mound and untied his sack. Throwing it open, silver and gold sparkled from within like moons and suns.

Bit by bit, Gobba adorned himself in shiny, re-piercing old scars with jewellery through his nose, ears, and eyebrows, slipping rings over his fingers. Many of the Sticky Bark Combe boggarts gathered to watch as Gobba wound medallions around his scrawny neck, tight enough to not slip over his narrow shoulders. So much neck-shiny that it made his back ache.

When the crowd had grown large enough, Gobba deemed it time to show the best shiny ever. He unveiled the coronet of Dukedom. *Coronet, pah. Crown! It is a crown.* Heavy and oversized, Gobba forced it to fit anyway by tucking his ears under the rim to pad it out. Finally, he cast a handful of rose-coloured buttons into his audience. Kicking up turf, a mad scramble broke out.

Disturbed by the commotion, a boggart emerged from the grandest of all the wooden huts. Younger and bigger than Gobba, skin still smooth, he wore a human-sized breastplate, shiny and silver although badly scratched, which covered him from neck to toe. With gold teeth, Chief Nob snarled.

*Chief Nob looks positively poor,* smirked Gobba from his mound. The old boggart pointed to the chief; the crowd looked back. "I have the shiniest shiny a boggart has ever seen. Not given to me for being a pet, not for being a toy. I stole it! Does Chief Nob match me?" Green faces looked back and forth with a hush-shush of mutterings. Then a chant started to brew, simmering softly at first and then boiling into shouts, "Chief Gobba, Chief Gobba, Chief Gobba."

"By Chief Nob's rules, the Right of Shiny, I should be your new chief. But I am old and wise and merciful. Chief Nob can keep his position. I will have something even better." Although his audience clapped with wild abandon, their faces were screwed with confusion.

"Never has a boggart shone like the sun. I demand a new name. Call me King Gobba. I will lead us, teach us to embrace the life of vermin. Vermin thrive, fester around the edges, worm deep into the cracks until they cannot be removed without risking the toppling of the once healthy whole." Whoops and cheers from the mob, younglings somersaulted in the air. But many of the listeners looked on blankly. But not, most importantly, the old ones. The aged eyes in the crowd sparkled with something they hadn't felt for decades. Something *childish.*

<hr/>

A tingle shot up the length of Gobba's throat. He wheezed. All the bumps and burns and bruises had taken their toll and the coup had turned exhausting. But as he stumbled, this time many hands reached out to catch him.

"King Gobba must rest. Talk more later," said a young one, well trained in obsequiousness. *Yes, you will do well.* A host of boggart pups hurried around their King and carried him on their shoulders to Chief Nob's wooden hut. Boggart women squealed. Gobba sniffed the air, relishing the stink of musk and the thrill of power. The mob laid Gobba on a straw bed. Happy faces smiled down on him, not in superiority but reverence. All except one. Gobba saw Nob swaggering past the younglings, hands hidden behind his breastplate, undoubtedly fondling a stiletto. With confidence, Nob strode to the straw bed that he used to own. A sneer worked its way up his cheek.

King Gobba clicked his fingers. "Pull out your knives young ones. You are the royal guard." A chorus of metal scratched against course rope belts. Nob's face fell, his hands pulled away from his breastplate, empty.

Looking around the room, Gobba pondered how well his portrait would look hanging on a wall. Then he examined some of the young boggart ladies and noticed their bee-stung breasts. Perhaps he should decree they steal butter and drink it until their breasts swelled as squishy as that Lady Regina's from the carriage. Then they could learn to dance, just for him. *Hmm...*

"Chief Nob," said the King, long tongue licking cracked lips.

" Yes... King?"

Gobba narrowed his eyes. "Sing me a lullaby."

Dark green skin turning a few shades paler, Chief Nob swallowed, coughed, hacked a glob of phlegm. Only then was he ready. He sang "The Boggart and the Lusty Barmaids' with a voice far more horrible than the nightly fox screams.

*That voice should be banned by law,* mused Gobba. But the King felt entertained enough. Why, watching Nob sing made him laugh. *Perhaps I will make him my jester.* Even with that cacophony in the background, exhaustion finally took hold. Gobba found himself fighting sleep, aching to keep his eyes open. *Why sleep, when being awake is so damn fun?!* But, somehow, sleep seemed to call him, to soak into every ounce of his boggart-self. For the last time in the mortal realm, King Gobba's eyes closed. He would take his title to his grave, destined to be the first to visit Avalon in centuries.

# CHAPTER ELEVEN

# LOOSENING GORDION

*Somewhere in England, 1855 A.D.*

"We go away from the river, away from roads and rails," Artos said to the anarchic crew comprising his trading caravan. "We follow the leyline until our eyes recognize not a place in Britain."

On they went, a merry band of Fey and human craftsmen, strolling to the tune of fife and drum, gorging on beer, cider, and fairy dust. Soon, drunken songs and riotous laughing added to the percussion of the swaggering delegation, on their great adventure to find the last ancient grove.

The summer turned out brilliantly, a sky of spotless blue with a white sun that embalmed all with a deep, relaxing warmth. Flowers bloomed every shade under creation, sweet pollen and meadow grass flavoured the air. It was a dreamy time, an endless trek across the British Isles; a time that rivalled Artos' recollection of his stay on the fairy isles. Less fornication but more companionship and hilarity. A band of jolly travellers gathered the attention of all they came across, a famous circus-carnival of performing Fey and magic.

Hangers-on followed, and an entourage grew. Landowners, and some of the few remaining lords and ladies, sent messages of invitation ahead. Stands were built so crowds could come together and watch performances. Whole villages watched, serving fine rural fare. Artos had never felt in better cheer than with this happy, sprawling bunch.

One evening at the end of that glorious summer, during a spectacular sunset, the procession settled, as they always did, beside the faint leyline they followed. Such a joy this summer had been, Artos didn't even mind if they went home unsuccessful in their task. *This is how we bring people together. In celebration, feasting, and music. How could I have forgotten this?*

Throwing off his boots, he took in the scenery as the camp made merry. Toes clenching the grass, all around spread a wind-beaten plain, not a farmstead or railway in sight. It was an exciting moment. Murmurs went through the camp, questions about their location. Nobody knew where they were. Anticipation scintillated the air when the sun finally set and left them in darkness for a good night's rest. *Are we, truly, lost? Are we on the verge of entering Old Albion?*

Despite how he had tried, when his fellow travellers woke to a bright, fresh morning, Artos had not slept a wink. Not in the least bit tired though, he thrilled at the potential of this new day. Over a breakfast of salted ham, bread dipped in dripping, and chicken eggs donated by curious farmers and village folk, under the gaze of an unimpeded sun, the wanderers identified their next destination; a line of trees silhouetted on the horizon.

Moving quicker than they had been, in mere hours those tiny silhouettes thickened into a wood, wrapping them on every side. Scattered trees tightened. Eventually, movement became difficult.

No clear path was now visible through this unnaturally thick forest. Artos, wild-eyed, felt the breath of untamed land. *Yes, this is the right way...*

Proceeding onward, they packed together, pushing carts over rough ground. Occasionally, they had to bring up axes and chop their way. Progress slowed. However, the mood remained joyful. Fey cheered at the prospect of seeing their ancient forebears. "Soon we will bind our worlds for mutual benefit," Artos told them.

Deeper into the forest they went. Ever so slowly unease started to seep into the humidifying air. Day and night became meaningless in the perpetual forest twilight. Time itself seemed to rush by, greying hair, creasing skin. Or was it just a trick of the light, the effect of the shadow-filigree under the canopy of leaves and branches?

Unseen things rustled. Periodically, an unsettling popping echoed through the trees, its source beyond sight. Artos recalled the moment, millennia ago, when he had met Andraste in Fey Forest, shimmering in vibrant, healthy green. But not here. In this place hung a sickly, yellow haze, almost like a London peasouper. Worse, the haze thickened as they went. Every so often, Artos found himself wiping a film of yellow from his eyes and mouth. No song or laughter accompanied the caravan now. It was silent, tense.

Suddenly, Artos heard a scream from the middle of the caravan. He rushed over to find a cluster of elves, nestling on a pile of sacks in one of the carts. They held out knives at shaky arm's length. Around them buoyed dozens of floating spheres, shimmering with fluidity; green boils in the yellow mist. An elf got too close. The nearest sphere dilated then burst, splattering anyone near enough with a sap-goo that mixed with the haze-grease. Harmless though they seemed, they spooked the whole mission. Where were the sprites? *What perversion of forest beauty is this? Gods and magic have cursed this place.*

Sucking at their boots, the ground churned into gluey mud. Eventually, the horses and heavier carts had to be abandoned. By now, everything was just a chokingly tight forest. With no other choice, they continued. Deeper and deeper into the forest they went. The haze congealed, liquefying into a humid brew of yellow and green.

Doubting his vision, unease tearing at his composure, Artos unclipped his spear, using it as a staff as he led the way. *We have arrived in some type of hell.* A rising chattering noise taunted from behind the trees. Claustrophobic vegetation eventually halted their progress completely. Everyone sweated, gasped for hard to come by breath.

The plant life here had become a sheer monstrosity, writhing with hundreds, thousands of snapping maws on every plant surface. A constant drone of gnashing teeth! Branches and stems twisted at natural and unnatural angles, everything engaged in a cannibal frenzy. Vines, like thick purple candles, sweated in self-devouring bursts. Green boils strained from great, rubbery buds. Rough-skinned shrubbery and fibrous stems pulsated with veins, reminding Artos of the bloody innards of a gutted foe or butchered animal. But this was worse. Nothing he had ever seen could compare to this repulsive perversity.

With the alacrity of snakes, vines lashed out, needle teeth, sharper than razors, tore at suits and jerkins. Screams all around. Chattering, gnashing all around! Everything blurred into carnage. It seemed the taste of blood had awoken the whole forest. Plants swarmed and surged. Purple stems erupted from the sludgy ground.

"Fight it. Burn it. Hack it away," yelled a discordant chorus.

Anywhere and everywhere, musket's snapped fire into the chaos. Blades of all sorts whipped out in a primal urge for survival. Artos stabbed with his spear, the god-killing artefact causing the plants to recoil.

"Use magic. Magic seems to work. Anything you can think of!" How he wished he had brought his Hymn Whisperers with him. But then, it wasn't supposed to be like this...

Electric arcs burnt through the canopy; impromptu lightning charmed from the sky by elves. Spouts of fire, cast by sprites pooling their thimblefuls of magic together, scorched the thick, dense mass of cursed vegetation. Knockers stuck their black powder-concoction into hollowed-out iron balls, lit fuses, and ripped the forest apart.

Somehow, beyond all sense and reason, a dozen of Artos' followers survived. Showered by ash remnants of vegetation, they managed to fight their way through to a clearing of sorts. Here, giant purple stalks climbed high, secreting a luminous jelly-web over the canopy. It bathed Artos and his remaining band in an eerie blue light, the jelly drooling down over all the gaps in the vegetation to trap them. Twisted shadows of feral creatures scrabbled through the clearing. On noticing the intruders, they began cackling excitedly, spinning and rushing in fits of madness.

In the centre of the clearing rasped the grey body of a woman, ruffled black feathers sticking out in patches. There was something to her harsh, raspy breaths, something which provoked images of ravens in Artos' imagination. *She is who I am looking for.*

He could feel her in his mind. A living sadness, a tragedy that stirred pity in his soul. This, here, was one of the great goddesses of his people, a queen of goddesses even; Morrigan, patron of many, many things. There was no greatness left, though. Morrigan's empty black eyes conveyed utter defeat. This was what remained of the wild Fey, of Old Albion.

Crouching by her side, he shared her feelings of hopelessness. But he couldn't take it. Not him. It built as frustration in his gut, found expression as water in his own eyes. "You fled the world to live in a sacred grove, followed by the wild Fey. Many gods did. I thought the Puritans had hunted you all down. What has happened, here? What is this...abomination?"

She didn't move her crusted lips, but Morrigan's words gathered inside Artos' mind. "Forgotten, we corroded. The Fey have diminished. A worm in the apple."

A waft of decay. Artos gagged. A deformed creature, scrawny and bulbous with tumours growing all over its body, skittered towards him. It gargled in a high pitch, perhaps trying to communicate with what passed for its language. Lips stretched around the tight pucker of a mouth. It smiled an array of needle-like fangs, layers of them. Artos didn't know what to say, slightly moving to allow the creature closer to Morrigan. The thing stepped forward, regarded Artos for a moment, before it turned to Morrigan and feasted.

Frenzying from all parts of the corrupted forest, foul things swarmed over Morrigan like piglets desperate to suckle from their mother. Morrigan's voice returned to Artos' mind. "Inhospitality and faithlessness are all that is left. See the truth of the Fey? And yet I heal, only to be consumed again every day. Because of the Crone, we are forced to suffer this slow death. End this old world, Artos, for the sake of mercy. I once held sovereignty over Revenge. Help me and claim my power."

"You bid me remake the world?" In horror, Artos watched the degenerate Fey feast on all that was left of their god. Around them, vines pulsed, and the ground shuddered. *For all these years I have blamed Andraste for abandoning us. I was wrong. Not only should I have crushed the gods, but everything to do with them. I led honourable, brave tribesmen to defeat. Now, I know why. The Fey, those parasitic things feeding off the emotions of true warriors, true Britons, and to what end? Defeat, despair, degeneracy.*

"This land is a mistake," Artos said under his breath.

Twirling his spear in figure eight, he yelled to his entourage. "We burn this place to the ground." The air whistled as he stabbed the spear-point through the skull of a withered Fey before withdrawing. With lightning speed, he stabbed another, then another... The creatures scattered, chattering into the waxy shrubbery. Behind him echoed a few stray cracks of gunshot. It wasn't of those obeying his orders, though. It was a deliberate call to defiance.

"No, Artos. We would follow you into Hell, Christian or otherwise, but we will not lay waste to the Last Grove," said a knocker.

Breath heavy, shoulders rolling, without turning Artos spat. "Fine. I will do it myself." Unceremoniously, he jabbed his spear into Morrigan. The whole forest winked black and white. She gazed into her killer's eyes, her last words echoing in Artos' mind. "Thank you. I leave a gift." For an instant, she appeared young and utterly, achingly beautiful.

Corrupted trees and vines shattered into a blizzard of fragments. From the collapsing trees, withered Fey sprung at the survivors of the trade mission, picking and tearing at whatever they could, only to be smeared across sludge-earth by bullets and swords. Knockers quickly assembled crank-turned guns and sprayed bullets across the grove. The men and women in Artos' entourage fought as valiantly as they could, but the swarm began to overwhelm them. Confusion reigned. A voice called, "Kill Artos, he has murdered our goddess. He is cursed!"

Artos slid his hands into the ash and green dust of the fallen goddess, letting it run through his fingers. He didn't see any boggarts here, though, not like when he had done this two thousand years before. What he did find, under the faerie dust of a god's ashes, was a puddle of lime water and a gloopy dollop of, already prepared, woad. His *gift* - the true Artos, the true Albion.

While chaos consumed the forest, Artos ripped off his once-fine jacket and shirt. Slaking his finger with lime, he ran it through his hair, spiking it like the horns of a demon. Then, he rubbed woad into his skin, over his face and torso, feeling the sting of the medicinal balm contained within. Licking his lips, snorting in a great huff of ire, he stood, with his spear, and roared.

He smelled of warrior, tasted of warrior, sounded like a warrior. All would know him as dangerous just by looking at his warrior visage. Now, it was time to *feel* like a warrior. He waded into the sludge and chaos as the power of the Goddess of Revenge soared through his veins.

Chunks of flesh were blown from his body by guns and other fiery knocker-contraptions. It hurt, but the pain felt good. Those blemishes healed quickly, regrowing in rolling heaps of white bone and pink muscle. Closing in, getting eye to eye with opponent after opponent, Artos fought his way through man and Fey alike. All he wanted was slaughter. Slaughter against the weakness of New Albion. *All of them, weak.* Not one gave him a challenge. So many died on their knees. Others ran off into the forest, only to be devoured. It was all they deserved.

When all around lay dead and dying, Artos collected Morrigan's remains into a sack, after emptying it from the leftover trinkets of the trade mission. Any remaining carts he came across, loaded with all their tools and alchemy to share with the faerie grove, he set ablaze. He watched how the flames rushed like a demon over the corrupted and broken forest, all-consuming.

"It is time to erase the prison of history," Artos said to the crackling fire.

Wandering away, the sludge clay-like under his bare feet, he heard the caw of ravens. He glimpsed three of them through the tattered canopy, circling in the sky. Beckoning to one, mimicking its caw, it spiralled down into his outstretched hand.

Gently, he kissed the bird on the tip of its head, before snapping its neck. Carefully, he plucked out both eyes and ate them, swallowing in one go.

Now, he could see through all nearby raven's eyes, sharing their panoramic view of the surrounding land. He would find his way out and claim the mantle of a true God of Revenge. Then, he would rip the Marsh Worm Mile from this corrupted world and rule a place of warriors, free of Fey, in a new Avalon worthy of his godhood.

## *Marsh Worm Mile, 1861 A.D.*

Shammy bowed and refilled a goblet with ancient, alcoholic ambrosia. The well-to-do patron nodded and smiled groggily. She replied with an empty smile of her own, feeling too uneasy for real joy to lift her mood.

These celebrations caused her to pause for thought. She couldn't quite make sense of it all. The Crone lay silently upon the church altar, tied with many-knotted rope and bound with cloth, the seams inside-out. Her dead eyes gave off no emotion. She just peered, unblinking, at the ceiling. But there was nothing up there. Wasn't she supposed to be a magic-goddess-fairy? How could she be so silent in all the... *madness*?

Madness! All around Shammy slumped the bodies of prominent Londoners, lulled into a stupor by excess, lost in faraway fairy dreams. Bizarre how blue-faced urchins, or perfumed girls, swanned among them like servants, tending to their every whim, instead of conniving a plan to pick their pockets.

The church hall now resembled a junk shop of the mysterious and magical, or a hall of oddities, or a freak show! Donations from archaeologists, historians, and adventurers made the place a cornucopia of legend, a museum of Old Albion. Much of it counterfeit for sure, but Artos said he had never felt the thrill of so much magic in one place. *It is not the 'truth' but the believing that matters.* Apparently.

Shammy had passed the time by letting her curiosity run rampant. Glass jars lining shelves held grim, sometimes pickled, artefacts of ancient and urban lore. The disembodied 'Hand of Glory,' said to open any lock, floated palm open. *That would be handy for making mischief, for sure.*

Odin's eye, lidless, stared from another jar. None could hold its all-knowing gaze. *Too creepy.* Dragon scales and teeth, hydra blood, phoenix feathers, a unicorn's horn, and other fantastic odds and ends cluttered up any free space. Shammy decided that she hated them all, except for the phoenix feathers, with their pretty, fire-mimicking pattern.

Pieces of rock, pebbles, and marbles lay scattered against the interior church walls, made from toad, adder, and other healing stones, along with minerals that were said to be fireproof and some which sang songs of the sky and the sea. Among these were pieces of mithril, adamant and other magical substances, invulnerable materials from a lost age.

Woad Warriors inspected the bounty too, with amazement and suspicion. One tall, thickly muscled warrior, called Miles, with a belly gone a bit fat swaggered with braggadocio, lording it over his fellows while wearing Goshwhite, the fabled helmet of King Arthur. Gentlemen and urchins alike grabbed weapons and sparred against each other, or bashed the relics against a multitude of legendary suits of armour. Caladbolg, a blade so strong it could sheer the tops off mountains, rang harmlessly against shining green plate-mail, an armour of invulnerability. The magic blade, Fragarach, 'sword of the wind,' summoned gusts that sent any sparring partner scurrying to the floor. Other's toyed with Excalibur or Caliban. Artos amused himself with a few swings of the 'Sword of Attila,' ravisher of the Roman Empire. Victor could be seen thrusting the unstoppable spear, Brionac, against a supposed shield of adamant, shattering it into a thousand pieces. *Scratch one fake off the list...*

Eventually, as initial excitement dwindled, Artos and his warriors settled to feast around two cauldrons, these being artefacts too. One was the bottomless Cauldron of Dagda, ever filled with delicious stew. The second cauldron, of Dyrnwch the Giant, refused to warm its contents for cowards, instilling fearlessness into already brave men.

Warriors periodically poured Dagda's brew into the giant's pot and feasted from it. All claimed their stew to be piping hot! Shammy had her suspicions.

They feasted on ambrosia, followed by silver and gold apples, all toasted with gallons of dark mead. Drunk and full men and women played with jewellery and covered their fingers with magic rings. A particular ring gifted its bearer with the 'tongue of a poet.' Although that ring was taken away and hidden by a particularly bawdy group. Other rings magicked gold or sent the wearer blinking away, invisible to all.

Merry and sated, those with talent blew, plucked, and beat instruments of legend. Flutes, horns, harps, drums, and even a conch shell, became an orchestra of mythology. Such a celebration of magic had not taken place for thousands of years.

Throughout the feast, the Crone remained utterly passive. Knowing full well that her thoughts alone could be deadly, Artos had ordered none to interfere with her, 'let her soak it all up before the final sacrifice of the Old World.' Yet, even though he stood on unsteady feet he swaggered, unable to resist one last slurring gloat. It caused doubts to grow in Shammy's mind. Danger pulsed ever stronger in that magic-heavy air.

"Doomed Goddess, look upon me," Artos yelled, face so flushed it showed even from under the woad. Goblet held high, he continued, "I am the final conqueror of this land, already built upon the bones of conquest. I am ready to mine the lost memories and magic which are trapped underneath. From down there," Artos stumbled, pointing to well-worn tiles on the floor. "Avalon calls to me, a shadow of a whisper under the earth, but sharp and humming, like the gust after a blade swiping the air. A light on the edge of seeing, a truth in a sea of dark unbelief. You are part of this great breaking of everything."

It was the strangest thing. Though her eyes remained motionless and empty, a slight smile cracked across the Crone's face. She spoke, strident yet calm. "Listen, blowhard. I planted the seeds of Avalon down the well the day you returned to Britain, after your cowardly flight to the fairy isles. Down there, in the darkness of oblivion, a boggart tends the rebirth of Albion. Remember boggarts? Pesky things you lacked enough power to control. Avalon does not call to you; it answers to me."

"Bah. I have my warriors, my magic, my godhood!" yelled Artos. But to this, the Crone held her smile and never said a word.

"To hell with you, then. Let your boggarts know that I take your mantle of Fate. They will obey me in my new Albion. Watch as Fey destroys Fey." Artos dismissively waved his goblet, spilling a golden liquid. "It is time to light the fires and burn away the shameful past." Revenge, slow-roasted for nearly twenty centuries, was his. 'Fate' would be sacrificed and, in the void left over, he would build the Albion of his dreams.

Through his preoccupations, Artos failed to notice a pretty, young girl, made up in rouge and finery, slip through the large church door and away into the street.

The black flames of prophecy crackled as they consumed the pyre of relics. Fuelled with the energy of ancient manna, many of the artefacts ignited into soaring fireworks of inky void, smashing stained glass windows and leaving gaps of abyss in the towering, empty frames. Above the fire, hanging from silver chains and knotted rope, the Crone shrieked and wriggled, leaking green effervescence from her eyes. Everything thrummed with anticipation. A rising volume of shouting rung from the square, outside.

Woad Warriors cheered at this great remaking. From now on, only one God mattered; Artos, the God of Victory, Revenge, Fate, and now of New Beginnings. Marsh Worm would be reclaimed, made into a new Avalon for true warriors of Albion. History would be restarted, and shaped the way it should have been. It will be like Rome had never happened. Yes, Artos would build an Albion, an Avalon on the ashes of thousands of years of choking superstition.

The church did not, however, just contain those loyal to Artos. Gentleman and ladies, collectors, curators, adventurers, the donors of his artefacts, all now stood aghast, on the edge of whatever intoxicants consumed their senses. Murmuring sentimentality played with the lingering sensations of green powder. This eased men and women into tearful states over the loss of such ancient treasures. Now the euphoria had dissipated, and it all seemed so wrong. Artos seemed... dangerous. *This man has gone too far.*

"Stop this," shouted one of the dandies, a fat man well feasted on the spiced delicacies of imperial trade routes. The chants of Woad Warriors, though, proved hard to overcome. The man shouted louder. "I will have nothing more to do with this. You are a monster."

Not even turning to face him, Artos spread his arms like wings and roared, as a rainbow burst of huge amounts of magic wrapped around him, laced through him, permeated every part of him. Yes, he was now the font of all magic, all gods, all...myth. "It is time to kick off the barnacles and cast adrift in our own sea. Time for the spilling of blood, for the sacrifices. Welcome back old friends, come to your God of Victory made anew."

From the shadows, springing from nothingness, came boggarts, not green but made of flickering shadow visible to all, sinking their teeth into Landed necks and savouring the juicy flesh of London's wealthy. Screams made a cacophony and Artos yelled even louder.    "Leave or die!"

<hr />

### Avalon, 1861 A.D.

With one hand on his hip, Gobba shuffled forward, his back hunched. Sol suspected that much of this was put on but followed anyway. What else was he to do? There was something relaxing about this place, once he allowed himself to get used to it. Could he live down here eating apples every day?

"Boggart King, look up there. Squint and spy on the emotions of what should be your domain." The creature pulled at Sol's jacket, grinning toothlessly.

Starring up, through the apple-scented abyss, a round disc of light, barely more than a pinpoint, twinkled dimly. "It's the old well. I know it."

"From up there, instead of warriors, only unwanted things were sent to Avalon. And when no one cared about it anymore, it turned dark. Been a bit of a burden, taking care of it all. I just had to believe in it a little bit. Hard not to since I live here. I was just told to keep it going until you arrived. *If* you arrived. Bored to tears, I am."

"But what do I do with this place? How do you know I even want it?"

"Old Lady said it. What Old Lady says seems to be what happens. Eat some more apples and have a little kip." Gobba looked at Sol, waiting for a response, but the young man stood silently, his thoughts elsewhere. "Well, you do what you want. I'm going catch my well-earned everlasting forty winks. I been promised forever dreams of when I was young and virile. I suggest you get rest before all the boggarts come running to help you."

All that was lost to Sol. He was imagining what was going on, up there in the Mile. For the first time in a good while his head was clear, his thoughts untainted. If he concentrated while staring at that point of light, he could even get the sensations of the Mile. Victor, he was drunk, broiling anger inside his chest. But there was something darker too, a hatred...But not for Sol, for faerie. He actually *hated* the Fey. Victor's thoughts concerning Sol centred on sadness and confusion. *I miss you too, my long-time friend.*

Allowing his mind to wander to Shammy, Sol pulled back once her sorrow exposed itself. He just couldn't bare the guilt.

*Damn Artos. Damn him!* How was that bastard feeling? But Artos was a void, impenetrable. No surprise there.

However, when Sol thought of the others he knew, Paul, Blunt, and even Rozzer Jim, it was prickly anxiety, overwhelming above all other emotions. Something dangerous was brewing. Something horrible. He wondered, could he push this experience forward, into the future. What lay ahead? He held his breath, strained until blood thundered through his ears...

Sol gasped, his shoulders slumped, his knees buckled. All energy drained from his body.

Unable to penetrate the veil of the future, Sol had managed to tease at the sensations of upcoming events. A creeping, shuddering dread slowly spread through him. He tasted blood. He heard raised voices and fighting. In the future lay terror and death.

Needing nothing more than a chance to rest, Sol made his way to Gobba's hut. Inside, the old boggart was already sleeping. A deep peaceful sleep, for sure. Gobba didn't twitch or snore. He didn't make a sound at all.

Knowing what was coming, Sol knelt by the ancient creature's side and placed a hand on its bony chest. Absolute stillness. Absolute silence. A great grin on his face as if enjoying the most fantastic dream. Despite only having met Gobba a short time ago, Sol couldn't help the swelling of a few tears. In this empty land, the sadness of loss magnified tenfold. Although, he suspected the boggart was enjoying a dream-blessed afterlife better than this empty Avalon place.

Unearthly, hellish, demon-squeals devastated the lingering calm. Rushing back outside the hut, Sol watched as a column of boggarts, excitedly screaming, yipping, cursing fell from the pinpoint of light. At least a hundred of the things hit, without impact, the black ground, before springing up and circling the hut, always jabbering on.

Sol pinned his hands over his ears. "Shut it, will you!"

Just like that, silence returned. The creatures fidgeted while squinting Sol's way. One of the boggarts wore a flat cap, a young, spruce thing with pockmarks all over its face.

The creature responded to Sol's questioning look. "I'm here at your service, milord-highness-imperial-ship. Anything I can help you with?"

Sol just watched, slowly shaking his head.

"Well, they call me Jobba, a great, great, great, great...How many greats? Many greats, great-grandson of Gobba. We all is his offspring or tribe, somehow. Tell me what to do, matey, and we'll have it done since you is our new king."

When Sol turned his attention away from Jobba, back to his personal boggart horde, the creatures all sat cross-legged, in neat rows, awaiting his command.

"The world above has left the Fey and Avalon behind it. It is time to reclaim our place as myths and tie up all the loose ends of fate for good." Reaching up to that pinpoint of light, Sol felt the darkness throb around him. That pinpoint winked, then spun larger.

"Let's make our beds and go lie in them."

<hr/>

# CHAPTER TWELVE

## CUTTING THE KNOT

***Old Well Square, 1861 A.D.***

"Valeria, look, there it goes again," the old knocker called Blunt, looking out of the bedroom window, said to the painted lady-elf. She rolled her eyes. But *this* time Blunt was sure the shadows flickered *unnaturally*. Blunt could feel it, a bad spirit or essence lingering will ill intent. Lately, that spirit seemed to possess every nook and cranny of Old Well Square.

"Hangover, my lovely?" Sitting on a stool, Valeria preened herself in front of a mirror and touched up irregularities in her makeup.

That could well be part of it. It wasn't *just* the gin though. That stabbing behind his forehead, a migraine residue made worse by the midday glare, didn't help either. Old Well Square, after all, was a mess of ever-moving shadows, a slum of market stalls, slumping hovels, and ill-set lines, coalescing around the grander shadow of the church. Despite appearances, Blunt knew how the Square *should* feel.

The sun beat oppressively. Ne-er-do-wells at street corners squinted past the sweat baubles on their brow, eyeing all the comings and goings with studied focus. Normally they looked for every opportunity to make a bit of coin however it presented itself, yet even they seemed distracted. Today, everyone seemed to scent that *something* was in the air.

The Square thrived, the way weeds thrived, with beggars, hustlers, and buskers, poor sods scraping pennies and selling trinkets, human and Fey alike. Ladies and lady-boys swanned and minced, sprayed stinging-sweet perfume and courting custom. And above them all, the church cast its shadow. An ominous pillar of pure darkness joined hands with a blackness rising from the well. Chewing up the light at the edges in blasphemous silence, it seemed to spread at a miniscule pace. Just looking at the damn thing twisted Blunt's queasy stomach. *But the shadow was growing, wasn't it?*

Then again, maybe it was his old, drunk mind playing tricks after all. At just that moment, the whole damn square blinked a bright, venomous green. It blinked again, black became white, white became black, then everything blinked the colour of abyss. Grabbing the nearby mess bucket, Blunt threw up.

"Tell me you saw that, right? It is Artos, I tell you," said the knocker to the painted elf, trembling hands wiping his mouth with a rag. He swigged his mouth with a cupful of cheap gin.

Valeria got up on her tiptoes and kissed Blunt's cheek. A wet 'thick as thieves' kiss. He nearly swooned from her miasma of reapplied perfume. "You're always on about that, my lovely. So, he beat you in a fight? Let it go. Hush your conspiring.

Parliament will hang him high if he causes too much of a nuisance, mark my wise words, my lovely. What can he do against all the mechanical bits and bobs of our new age?" She smiled her carnival smile.

A synthetic-crazy kind of pretty, Valeria was made up like street artists had run a riot over her face. Again, she kissed Blunt, this time on his lips, her tongue salacious. She pulled away with a big 'mwuah.' After that Blunt couldn't help but smile.

"I swear you're half nymph! Just keep your eyes open. Something ain't right. Today, something's different." Blunt sighed, then looked out the window again squinting through the sunshine.

"Watch yourself, Blunty. Don't stare too hard. The law's about. You'll make them stick their piggy noses in looking all suspicious like that." Valeria nudged Blunt with her elbow and nodded toward the Peeler swaggering through the crowd just below.

Rozzer Jim, the joke of the local pubs, tolerated and indulged throughout the Marsh Worm Mile for fear that, if he were replaced, someone competent might actually do the job. The constable motioned at his eyes and drew a line with his fingers toward Blunt as if to say, 'I'm watching you,' before he waddled and sweated onward in the oppressive heat.

Perhaps it was going to be a normal day after all. As normal as they got around Old Well Square anyway. *Too many pleasures are turning me crazy*

The world blinked again.

Differently this time. Everything turned to night and stuck that way. Scratchy white lines appeared superimposed over the

Square. Smaller, white-outlined details exposed something that... *wasn't there.* Ugly man-things, boggarts to all that knew the old ways, watched him, watched everyone.

Blunt assessed the crowd's reaction, making sure it wasn't just him, making sure he hadn't, just that very moment, imagined something that wasn't there. He spied a little lad down below, whose concentration had seemingly broken while he tugged too hard at the pocket he tried to pick. Others stopped their touting and browsing. Old Well Square became an alien place of stillness. The only moving parts at first were lips and tongues, slowly forming whispers. The undercurrent of gossip quickly turned from ripple into wave. Valeria pressed closer to Blunt to share his vantage place.

"See up there?" Blunt pointed at outlines in the sky, at ghosts of weird, twisted trees which dwarfed the wretched shanty structures of Old Well Square. Rows and rows of boggarts looked on from every branch. All of them just watching...but then the boggarts moved as one.

With disconcerting stop-start motion, the things raised their arms. White-black flickering shadows stretched from their feet, cones in ever-increasing broadness spreading over the Square. Shadow hands snatched tentatively at hats and bonnets, knocking them off people's heads like gusts of wind. A few locals giggled, apparently thinking it was all some type of magical entertainment.

Spreading further, the shadows groped with greater tangibility. A woman screamed then squeaked, her voice choking under the outlines of the hands crushing her throat. People rushed away, abandoning her in an island of darkness, her edges glowing white and her insides fading into transparency. More screams, then she simply vanished, her remains smudging the ground like a shadow stain.

"Fight them," yelled a disembodied voice. It could almost have been a voice from beyond the ether, frazzling in the ears of the Fey-touched inhabitants of the Marsh Worm Mile.

Noise jerked Rozzer Jim into fumbling action. All fingers and thumbs, the constable pulled out his pistol, pointed, and fired. Old Well Square cracked with gunshot. The nearest boggart fuzzed into nothingness.

Roaring joyfully, the crowd revelled at the excuse to unload their knocker-made hand cannons. A few painted ladies whipped derringers from between breasts or from under garters. Gunshots blistered brickwork; splinters cut into the crowd. The boggarts rippled, not quite fully tangible yet. All the time, the shadows from the church grew and grew.

Blunt grabbed Valeria's arm and ran down to the Square. Stampeding over the unfortunates lining the stairwell, the pair slipped through a side door into well-sheltered alleys, made into tunnels by leaning houses. Behind them, Rozzer Jim screamed his head off. "They're making them all disappear!"

Valeria's make-up ran awash, ghoulish around her eyes. "The magic's gone bad."

"It's Artos. I told you, he has a hatred for us now." Blunt edged to the alley's end, anxious to spy on events from relative safety.

Sounds of heavy boots spanked against the tight alley's confines. Light shifted. A boggart appeared against a wall like the outline of chalk graffiti. Its shadow hand crawled across pock-marked concrete. Blunt squeezed Valeria to his chest, protective instincts fired his actions even as the shadow hand snatched across the elf lady's multi-coloured curls. Rozzer Jim suddenly appeared; his face melted with sweat. Swinging his truncheon, it battered solidly against the shadow and sent the boggart flying.

Holding Valeria tighter than ever, Blunt prepared to run back into the Square, away from even more boggarts, now materializing behind him and cutting off his escape route. A shadow hand lunged to grasp around Blunt's beard. Another shadow hand grabbed Valeria's slim throat. Hands of darkness crept from every shaded place. Punching the air, the shadows, everything around him, Blunt knew the odds were against him.

But then a boggart screeched. Against the haphazard outline of twisted black-and-white forests shone a new colour. A vibrant healthy green. Now, a green shadow hand, casting its own spreading green shadow, wrenched back an offending boggart's wrist.

"I banish you," said the green shadow, with a voice of odd familiarity. At once, with a million tiny sparks, a dozen boggart outlines shattered and sprayed white across the alley. Light droplets remained where they fell for a few seconds, fading eventually until only the tattoo of residue-brightness speckled across the vision of any witnesses.

"What is that?" Rozzer Jim pushed himself as flat as he could against a wall. His rosy chubbiness had drained into a damp pallidity. "I'm leaving. I've had enough."

For an instant, a young man stood in the place of the green shadow. A wiry man, bright-eyed with cunning.

Valeria gasped in shock. "Sol!"

"Sol, my boy. You're a sight for sore eyes," said Blunt.

"No questions, please. Listen! Any boggarts you banish or kill I can control. Just know that magic is alive and well and that it's time to reclaim what is ours. It's time to finish Artos for good," said Sol, his body already flickering away into green shadow. In his place sprang a dozen, very green, boggarts.

Valeria and Blunt, looking into each other's eyes, nodded.

"I dare you to kill the bastard, Artos," whispered Blunt.

"I double dare you, my lovely."

<hr/>

The preparations were rapid. Sol sent Jobba, and any loyal boggarts, throughout the Mile. Scratching fairy eyes on walls, the creatures created a trail that would lead to Old Well Square. More so, they screeched at anyone they saw to join the riot in front of the Church.

Knockers in overalls descended on the Square, sweating in the heat. With ink-stained fingers, and smelling of spices, alchemists, and magic users of all kinds followed the fairy eyes through any number of the maze of threaded alleys. Once the energy of curiosity saturated the air, all faerie would be virtually unable to resist having a peek at what was transpiring.

With an atmosphere turned almost carnival, children thrilled to the chants of Fey, fidgeting as parents pulled at their collars to get them off the streets. Above, an air balloon hovered, armed with magic-weavers and Brown Bess armed sharpshooters. People smiled. Sol's shadow smiled, although no one noticed.

But then the light flickered again, and everyone silenced. A column of lightlessness now rose around the church, churning the light away without a sound. Rectangles of black- were thrown from all the windows surrounding the square. With hushed breaths, a thousand pairs of eyes hid behind those windows, praying and counting their blessings.

The monumental forest of a twisted Fey-world was superimposed over the sky. Across every wall and surface, the scratchy outlines of wicked trees and Artos' wicked boggarts clashed with the green-outlined boggarts loyal to Sol. Boggart versus boggart in tumbling, swinging, screeching cat-fights.

Blunt now stood with his fellows, in a perimeter around the well. Groups to his left and right armed themselves with guns and blades. More boggarts flittered en-mass into existence, at once superimposed over everything too. A few mechanical grinds from knockers and their weapon contraptions did nothing to dissuade their presence.

The army of unlight struck again. Tendrils of negativity sputtered from the shadow-boggart ranks, spears of oblivion threading through the air, lashing against the languidly floating air balloon. It went down in slow motion, a giant jellyfish flopping onto the crowd. Boggarts waved their arms, urging their shadows to spread further, banishing life. Everything they touched sunk into puddles of darkness. They were getting stronger.

Rozzer Jim backed away and pushed into Blunt. "I ain't cut out for this," he squealed, small eyes straining around swollen pupils. "I'm sorry. All the best." He wobbled away, heading for any available escape route. The old knocker ignored him as he gritted his teeth and rushed into the fray. With violence, Blunt threw people aside, tunnel-vision fixed on the church door behind which *must* have been Artos.

Just then, the door opened slightly. It was Shammy, running anxiously from the horrors within, seemingly more horrifying than the sights which greeted her in Old Well Square. The sight caught Blunt by surprise. He halted his charge.

A chill passed over him. At once he knew that eyes of unlight had targeted him. *One last crack. Come on, old dwarf. Old dwarf. Come on.* Urging his legs and heart to piston and pump, he started to run to the church again, even as a palpable feeling of 'draining' numbed his limbs. Everything he saw flickered in the darkness; breath choked in his throat. *I'm too old. A knackered knocker...* Just as his legs gave way, he heard Sol's voice. "Welcome to Avalon, brave warrior. Join my army and banish those bad boggarts!"

Louder now, calling to the part of all faerie that remembered Avalon, Sol sent his messages across the whole Marsh Worm Mile, a wind voice from every nook and cranny. "We must all join in the chorus. Banish them from this world! Shout it from the rooftops! 'I banish you.' This is the call of Avalon, taking claim of what belongs to it."

Louder and louder, magic chants fought against boggart-shadow light. Another burst of light inspired hope as boggarts shattered. Sound warred with Light. And slowly, bit by bit, the weird, wicked forest shone green. Twisted, unnatural trees seemed to wither, replaced by visions of oak and apple trees, growning before everyone's eyes into a grove of brilliance and splendour; a semi-transparent vision of a mystic land that could be seen but not touched.

Guns cracked and choirs sang, people clapped and stamped their feet. All joined together in a tuneless sprawl, impossible to ignore. A hundred staccato rhythms played, overlapping into a raging cacophony.

Then the remains of the twisted forest crumbled and tore. Luminous rain fell in sheets, droplets settling and fizzing out into dark nothings. With greater volume came greater confidence. From everywhere now, shone green light so bright that, for a while, no flaw or blemish showed against pocked faces or rotten buildings. Shadow was banished. The people of the Marsh Worm Mile had won!

Then, the doors of the church slammed open.

◦➤❙⠿═════ ══❙❘❧◦

"He is mad!" screamed a man dressed in finery, his high collar twisted, his smoking jacket creased as if just put on, while crashing the church doors open with a mighty shove. From the Square, Shammy watched the rush of blood-smeared, hungover men and women escaping from the church, colliding with the tide of faeries pouring from the alleys. Skittish and hoarse, all wove their terror with their voices and movements. From stained windows emanated a glow of pure black which seemed to smudge against the edges of the world.

Buzzing in Shammy's ear, a sprite tugged at her hair. "'Tis a reckoning. It's not over. Get out." Urgency prompted Shammy to follow the gentle pull until she saw a wall *blink*. Two evil eyes opened...but they didn't look *that* evil, all warm and brown and peering back. *Sol's eyes!*

'*Get out,*' whispered a voice she hadn't heard for what seemed a lifetime.

With thunder, the church now unleashed a raging tribe of warriors, their spears humming and thirsty. Victor was at the lead, roaring, a feral demon unleashed.

Bodies pushed around Shammy. Gunshot cracked across the Square; mistletoe and oak flavoured the air. For a moment, Shammy covered her eyes to block out the violence. She allowed the stampeding crowd to carry her off as if a piece of driftwood carried on the sea. It was her chance to give up all responsibility, to become passive. Just dwelling on that thought released some of that built-up tension. But how could she shy away from this?

Once, she had climbed, with Sol, to the highest heights of London. When just a girl, she had scrapped with the gangs and lived a life of bruises and bravado. Some said she had the brains of Sol and the fighting heart of Victor! Though not for a while. Not since she had... *grown, matured*. She bit her lip until she tasted blood.

"Beg your pardon, mate," she grinned and winked, snatching at a passing elf's belt and grabbing one of many blades, this one a razor-sharp hunting knife of sorts. The elf tipped her hat and grinned back.

Though, no cocky act of showmanship could stop the fear boiling inside Shammy's stomach.

◦✣◦〈▥▬▬▬ ▬ ▬ ▬▥〉◦✣◦

Woad Warriors clashed with a throng of faerie. They fought with invincible madness, weapons and shields cutting, thrusting, and shoving. Drunk on magic and fixing for blood, they were the hunters of she-wolves, the sackers of Rome, the spear-point poised at the heart of the World Empire. Even though the faerie swarmed against the warriors and managed to wound a few, broken bones and torn skin re-knitted right before everyone's eyes. Eventually, the faerie were pushed back, leaving a ring of cleared space around Artos' 'tribe.'

Forming into a shield wall, the tribe pushed onward, spearing all who strayed too close. "Only room for warriors in the new Avalon," spat Victor, under a hail of stones and fire pebbles.

The crowd loosened around Shammy. At the edges of the Square, many of the beings loyal to Sol simply slipped away unnoticed. More out-and-out sprinted to safety. Resolve was dwindling. Yet, a brave core held their ground, determined to go down with the Marsh Worm Mile, if that's what fate intended.

"*Run. What's done is done. Better for this to be a nightmare than a reality,*" urged Sol, in a whisper Shammy knew was for her alone.

"You know me. I only run if it's a good laugh, and I ain't having any fun today," replied Shammy to the voice in her head.

Cheering in the periphery, Rozzer Jim had returned with help! Suddenly, a dozen peelers, with their blue top hats, shoved through the crowd. Behind them marched a contingent of red-coated soldiers. Professionals, rigid in a time of crisis.

As the centre of the crowd parted for the redcoats, it tightened again around Shammy. In disciplined, stilted motion, the redcoats formed their battle line in the newly created space. They faced the shield wall.

"Present arms," went the order. The fifty or so soldiers levelled their Brown Bess rifles. The moment hung... Artos pushed through the shield wall of his warriors, his eyes glinting, his lips thinned. He snarled like a rabid dog, then spoke to the redcoats.

"I recognize none of you! You build with columns and subjugate the world. A world I no longer wish to be part of. Today, we settle old scores. Today, the Iceni defeat Rome without the faerie rot in our hearts. Anyone who isn't with me must leave the Mile now, or die." His voice quietened; his tone intensified. "This is a final warning to all." Stepping back, the shield wall slotted around Artos. As one, the warriors stepped forward, snarling, some frothing at the mouth as a contagious berserker rage rippled through their ranks and took hold.

"Fire...," shouted a redcoat.

Musket balls shattered wood, blood spiralled against the side of the church, and many warriors dropped. Shammy strained to see through the crowd blocking her way. Tiptoeing to peek over their shoulders, she gasped. Victor lay on the dirt holding his stomach, red bubbling from a wound and turning his woad-stained skin purple.

The remaining warriors continued their slow stalk forward as the soldiers tore at their paper cartridges and loaded the gun pans. But something agitated their ranks. Men started murmuring as they watched fallen warriors pick themselves up. Victor, the biggest, re-taking his spear as his wounds folded over and healed.

Bloodlust was now upon him. "Charge," Victor roared as he surged ahead of his shield brothers. Just behind him crashed the wall of wooden shields. Bayonet met spear in a chaotic melee.

From Shammy's point of view, it was just a flail of arms, shields, and metal, blues and reds. Behind them, the church continued to ooze out its black flame, wisps of that blackness twirling upwards, condensing, rising like a tower above the Marsh Worm Mile. It seemed like the end of the world. But was it?

"Sol, I know how to get Victor back with us. You know he'd never hurt me. He'd never ever let anyone hurt me. Not you, not even Artos." At that, Shammy raced into the battle, ducking blows, dodging kicks, running as fast as she ever had. She held her hunting knife so tightly that her hands ached, and her knuckles turned white.

<hr />

Disappointing, how the soldiers fell back, some dragging their colleagues, others throwing down their rifles and all-out routing. Although he couldn't blame them for fleeing inevitable death, Victor felt that warrior fire inside ache for more. Perhaps only a half dozen fell to his spear and shield, in exchange for a mere slash across his stomach with a bayonet. That slash had already healed.

Now that the humans had gone, Victor would have to sate himself on the faerie. Already his brothers had turned back and reformed around Artos. The Woad Warrior beckoned Victor back to their lines.

About to take his place at Artos' side, Victor suddenly stopped. Above him, between two windows, a wall had winked at him. Then a dozen pairs of brown eyes popped up on every wall around him, wherever his gaze settled, before closing their red-bricked eyelids and hiding away.

*"Stop, Victor, my...friend."*

Woad warriors charged into the Fey. Battle resumed, but Victor hesitated and looked on. A feeling of dizzy distance muffled his warrior fire. Black flame now lapped around his feet, scarring empty void whenever it touched the ground. Still, the battle raged, on this cliff-edge of past and present. Fey fell in great numbers, tossed aside, stampeded. It was a massacre. In the middle of it all, a berserker Artos slaughtered any who dared come close.

*"Look, Victor, at the man you follow. He has been twisted by fate and disappointment. He only brings death. He cannot be anything else but a God of Destruction."* It sounded just like Sol.

Victor's shoulders and chest rose and fell with each deep breath. He spat blood onto the ground as a mark of resolve. "Witchery." Leaping into the fray, he submerged into the violence just as another figure launched from the fight. Like a cat with claws bared, right up at Artos, Shammy bounded from the shoulders of others. But, like swatting a fly, Artos spun and caught her with his elbow. Enraged as he was, he stamped down onto Shammy's chest, pinning her like prey in a trap.

*"Now look, Victor! Look at Artos! What is he doing? What will it take?"*

With grunts, Victor effortlessly shoved Fey and woad warriors aside. Never had he felt stronger. Never had he felt such brimming exhilaration. But Sol, he wanted to ruin this feeling, too. Victor stifled a roar and clenched his jaws. His spear shook in his grip until it snapped!

*"Victor. Do it now, Victor!"*

Artos stood over Shammy, his spear poised. "I hate you," she said, winded, a voice only of breath. With what little she had left; Shammy jabbed her hunting knife into Artos' shin. The man's leg twitched for a drawn-out second, then snapped away in a lightning moment of intense pain before snapping back into Shammy's face. The world grew dim at the edges.

Bursting across Shammy's field of view, a cannonball of woad and muscle collided with Artos. *Victor!* He threw all his strength into every punch, hitting Artos twice as he straddled him on the ground.

"You bastard! Why did you hurt her? She is all the happy things in the world."

The God of Revenge twisted, finding leverage enough to jerk his legs up and over Victor's shoulders, locking around his throat, pulling him back. Both men scrabbled in the dirt to get to their feet as the clang of battle started to hush around them.

Artos crouched, his eyes locked on Victor's, his spear dancing back and forth between his hands. Victor stood stiff and tall; his hands reached out. "You would fight me, though I have no weapon? If I'm a bear, let me fight with claws." By now, the surrounding fighting had ceased completely. Combatants turned into spectators, all paying rapt attention to what Artos would do next.

A motion of Artos' eyes directed one of his men to throw a spear Victor's way. Catching it, Victor held the spear out to mark a target on Artos' chest. He knew Artos couldn't, and wouldn't, back down now, not in front of such an audience. Even if Victor had wanted to put a stop to this fight, he couldn't either. An example had to be made. Only one warrior would survive this duel.

Artos jerked left and sprang quickly from Victor's flank. Victor sidestepped the other way, bringing up his weapon's shaft to counter an expected blow; but it was a feint. Artos surged up from a crouch, supernaturally agile, shifting his weight to the other foot, his ancient spear piercing Victor's left shoulder in one quick stab. Instinctively, Victor stepped back. Only a flesh wound. Artos was toying with him.

Artos smiled as he circled, arms spread out to his side, spear-point tilted away from the action. Every twitch made Victor flinch in expectation of an attack. He wouldn't run though. But he couldn't let himself be hacked to pieces, bit by bit. Not a slow death. He would not be made sport of! For Shammy, then. He would die for her, protecting her. But more than that, he would die fighting, and everyone would see and know that 'Victor, the Bear of the Mile' was never a coward.

Dipping his weapon, Victor lunged forward with such force, that he again collided with Artos. A sickening smack echoed across the Square. Both bodies stumbled back. For a moment, it looked as if Victor had somehow disarmed the Woad Warrior until the crowd saw the wooden shaft sticking out from the big man's chest.

Victor tasted copper. His strength vanished and he sunk to his knees. At this, utter silence took hold of the battlefield for a few moments.

"It saddens me, my Bear, that you will not join me in Avalon. But no tale of gods and heroes was ever told without a betrayal." Victor's blood coiled down Artos' spear. Other warriors watched silently. First one, then another, then all of them dropped their weapons and stared at their bloodstained hands.

<hr />

Spluttering, her cracked ribs grating and stabbing like nails in her chest, Shammy pulled herself along the dirt, determined to go down fighting by Victor's side. Somehow, she had lost herself, failed to see what was really going on. She had let other people define her. Even believed them. But, deep down, Shammy knew what she was. Not a caged tigress whose purpose was to be admired. Not a fat, well-kept house cat with a fluffy, shiny coat and happy, trilling purr. She was an alley cat. Blessed with luck from Sol and protection from Victor, but an alley cat nonetheless. And an alley cat hissed and bit until the very last.

With a scream, Shammy stabbed her knife down into Artos' foot. Artos twitched instinctively, the pain enough to distract him. One of his hands grabbed at the blade in his foot while he took a grip of his weapon still lodged in Victor's chest.

*"Victor, his spear, the last relic left,"* said the words on the wind.

⚬━━━━━━━━━━⚬

Even though he felt dried up, brittle like a brown autumn leaf, Victor expelled his pain with a bellow, and yanked the spear, a whole yard of its wooden shaft, from his chest. Artos' grip faltered as he reached for his footing. Letting the dead weight of his heavier body push back, Victor pulled the spear free. With violence and force, he pressed the shaft back, shoving Artos against the old stone well, even as it disintegrated under the black flames still spreading from the church.

Locked under Artos' chin, the blunt end of the spear pushed painfully upward. Victor pressed into it with everything he had, eyes bulging as he roared against the pain. His veins stood out in relief across his entire torso.

Froth flecked Artos' lips, his own eyes bulged red and wild. Then, like the bear Artos had named him, Victor stood tall, pulled the spear away, and spun it around to levy the business end. Spear pointing down, bellowing to the point of insanity, Victor stabbed with all his might, through Artos' chest and into the flickering stone of the old well.

*"Now, run! Leave the Marsh Worm Mile. Run, as quick as you can, with Shammy."*

Barely able to stand, Victor looked at his wounded friend, now on her hands and knees. Her eyes shimmered with something akin to awe. It might have been the woad, or perhaps a spell from Sol, but Victor dug deep enough and found the strength he needed.

Stumbling toward Shammy, black flames spread like vines across houses, lacing around warriors and Fey alike now, holding them down as they faded away. It was happening so quickly. Victor wasted only one moment checking on Artos.

Slumped by the well, Artos rattled for breath. His hands dug into the earth even as they interlaced with the black flames of nothingness. His spear stuck him to the well. *Was it enough to kill him?* Artos caught Victor's curious eyes. He blinked, before resting his head back against the well and... smiled.

With pain burning white behind his eyes and energized by a magic-buoyed will, Victor slung Shammy over his shoulder and drunkenly swayed into the tunnel alleys. Fey made way for him, all bowing their heads, seemingly accepting their fate as one with the Faerie Borough. *Or did they know something he didn't?* However, one presence loomed large and blocked the way. It was Shiv, bloody and holding his spear.

"You ruined it all. This ain't the way it was supposed to be. Now, look at you." Levelling his weapon, Shiv's eyes narrowed. "I'm going to..."

He never got to finish. From the very walls of the alley tumbled...apples! A veritable avalanche of apples from all angles, thumping against Shiv, knocking him senseless over and over, forcing him to drop his spear and protect himself.

With no time, and in too much pain to savour the unexpected turn of events, Victor hurried on, his insides tearing as he did. The black flames spread behind him; a constant erasing inching ever closer.

Almost out, by the river Thames now, with Shammy's weight stealing his breath. Victor could only shuffle. Utterly drained of strength, his chest seemed to clench his lungs closed. He couldn't make it...He was going to fall...

A pale hand stretched from a wall, straight out of the stone, and shoved Victor those final steps onto the docks before he collapsed. Behind Victor, the void flames took an ultimate, final grip around the boundaries of Marsh Worm Mile.

⟡⟨⊪⊫══ ═══ ═ ══⊪⟩⟡

Emerging from a wall in a bright green blur, Sol caught Shammy before she hit the ground. Victor slumped, laying down as people spilled around him. Diligently though, none trampled over him, even in their frantic attempts to escape the shadows consuming the Mile. A great cracking echoed across the horizon. Shammy screamed, even as she clung on to Sol when the raging blackness unfolded from the alleys.

Holding her by the shoulders, forcing her to look at him, Sol said, "Don't worry. Avalon is not for those beyond the reaches of our borough." The blackness spun inward to a point, seemingly creeping up Sol's face, crawling towards his eyes, winking away into Sol's pupils. Dreamlike, unreal, Shammy inhaled as deeply as she could before the pain in her chest brought a modicum of reason to her mind.

"It is my burden now," said Sol. "Instead of Artos stealing us all away into a world of bitter hatred, I have replaced him. As a Fey-child of Fate, I will be the one believer with enough faith to know the truth. The rest of us will remember the old stories as nothing but myths, harmless tales to stir the imagination."

Shammy looked over Sol's shoulder, tears budding in her eyes, the pain still cutting into her chest. Everything had changed. In place of the Marsh River and the Marsh Worm Mile now spread an empty field, which abruptly ended at the skeletons of new builds on London's periphery. *Gone. A memory.*

"I need to find a place where I can set Avalon free. London will soon forget that faerie and old gods lived just next door. Everything will become myth. But we can help each other to remember if you wish it. I could leave a tiny piece of magic for you, Shammy, so we will never forget each other or Victor."

Joints stuttering like an old woman's, shock trembling her very bones, Shammy slid from Sol's embrace and crouched beside Victor. Silent, still Victor. "I don't want to forget everything."

"I can feel him still, Shammy. In the Avalon of my mind. He fights with the Fey now, resisting with them in a place that looks exactly like the Marsh Worm Mile. Artos is re-forming his woad warriors for tomorrow's battle. A battle without death, a battle for eternity. Perhaps *his* perfect afterlife. But it belongs to all the Fey peoples, a place which this modern world had long moved on from. I need to take it away to keep it safe."

All around, a crowd had gathered. It was those humans who had escaped the Mile. Taking tentative steps towards

Shammy first were the littlest orphans, faces full of fear and confusion. Hot liquid swelled in Shammy's eyes, a simmering of sorrow. But the tears didn't fall immediately. She opened her arms to the children and put up with the pain as they hugged her tightly. Only then, when they couldn't see her face, did she allow herself to cry.

"Sol," she whispered weakly. "You're leaving, ain't you?"

"Remember the many tall tales we always heard the sailors bleat on about, for all those years? Of huge open lands across the sea? There must be some places where the old-old world lingers."

"First, Sol, before we do any of that, we must bury him, right 'ere...Victor deserves something. He is a hero."

Nodding, Sol dropped to his knees and, with his bare hands, started scrabbling away at the grass and earth. Soon others joined him, flinging up tufts and sods for hours until everyone's hands were red, grazed, and raw. A hole, almost six-foot deep, waited to return Victor to the soil.

Some of the older men, and a few of the orphans, took out their hip flasks and spilled a drop before swigging their remembrance. A few drew crosses on their chests. Many wept their goodbyes or just stood silently. Victor was the symbol of all their losses. The last remembering of when myth walked the land of England. Shammy tightly held Sol's hand, refusing to cry again in front of the orphans flocking around her.

On the docks, beneath the forest of funnels, masts, and cranes, Shammy and the orphans came to see Sol off. Afraid to let go, she gripped his jacket until her hands ached, just as the youngest of the orphans gripped the shabby silk of her dress. Her recent wounds had, luckily, not led to anything serious. Remarkable. It was as if some magical doctor had visited her while she slept.

"I'll be back, Shammy. Not too long, I hope."

"I don't know what to do, where to go. How can they all depend on me? Their memories have been wiped like chalk from a board. All they remember is streets, but no magic, no Victor..."

Sol prised open Shammy's grip with his free hand. He held her hand and looked into her eyes. It was obvious that those warm eyes brimmed with deep affection. But it was different now. They had grown up. It was time to cut the apron strings of the past.

"You'll get by. More than just get by. I know, and I'm the boggart King. It's always handy to know people in high places."

Swinging her arms around him, Shammy held Sol close and rained kisses on his cheek between every sob. Until, when she finally pulled away, Sol's shoulder and face were somewhat damp and humid. "I dare you to stay, I double dare you to stay," her voice scratched and thin.

"Shammy, I spied something," said Sol, calm as you like, pointing down to a bit of mud congealed on the boardwalk. "Look, it's glinting. I bet it's valuable?"

Snatching it up, Shammy saw it was a mucky gold coin. "It's a sovereign." Her wet eyes blinked with surprise.

"Stroke of luck. Told you I'd leave a bit of magic hanging around." Sol beamed broadly, waving a hand like a dandy and taking a bow. Abruptly he turned away, forcing himself to walk toward the bustle of sailors, to find a ship going somewhere, anywhere.

On the riverfront, only once a big, rough bunch of dockers had jostled past him, did Sol look back. He watched how the orphans danced with glee as coin after coin seemed to magically appear between the planks of the boardwalk. Also, and for his eyes only, he watched a green child-sized figure pick the pockets of a passing gentleman. The figure looked back with gas-lamp-yellow eyes.

Doffing his flat cap, a toothy smile splitting his face, Jobba soon went back to his mischief. *Perhaps there had never been such a happy creature before?* "Look over them. Do whatever it takes," said Sol to the wind.

Turning away, he pushed further into the crowd, determined to be the master of his own fate.

# UNBOUND

The flames had all but disappeared. Boggarts crawled over her, the nasty things. Yet, these were her saviours. They knew where their bread was buttered. Still, it was a mark of how low she had fallen.

They chewed on the knotted ropes, and dragged her from the bindings, before slinging her over several shoulders and carrying her into a clear space. Well, all the church was a clear space now, a burnt and gutted husk. Chattering among themselves, anxiously fidgeting, the boggarts were uncomfortable about something. The Crone didn't know what was going on, what with being tortured and bound. However, it took her only a few moments to come to her senses.

"Yes, I see. We are not where we once were, yes?" Nodding frantically, the boggarts bounced on their tiptoes. "We are back in Avalon! How I have longed for this. So, you want to go and 'play,' yes?"

Squealing with excitement, the creatures exaggerated their nodding and bouncing.

"Well, help an old lady to her feet, then scamper away into the fray. May your days be bloody good fun."

In a split second, the mass of boggarts surged towards her, jolting the Crone around as they pulled her, shoved her, and wrestled her to her feet. She thought about whispering some syllables of fiery torment at their rough-housing but then reconsidered. How could she blame them for feeling utter joy at this homecoming? Anyway, she had managed to get to her feet. She waved the boggarts away, shooing them as one might a cat or dog.

Witnessing this, the boggarts leapt towards the church door, swarming out into the Square. But they didn't stop there, they continued running, disappearing into the maze of Marsh Worm Mile's streets, hunting the echoing sounds of battle.

*Now that's odd. Why is the Square itself so quiet?*

<hr>

The Crone hobbled about the Square. None would be able to tell, but she smiled under her hood. Trees had already sprouted underneath the houses and the church. Branches were pushing and slow-punching their way through windows and walls. Better than that, the first few apples had started to spring on the sturdiest trees.

It wouldn't be long until the Square was swallowed up within the fist of a wild forest. That would be something. That would mark a true turning of the wheel.

Elsewhere, the resounding clangs and war cries raged from every direction, the everlasting battle having moved on from the Square into the surrounding streets. Artos and his warriors clashed with the faerie, unending viciousness looping over and over. While the big warrior, Victor, once Artos' prodigy, now fought against him too, with a few dozen red-coated men with thunder-sticks. And weren't they having their own bloody good time!

They died, bled, cried. Some prayed. By now though, all had realized that death did not exist here, at least as a finality. How long would it take for blood-lust to become boredom? How long would it take for all, Fey and human alike, to realize the futility of war in this place? In Avalon, battle was a joyous sport, something of no consequence. There was no point in harbouring grudges, no point in factionalism. Once warriors tired of fighting, they would turn their minds to other things...

Feasting, drinking, sleeping. Rutting. Even loving. For now, the men and women of Artos' tribe, the redcoats and the amorous Fey, fought. But the Crone knew too well that, in the end, realizing they couldn't kill each other off, well, then they would decide to create something instead. After all Cerridwen, the Goddess of Fate, had seen it all before.

**The End**

# AUTHOR BIO

James K. Isaac was born and raised in Lewisham, London, spending his youth at play among the dense, vibrant, and sometimes challenging streets. When on mischievous voyages of urban exploration, he found quiet corners to play gamebooks and read Dragonlance novels. He has a MA in Ancient History and knows a few obscure things while misunderstanding many more, apparently, obvious things. James has always appreciated cats, animals of great character.

He has traveled much of Europe, East Africa, and China, worked on a kibbutz in Israel, and at the famous 'First Emperor' exhibit in the British Museum. Living in China for a few years, he taught and lectured on English and Mythology before returning to London to continue teaching there.

A little whiskey, a bit more wine, too much coffee, sandwiches, and boxing are among his hobbies, though his greatest passion is for stories in any form. He has had several stories published in fantasy and sci-fi magazines and collections and self-published his own short story collection. He also creates interactive fiction and story-based computer games. All of these can be found on the web under James K. Isaac or 'The Numbered Entity Project.'

Not sure I want this. Part of me always feels that seeing an author distracts from their story unless it is a biography. Of course, the mileage may vary.

Printed in Great Britain
by Amazon